Ploughshares

Fall 1992 Vol. 18, Nos. 2 & 3

GUEST EDITOR
Tobias Wolff

EXECUTIVE DIRECTOR
DeWitt Henry

MANAGING EDITOR & FICTION EDITOR
Don Lee

POETRY EDITOR
Joyce Peseroff

OFFICE MANAGER
Renee Rooks

ASSISTANT FICTION EDITOR
Debra Spark

FOUNDING PUBLISHER
Peter O'Malley

PLOUGHSHARES, a magazine of new writing, is edited serially by prominent writers and poets to reflect different and contrasting points of view. PLOUGHSHARES is published three times a year at Emerson College, 100 Beacon Street, Boston, MA 02116–1596. Telephone: (617) 578-8753.

STAFF ASSISTANT: Phillip Carson. ASSISTANT PROOFREADER: Holly LeCraw Howe. FICTION READERS: Billie Lydia Porter, Karen Wise, Sara Nielsen Gambrill, Phillip Carson, Holly LeCraw Howe, Christine Flanagan, Win Pescosolido, Paul Brownfield, Michael Rainho, Erik Hansen, Molly Lanzarotta, Thomas Olofson, Thom Shaw, and Kathryn Herold. POETRY READERS: Renee Rooks, Jason Rogers, Karen Voelker, Tom Laughlin, Jenny Cronin, Tanja Brull, Sandra Yannone, Rafael Campo, Mary-Margaret Mulligan, and Ed Charbonnier. TYPESETTING: Gian Lombardo and InText Publishing Services.

SUBSCRIPTIONS (ISSN 0048–4474): $19/domestic and $24/international for individuals; $22/domestic and $27/international for institutions. See last page for order form.

UPCOMING: Winter 1992–93, Vol. 18, No. 4, a special fiction and poetry issue featuring works by emerging writers, with Christopher Tilghman and Marie Howe as the editors, will appear in January 1993.

SUBMISSIONS: Please see back of issue for submission policies.

BACK ISSUES are available from the publisher. A listing is printed on pages 221–226. Microfilms of back issues are available from University Microfilms. INDEXED in M.L.A. Bibliography, American Humanities Index, Index of American Periodical Verse, Book Review Index. Self-index through Volume 6 available from the publisher; annual supplements appear in the fourth number of each subsequent volume.

DISTRIBUTED by Bernhard DeBoer (113 E. Centre Street, Nutley, NJ 07110), Ingram Periodicals (1226 Heil Quaker Blvd., La Vergne, TN 37086), and L-S Distributors (130 East Grand Ave., South San Francisco, CA 94080). PRINTED by Edwards Brothers.

PLOUGHSHARES receives additional support from the National Endowment for the Arts and the Massachusetts Cultural Council. Major new marketing initiatives have been made possible by the Lila Wallace–Reader's Digest Literary Publishers Marketing Development Program, funded through a grant to the Council of Literary Magazines and Presses. PLOUGHSHARES also acknowledges a generous software donation from Lotus Development Corporation's Philanthropy Program. The opinions expressed in this magazine do not necessarily reflect those of Emerson College, the editors, the staff, the trustees, or the supporting organizations.

Contents

INTRODUCTION
Tobias Wolff   5

NONFICTION
Susan Bergman, *Imago*   7

FICTION
Mary Bush, *Rex the King*   18
Dan Chaon, *Fraternity*   36
George Cruys, *Cadet Barnes Learns the System*   51
Andre Dubus, *Woman on a Plane*   64
Stuart Dybek, *A Confluence of Doors*   68
Paul Griner, *Grass*   73
Susan Hubbard, *An Introduction to Philosophy*   94
Robert Olmstead, *Kennedy's Head*   104
Susan Power, *Moonwalk*   112
Mona Simpson, *Van Castle*   132
Sharon Solwitz, *OBST VW*   151
Jessica Treadway, *Down in the Valley*   163
Christopher Zenowich, *Po Lives on the Y*   182
Vassilis Tsiamboussis
    (translated by Martin McKinsey), *A Pat on the Cheek*   199

CONTRIBUTORS' NOTES   200

ABOUT THE EDITOR   203

PLOUGHSHARES BOOKSHELF
The Stories of John Edgar Wideman by John Edgar Wideman   204
Goodnight, Gracie by Lloyd Schwartz   208
City of Boys by Beth Nugent   208
Two Trees by Ellen Bryant Voigt   211
The Lover of History by Jonathan Dee   212
Gilgamesh by David Ferry   215
Anne Sexton: A Biography by Diane Wood Middlebrook   217

PLOUGHSHARES BACK ISSUES   221

Ploughshares
Patrons

Tobias Wolff

Introduction

My first thought in editing this issue of *Ploughshares* was to put together a collection of autobiographical and fictional writings that tested the border between those preposterously rough groupings. And the very first piece that crossed my desk, Susan Bergman's "Imago," confirmed me in this intention. "Imago" is a brilliant family portrait whose narrator claims the authority of history even as she helps herself to the dramatic devices of the fiction writer. Hitler makes an appearance. There's even a ghost, or spirit, that abides in a painting. I put it aside and waited for more.

But that was the last of its kind. Over the next nine months almost every piece that came to me was either straightforward reportage or imaginative writing that chose not to concern itself with self-conscious questions about its own nature and relationship to other kinds of writing. And so I was forced to surrender the principle by which I'd hoped to organize the issue, and look for another. The New Fiction—something like that. I thought I might be able to find a signature tone or ethos, especially among younger writers, that would set them off from the rest of us. Here, too, I was frustrated. I could find no subject or perspective common to the best of the work I was reading. I couldn't classify it.

And that, of course, is as it should be. Good writing resists classification, breaks it down. The closer we look at any literary category—Modernism, Minimalism, Post-Modernism, Neo-Realism—the more meaningless it becomes. Are

Hemingway and Faulkner and Fitzgerald really doing the same thing? John Barth and Donald Barthelme? Do they share the same aesthetic or political ideology, express the same vision of the world and our place in it? In a pig's eye. These are terms of convenience for academics and pedants-at-large, to give them a sense of mastery over what is too varied and complex for their patience or understanding.

Then why did I choose the works I chose? In the end, because they interested me as stories. I wanted to know what happened, how things ended up. This appetite was in some cases stimulated by curiosity about the lives of others, which can be as voracious concerning avowedly fictional characters as for those dreamed up by the newspapers and called "Di" or "Leona" or "Trump," and illustrated by photographs to extend the illusion of actuality. I wanted to know more about the dying woman in Susan Power's masterful "Moonwalk," the numbly grieving, guilt-crippled boy in Dan Chaon's "Fraternity." And there were other elements that took my interest by force; the peculiar premise and atmosphere of Stuart Dybek's "A Confluence of Doors," the puzzled, digressive, deceptively naïve voice of the narrator of Robert Olmstead's "Kennedy's Head." Every piece here had, for me, some quality of tone or narrative virtuosity or moral power, some piece of previously suppressed evidence in the human case, that I was unable to ignore.

It goes without saying that another editor would have put together, from the same available manuscripts, a different issue. I can only hope, Dear Reader (Perfect Judge, Angel of Mercy, Shadow of Death), that your excitements coincide sufficiently with mine to allow you some of the pleasure and wonder I have felt, reading the pages to come.

Susan Bergman

Imago

When we ran out of money, the paintings worked like magic. My father would take one down from the pair of nails it hung on and would carry it—his face close to the portrait's face—to his creditor's car. He told the few facts he had been told about the artist's life, a name changed from Hinshaw to Henshaw, sent to Europe for formal training by the disapproving father of a Brown County girl, a barren witch for a second wife. Then, ceremoniously under the cloud of repossession or eviction, he would turn the picture around in the natural light before the man drove off, the "collateral" padded with a blanket, or propped in the trunk on top of the spare tire. It took those last months of my father's life when he was nearly frantic for financial reversal to get down to the bare walls. All the oils and the larger pastels, the portrait of the old black sailor and the one of the girl with the bow in her hair went to the landlord who already held most of the collection hostage for six months of unpaid rent.

The ownership of the pictures is still in question. Maybe my father did buy them finally, after failing to sell them to anyone else. Maybe he never let them go. He said once that he was planning to make a fair offer for the lot, and no one has ever come to claim the few we've kept in all these years. Maybe we have moved one too many times for anyone to keep track. The paintings were put into my father's care by two women dressed like men who lived together in Florida, and occasionally in Ohio in a house without the right kind of light, my father told me. They had bought the works as an investment and made him the paintings' agent. I remember the one woman's taper cut and the other's unnaturally white, evenly cut bangs. Both had flattened their breasts somehow, it appeared to me, as I was working to grow mine, and so seemed unencumbered by what I had been taught were women's roles and duties. Prone instead to male cares, male freedoms, they were as dismissive of children as was suitable to men.

I must have been fourteen years old when we first drove to pick up the collection at the shop where the oil paintings had been cleaned and the pastels had been newly placed in huge gold frames with black velvet matting. Behind the glass I could make out cities with domed centers and rivers that narrowed under ancient bridges into the fog. I still have the drawing of the Chrysler Building, soaring toward the clouds, its confetti lights shining down on the trafficked New York streets. But most of the works were portraits of people exotic and woeful enough to be our ancestors, or even gods. What a gift, I thought, it was for a girl who wanted to paint to have a master's works to live with in her own house. Along the hallway walls upstairs, across from the dining-room windows, on the blank passages of living room, my father arranged and rearranged them. And now I would surely learn the angle of jaw, the lips' elusive edge, the shadow under the brow that made a flat page dimensional with life.

American Impressionism had not yet been commodified; the price list the women had printed seemed arbitrarily exorbitant for the relatively unknown Glen Cooper Henshaw. There were over one hundred works in all, to be sold as a collection only, and so they were never sold but moved with us from house to house like a troop of players jostled but unflappable.

Then one day in Atlantic City a black woman my mother had met at church saw in them the story of our lives. We did not believe her altogether then, but when I unpacked the few remaining pictures to hang them in the house where I now live I thought of that woman's warning, and wondered what I risked. It was the paintings that first drew her to my mother, Margo said. My parents regularly visited a racially mixed Baptist church that on Sunday nights brought in rock or jazz musicians with a testimony. The group would play then pass the plate, laying out a two-minute gospel in closing for the visitors lured in by the thick bass rumble that pulsed through the surrounding neighborhood. Margo was hiding out from her ex-husband, now openly homosexual, who had brought his lovers home. She had sunk temporary roots a block from the church where she had been delivered, as she told it, from a life as a Psychic that began when as a young girl her mother started charging for her "gift." Her off-hand observations had the ring of truth; they in fact came true. She didn't even have to touch a woman's hand to see her knot of suffering. Smell his breath, she told her mama, it's an omen. A man's boss is about to fire him when his children walk down this side of the street.

Gifts or perceptions, she read the images for clues, the spirit voices clustering in dreams. Waking signs had not yet turned off, though she'd given her soul to Christ. We had first seen her driving through town in an old school bus painted blue, in which she gathered unattended children and others of Atlantic City's early castoffs. One day the bus appeared on the street in front of our house and the pictures began to talk to her.

She had walked into the kitchen and started snapping the ends off beans until the whole bag was finished and washed and thrown in the copper-bottomed pot with new potatoes and ham my mother was simmering for dinner. They sat down after eating that night with their Bibles, marking the tissue pages gently so the ink would not run through, reading between passages the doctrine of predestination right on through to righteous liberty. *In Christ there is no Jew nor Greek, no male nor female, slave nor free,* I heard them read aloud, and believed it. The image of a different world rose up in me like the figures in the pictures haunted Margo. It was the first night she tried to sleep in our guest room that my mother heard her talking back to them.

In that room my father had hung the portrait of the painter's second wife. She was wearing a white gown with light brush strokes of lace along the collar's edge. She hovered in the center of a dark room. Only her face was fully illumined from a light source off to the left of the canvas. Her brown hair and the shadowy edges of her dress nearly blended in with the background so that she appeared bodiless, floating in the picture's space. Margo called her Carolyn when they spoke. The two sides of Carolyn's face were noticeably unmatched. One eyebrow was raised slightly, as if worried, and the other eye smiled, the two combined making her seem to mock and doubt whomever it was she saw. Wherever you stood in the room, her eyes followed you. They were not friendly dialogues between Margo and the painting but accounts of torment in marriage, torment from which even the dead are not exempt, torment to come.

Margo would lock the door and try to cast the painter's wife's spirit from the room, furiously, in the middle of the night, while the rest of us slept. Carolyn touched her face to wake her, and they wrestled through the night until dawn, the figure metamorphosing from woman to dwarfish man to the lizard-like shape in the lower corner of the canvas where the paint had begun to peel. She, too, had been a medium who for all her concert with the spirit world had not found her way under. She needed Margo, she insisted, to arbitrate her passage, but not until she spent the curse she carried like a longed-for child.

At breakfast one morning, unsteadily, falling from the middle of the night's vertiginous loops and whorls into our family chatter, Margo told us, "Images are the resting place of spirits." She could not butter her toast, her hand shook so. "You must get these pictures out of the house before it is too late." My father had already gone to the office, where he was working to lease land from farmers to drill oil wells. "She'll destroy your family, beginning with your husband, one by one," she said to my mother in a whisper. "The son next." She meant it. There was more Margo told my mother that morning, Carolyn's threats and curses foresaw much of what we have lived out. But my mother can't remember most of what she said, and I had crept upstairs to peer into the room with Margo's revelations fresh.

The woman in the painting seemed eerily calm, her skin loosely rounded over her bones. She stood as still as the dresser and bedside table I went in the room once a week to dust. Stiller than that. I looked for more. She was sneering now, her shoulders pinned back by the dark enshrouding her. I made the bed neatly, folding the sheet over the blanket edge while I kept my eyes from blinking by squinting hard.

The difference between Margo's range of cognizance and mine, which hours of attention could not amend, was a lesson in the many possible ways of seeing. Leonardo da Vinci found in the sense of sight eight parts, a family of attributes that contribute to perception, and so to interpretation: darkness, light, solidity, color, form and position, motion and rest, distance and propinquity. Each attribute in turn has its own qualities. Take the last pair's common traits: "Objects look closer than they really are when you're looking up- or downhill; across water, snow, or flat sand; or when the air is clear." You know this to be so. "Objects look farther away than they actually are when the light is poor, the color of an object blends with its surrounding, or the ground is undulating" (*Finding Your Way on Land and Sea*).

I overheard my children discussing a drawing one had hung on the pantry wall. The older one loved the way the lines went all the way to the edge of the page. "But there's lightning in the center of your house," he said. "That's not lightning," the younger one was adamant: "Those are yellow stairs!" The puzzle of interpretation starts in the kitchen before we turn five. We see one time the sudden illuminating flash, and another the irrhythmic path of our ascents and descents. Perhaps the light is poor, the object moving at too fast a rate. We are suspended in the unclear air where there are more than eight aspects of sight. Da Vinci accounts for the way the eyes take hold, and does not attempt to broach the subject of the mystical brailles and ciphers that remain beyond our view.

What Margo saw was triggered by the images on the canvas, by her intercourse with the unseen. I have no doubt that the windows of the visible open onto vistas of invisibility. Or that

Margo, because of her experience, must have sensed in my father's dissembling, in his wild unhappiness and stormings from the family table, the catastrophe to come which, in her own voice, was unspeakable. What she kept asserting she saw in front of her, speaking with the authority and intonation of the dead, was a woman's ghost she could not exorcize. The paintings needed to be sold at once, and something purchased to replace their power in our lives.

We could embrace the curse or turn away from it, invite blessing, or close and lock our gates. In this deliberate choice an image is often implicated, for standing in the way, for reminding us, for coaxing trouble, for transmuting the elements of salvation. Body and blood, voodoo, golden calf, grail, I have a pain under my seventh rib, ohmmmmm. The worshippers of Baal excoriate their limbs. Elijah builds his altar with twelve rocks. The worshipers of Baal call down fire, beg on all fours. Around the altar of the Lord, Elijah digs a trench the people fill with water. The prophets of Baal dance the Baal dance. Elijah cuts the ox in pieces and lays it on the wood stacked on the rocks. The prophets of Baal send up jaw-ripping howls. Elijah prays *ANSWER ME LORD.* "Then the fire of the Lord fell, and consumed the burnt offering and the wood and the stones and the dust, and licked up the water that was in the trench."

The disbelieving, too, are not immune. There is a spear that is said to have pierced the side of Christ. It hung in a glass case in the Hofberg Library in Vienna, Austria, where Hitler would stand some days for hours on end, inviting the spear's power to overwhelm him, worked by the spear's presence into a trance. Trevor Ravenscroft, in his book *The Spear of Destiny,* describes the self-eclipsing effects of the spear on Hitler:

> Adolph Hitler stood . . . like a man in a trance, a man over whom some dreadful magic spell had been cast. His face was flushed and his brooding eyes shone with an alien emanation. He was swaying on his feet as though caught up in some totally inexplicable euphoria. The very space around him seemed enlivened

with some subtle irradiation, a kind of ghostly ectoplasmic light.
His whole physiognomy and stance appeared transformed as if
some mighty Spirit now inhabited his very soul, creating within
and around him a kind of evil transformation of its own nature
and power (p. 64).

Hitler believed that Constantine had grasped the spear in his
hand when he conquered Rome in 312 A.D. The spear had borne
forty-five Roman emperors to triumph. He ached to possess such
destiny. To oppose God and win, to have the will to destroy the
very likeness of His image: His people. When he marched into
Vienna he took the spear into his possession. He prayed to that
spear, believing that the powers of evil flocked to him. The spear
was the site of their swarming. The spear hung without a flutter
of power on the wall of St. Katherine's Church in Nuremberg,
where Hitler knelt down before it. After falling into the hands of
the Allies the day Hitler committed suicide, the spear hangs again
under heavy guard in Vienna, an object of occult devotion.

A deacon in the Baptist Church bought one of the larger
paintings for enough cash to cover our heating bill, and another
for a short-term loan so my father could commute between New
York City and Ocean City. My father was sharing an office on
Wall Street with the other principals in his part-time current
venture. He played piano for an off-Broadway show at night. On
Sunday mornings he would pull into the parking lot just in time
to direct the church choir. He was perpetually exhausted with
effort, the near but not yet, any day now.

He was searching for a ten-billion-dollar loan for Mexico,
collateralized by oil, for which he had been guaranteed one
percent, or one hundred million dollars, for his finder's fee. His
partnership in the Red Parrot was nearly sealed, the redesign
drawn with leather banquettes and man-sized feathers. He had a
buyer on the hook for the Empire State Building and was flying
to Texas on Sheik ———'s private jet to confirm the commitment.
We were to pronounce his title *Shake,* not *Sheik,* he did not want
to catch us making that mistake again. *Shake,* Susan, he is not

Omar Sharif. At a folding card table in the downstairs family room, he had set up a telephone and makeshift file system, a rolodex and jar of monogrammed pens. He would draw the vertical blinds against the sun's glare on the sand. He did not want to look at the ocean, just now, he must sort through his small slips of paper for the phone number, where is it? My brother bounded down the stairs three at a time. "Nathan, you jackass, keep quiet in this house, as though an idiot could think with you pounding down those stairs." We were used to his temper, but not its accelerated vocabulary. Jackass? Nathan needed him to play the song he was going to sing for his audition, but not now. We knew our father could be soothed if he would come to the piano to play the old hymns, the show tunes we could sing with our hands resting on his shoulders.

As the deal flow quickened, the flurry of calls, wires, his take in the pipeline, somewhere, he borrowed a neighbor's van so we could all drive to Long Island to look for a proper house. The real estate would overlook the Sound. It was a clear, bright Saturday. After each mansion we reviewed in detail the gardens and pool, the outbuildings and maids' wing, extra bedrooms, linen closets, the arrangement of the furniture and artwork, where we would place ours, kitchen appliances, built-ins, the automated lights and alarms. We looked at the homes as those who have seen such luxury only from the outside would look, as visitors, with the pretense of deserving.

Not until we dropped my father off on a corner near Times Square, with one small sports sack of weekend belongings, did the houses seem unreal. What will you eat? I remember asking him. He was growing thinner and blamed his pace, his working through the night to finally close the deal. I will eat oatmeal, he said—to confirm his wholesome appetites, to convey his self-neglect? I knew he had only the money he had borrowed from his children in his pocket. We did not have enough between us to pay for his bus fare home. I will find you the perfect prom dress, he promised Abigail over his shoulder.

The images of that period of time in our lives have all been sorted through again and again, like a deck of cards, for what we had evidently, blindly overlooked. Then, the cards told tales of great wealth to come, great journeys that would shape great lives. What did the paintings know that we did not? In a short time the world would . . . just around the corner, behind that low-hung cloud, SUCCESS was planning to catch us up in its arrival!

That Christmas, the year of the hunt for adequate quarters, the year that I was married, the family arrived at our apartment early in the morning. I had made cinnamon rolls; we had a small fragrant tree. Tea poured, we sat on the floor to open gifts. My brother and sisters had made fantastic animals of clay, or woven bright yarns on lap-sized looms. I have no recollection of what I gave them. It is my father's gifts we talk about now. For each of us he had printed in his feminine script on large sheets of heavy paper the present he had not had time to purchase, yet. They were rolled up, and he had tied red ribbons around each one which he stood to hand to us, individually, with instructions as to the order in which we were to read the gifts aloud. My mother read hers first. He had given her a family cruise to wherever she wanted to take us all. Nathan was to purchase diving gear. Abigail and Anne had certificates for flight school, valid when they turned sixteen. I was to buy, at my father's expense, the camera my mother must have told him I wanted. He gave my new husband a Commodores album that we played over and over that day, my mother inviting my father to dance, and he obliging, keeping his eyes closed as he pressed her against his thigh and, with his hand supporting the small of her back, leaned her out away from him, then swept her back in close.

What we can't fathom looking back is the credulity that we presented on that day. For his sake we spent the afternoon planning, checking sizes, pouring over maps. It must have been our unacknowledged doubt that fired his extravagance (money was no object for the first time ever), our complicity. We wanted what he gave us—the high hope, the impossibility. None of us pressed him, by that time, or ever after, to come through.

It is not easy to let go of the picture of the family in a beautiful house filled with ancestral heirlooms, the great talent of the father and perfections of the mother, the children's careless laughter. We would have two more Christmases with Nathan before his accident. *First the father, then the son.* We burn the false images like graven idols, the relations we had to them screaming in the fire. Turning from a lie we can search for a true thing. Saying that truth aloud in front of the mirage, phantasms are defeated, but at what cost? It is as arduous a ritual to expel the replacement imagoes of victimization or ongoing demise that swarm like twelve-step jargon in familial air. Recover from the lie, and you must then heal from the truth.

To ward off her illusions my mother drove last year, eight years after my father and brother died, to reclaim the paintings from the landlord. We had lost them but had not escaped the curse. There was no reason not to try to get them back. She had sent letters itemizing the artwork and jewelry, the furniture and accessories that he had taken when he locked them out of their house, finally, the paintings of less value to him than the next tenant's cash. My father had been months away from dying then. There were doctor bills my mother was working to pay, but none of the anticipated gush of wealth. My mother had called to tell the landlord she was on her way. She had not consulted a lawyer, but one of the boys she'd taught in Sunday school was now a local cop and she had asked him for advice. He could not involve himself directly, of course, he told her, but would do whatever he could within the boundaries of the law.

She and my sister Anne, off-duty from her soap opera, a local legend, stormed into the landlord's offices, unannounced, and said they would not leave until he gave them back the pictures, NOW. Surely the inventory he had taken when he had put their suitcases on the street had covered any back rent. A play to his compassion. Her engagement ring, the ruby and diamond pin from her great-grandmother, the piano. Everything they owned. To his sense of fairness. Surely he did not want legal action. They had been too desperate then for any redress. "You don't want us to call the local newspaper," and other threats they thought of, "do you, Warren North?" On his intercom he told his wife, in the adjoining office, to please inform the police that he had two trespassers on the premises that he'd like placed under arrest immediately. "Ladies, that's the past. I have hung the paintings over the years in my rental properties," he told my mother, "in which my tenants pay their rent." Anne was not acting now, though her pitch was theatrical, the names she had for him coming easily, who didn't know the difference between art and the bottom of his shoe, whose children reveled in the mud outside like swine, whose wife's skinny neck . . . As they were shown in by Mr. North's wife the police held their handcuffs ready, stopping short of the offenders. A look at each other, before the younger officer looked down at his buttons, and away.

For my mother, who had lost her husband, and then her son, her things, her cache of memories to revision, her supposition of her own future health, the paintings were a tangible object that marked a missing time, and to her, had value for this, and value because she could have sold them, someday, or have given them back. For Anne, the paintings were a part of lost childhood. They were the one thing she could think of that might possibly—oh please God—relieve her mother's sorrow. Having been raised on delusion, if we are not vigilant, we cherish its perpetuation.

Whatever it was that Margo saw, and heard, and wrestled with—lightning or yellow stairs, demons or our family's deceit—we still combat. It is not specific to a single site. It is not flesh and blood, but the steady force of darkness: what we might look at and not see, what we might blindly desire. What we hold onto like crazy that eventually would devour us. Finding out requires a willingness to adjust our eyes to the light. The curse of the father, the way I heard it, visits the children. Visits. But it does not live here.

Mary Bush

Rex the King

1.

Come back, little Sheeba. That's Uncle Jack thinking he's
being smart, but I don't answer. I keep picking strawberries, my
fingers red as the berries so I get mixed up thinking I'm seeing a
ripe one to grab when it's only my own hand deep in the green
leaves. Twenty quarts, twenty-one quarts. One more and I'll quit,
I keep saying: One *more* and I'll quit. Sears, Roebuck swimming
pool in the catalogue, deep, up over my knees, deep enough to
lay down and swim. Ma says if we go over three hundred dollars
this year, yes. We'll see, Daddy says, and I count that good as
yes.

Sheeba, Sheeba. We're all ladies and girls, except for Mikey,
who's six, and Jack, who comes snooping around, nothing better
to do, like he does sometimes so that Ma finally tells him, If you're
gonna be that way at least do some work while you're at it.

When the berries are ripe, Daddy says. When the garden's
ready. That's when we got relatives, that's when we got friends
we never knew about. Daddy's off all day putting nuts and bolts
on the refrigerator parts when they come down the line while we
stay home and do the garden: me and Annie and Mikey and
baby Suse, Gramma and Aunt Bernesia and Flossie and today
Uncle Jack, behind me, not letting up. *You're turning into a big
girl, Sheeba.*

I don't answer that name. I don't answer no name except
Rex, the King, though I'm not really a boy, and I don't really live

here. I got stuck here by accident, back when the flying saucer broke down and landed in Sullivan's corn lot and they had to leave me while they went to get parts.

Sheeba, Sheeba, let me see your strawberries. Are they big and red and juicy?

Poor Uncle Jack, everybody says. Poor Uncle Jack, his wife died and he had to sell his cows and half the farm. Too bad, I think. Too bad he didn't have to sell the whole farm and go live in the poorhouse where everybody says he's gonna end up anyways.

When he keeps at it, I pick up the two quarts I got hid under a bushy plant and go over near Ma and set them down.

Them two's mine, I tell her. She's listening to Gramma yak away about what happened to the old priest when they found out he was drinking all the communion wine, the two of them wearing funny straw hats and their housedresses and Gramma in rubber boots so she don't ruin her shoes and stockings. Ma straightens up and looks at me. Her face is so puffy and red it scares me. She wipes the sweat off her face with the hankie tucked in her waistband. I'm afraid she's gonna have one of her faints.

Mamma, I say. You hot?

She looks down at the two quarts I got, then out at everybody picking in the field. Takes off her straw hat and fans her face. Her hair's stringy wet around her face.

You want to go in and get a drink? I say. We'll finish up without you.

Gramma straightens up then, looks hard at her. Don't you go having one of your fits now, she tells Ma. But I can see she don't mean it as bad as it sounds. Ma's got heart spells and can't take the heat or bending over, but who can stop her?

She looks at Jack across the field and makes a face like she's not too pleased. Jack, that's Daddy's brother. Everybody related to Daddy is crazy, Bernesia and Flossie too. That's what Gramma says.

I'm going inside for a minute, Ma tells Gramma. Gramma just

stands there and looks at her hard.

I pick up my two quarts and follow.

I watch her sit down in the parlor chair and I go get a wet washcloth to pat her face. I'm scared to touch her, cause we never get too close except when she's hitting me. But she lets me pat her face like it's something I always do. She's all splotchy red and hot and she breathes in little puffs and looks across the room at the picture hanging over the television: Saint Joseph sawing wood in his carpenter shop while a boy my age—that's Jesus—holds the board for him.

I get her a glass of ice water from the jug in the refrigerator. She holds it with both hands.

Cold, she says. That's good. She puts the glass to her cheek a minute. Then she drinks a slow sip.

Where's Suse? she says, looking around like maybe she brought the baby in and maybe she didn't, only she can't remember.

Aunt Bernesia's got her, I say. That's a lie. Suse is out crawling in the field, with nobody giving two hoots. A big old crow could come and snatch her away for all I care.

It's too hot for her, Ma says.

She's in the shade, I say. More lies, but who cares? I don't belong to these people.

I'm studying them for when I go back. I figure that's why I got left here so long in the first place: try to figure out these crazy people so we'll be able to take over. Though who would want to, from what I seen.

Suse starts wailing and Ma sits up in her seat like she'll go after her.

Go tell Gramma bring her in, she tells me.

At first I don't budge. I don't want that squalling baby in the house with us.

She's okay, I tell her. Gramma and Aunt Bernesia—

Bring her in the house, she says.

So I go bang open the screen door hard as I can and cup my hands to my mouth and holler out: Gramma, bring Suse in.

Gramma! Bring that baby inside.

Before I can say any more, Ma's behind me with the fly swatter, whipping me with it. Get out there, she yells. Who do you think you are, screaming like a fool banshee? What are the neighbors going to think?

I jump down into the driveway, holding the back of my leg where it's stinging.

We ain't got no neighbors, I yell back.

All we got is Sullivan, another dumb farmer, and all his drooling cows, and they don't count.

I could crown you, Ma calls after me, waving the fly swatter.

I already been crowned, I say. Me, Rex the King. But what does she know?

Aunt Bernesia's lugging the carriers, eight quarts in each hand, with Flossie trailing her, pushing the wheelbarrow stacked with quarts, the berries bouncing out of their baskets and down on the ground every time she wheels over a dirt clump or burdock root.

You done picking? Bernesia asks me.

I *was,* I say. But now I got to pick up what Flossie's dropping. If they ain't all smashed, I say.

She turns behind and tells Floss, Slow down. You're not in any race.

I'm going fast as you are, Flossie says. If you want me to slow down, you slow down. Then Flossie starts crying, which is what she does.

Mikey and Annie sit off to the edge of the field in the shade of the crab apples, their faces smeared red, watching the show. Gramma's down the row, tromping around in her straw hat and boots. When I see Uncle Jack moseying along the row with his hands in his pockets, looking down at the ground real happy, I know where Suse is. I start running towards him, making chicken calls to let him know I'm coming.

Ma wants Suse in the house, I say, snatching her up from the ground right under his feet.

Well I beg your pardon, he says.

Suse is heavier than an eight-quart carrier and her diaper's muddy from her peeing and sitting in the dirt. I try to hold her away from my body and run with her, and it makes her start blatting.

Oh Sheeba, you're hurting me so, Jack says.

2.

So we sit and wait. Aunt Bernesia's drove fifty quarts off to Walman's fruit store and Annie and Mikey sit out front selling what's left at the stand. We wait to fill up the canning jar with quarters and dimes and dollar bills so maybe by next week we can send away for that swimming pool.

I go out back and pace off the size of the pool again and figure how much sun it'll get over near the lilac bush. I learned swimming last summer when the church bus took us to the lake, but I already knew how. Put your legs out behind you, move your head from side to side, grab the water and go. I never sink like those skinny girls who do the crazy doggie paddle while the water goes up over their heads.

Water, swimming, that's the best thing I know. We got no water near enough to walk to except Sullivan's cow creek, all mud and manure, though I tried it once. I put my arms out in front of me and start moving them like I'm swimming while I walk around the circle where the pool's going. I can just feel the cool water on me. I look up at the sky while I go around. Swimming in water, swimming in air, it's pretty much the same thing, I think. When I dreamed of the spaceship, first it really *was* a ship, like the Santa Maria, with great big sails all different colors floating in the air. Then it turned into a regular flying saucer when it landed.

When you coming back for me? I ask the sky.

A dressed-up lady carrying a big white pocketbook is out front picking over the berries while Annie and Mikey watch her.

Annie hands the lady a quart, but she puts it back down and keeps looking. When she finds the one she wants—that I hope is full of smashed green berries and worms—she snatches it up and gives Annie a dollar bill. Annie counts out the change while the lady watches every nickel and dime drop into her hand. She looks relieved when the last nickel falls, and she takes her quart into the car, pats her face with a hankie, and drives off. Annie looks at me and shrugs. Mikey sticks his tongue out at the car chugging down the road. I hold up the jar and look at the money, wondering, We gonna make it? We gonna make three hundred dollars?

Then Gramma yells for me to come in.

Now what? I wonder. Don't tell me to cook nothing, I'm thinking. Don't tell me to wash no dishes or do any housework. Don't even try.

You stay inside and watch the baby, she tells me. While I go to fill your mother's prescription.

Prescription? I say. I look around the kitchen. Suse is crawling on the floor, over near the register, her diaper sagging. I go stand in the parlor doorway, looking. Ma lies on the couch, her ankles crossed, the back of her wrist across her eyes, the other arm on her stomach. I watch till her stomach rises up with the breathing.

I turn back to see Gramma snapping her pocketbook shut. She takes Daddy's car keys off the nail by the door.

Her diaper needs changing, she tells me, going out the door.

I stand inside the screen door. Prescription for what? I say to her fuzzy shape going down the steps. You better tell me, I'm thinking to myself. You better tell me something.

The sun got to her, that's all, she says.

I watch her pull the car out the driveway and listen till the engine sound fades away. I hear the flies buzzing on the porch and the whining of ones stuck in the flypaper. Then I smell the sharp medicine smell of the flycatchers, coming up from the heat.

I go back in the parlor doorway and watch Ma breathe. I count *nine, ten, eleven,* between her breaths.

What's wrong with you? I ask her.

She stretches open her fingers over her face, then relaxes them.

I had a little dizzy spell, she says. Did Gramma go?

She went, I tell her.

She lays there still as a dead dog.

I get a funny feeling in my stomach, watching her.

We picked eighty quarts today, I tell her, and my voice makes her stomach move. That's the most we ever got in one day, ain't it? I say, just to be talking, like the noise will make everything all right.

She flutters her fingers in the air, but doesn't say anything.

What you dizzy about? I say, real gruff, so she'll know I think she's just faking it.

How should I know? she answers.

I'm looking at her thinking, Tin cans. I got to get those two big ones I found over in Sullivan's trash heap. Get those cans and more wire from the barn and fix up my radar station so somebody will find me. I got to get away from these people.

I go pick up Suse and check her diaper. She laughs and tries to pull my hair when I heft her onto the bassinet. Usually I don't change diapers, but today I don't like the thought of her carrying a load around. I hold my breath when I unpin the diaper. Then I clean up the mess, straining to hear over Suse's gurgling if Ma's making any sounds.

I give Suse a bottle of apple juice from the refrigerator and she crawls under the kitchen table with it and curls up next to a piece of bread crust and a dirty sock.

I sit on the floor in the parlor doorway so I can keep an eye on the two of them. Ma's snoring on the couch. Suse sucks on the bottle, her arm flung out and her hand opening and closing around the dirty sock.

When she was born I had a fit at Ma. I didn't want any more kids in this family, but if we had to have one, I wanted a boy to play with, not another no-good girl. I stare at her fat head and think, *Sister?* That ain't no sister of mine.

And then I think how our house is like a hotel, with Daddy's two sisters living with us and now Gramma too and everybody in and out and hollering all the time and Uncle Jack coming around with his eyes going all over you and nobody saying nothing about it, and Ma's heart going bad. And it was bad enough, but then she had to go and have a worthless baby on top of it.

I look up at the kitchen clock; it hums. I wonder how much longer till Gramma comes home. As soon as she pulls in the driveway I'm heading for the barn for the wire, then out to Sullivan's trash heap.

I look over at Ma again, but her stomach doesn't move, and I get scared. I'm ready to jump up and go shake her when she takes a breath.

Goddamn you, I think to her.

Then a car pulls in, but it's Aunt Bernesia and Flossie and they come in making a big to-do, Flossie carrying on about the man in the fruit store, wasn't that Junior Menoni and didn't he say he was going to marry her a long time ago, and Bernesia saying, No, Flossie, that wasn't Junior Menoni, Junior Menoni passed on, back when the village took the lift bridge out, and Yes, Flossie I suppose he did say he was going to marry you but that was a long time ago, why you got to think about that now?

And Floss saying, What's Junior Menoni doing in the fruit store? Do you think he's looking for me?

Shhh, I tell them real loud, pointing to the parlor door. Ma's sick on the couch with her heart.

Shhh, Bernesia tells Flossie, and Flossie starts scratching her arms that are full of sores, and crying, Why you always got to tell me to shut up? What's Junior Menoni want with me?

Why don't you go sit outside on the swing? Bernesia tells Flossie and Flossie goes to the sink and gets a big glass of water and makes gulping noises while she drinks it. Then she bangs out the screen door scratching her arms crying, Ma, Ma, to her mother who's been dead since long before I was born.

What's wrong with your mother? Aunt Bernesia says. Where's your grandmother?

Gramma's in town getting a prescription, I tell her. Ma got dizzy from her heart being in the sun.

Bernesia lays a wad of dollar bills down on the kitchen table, next to the sugar bowl and some quarts of half-rotten strawberries that's got little flies flying all around them. Then she marches into the parlor and stands there looking at Ma.

Are you feeling all right? she says. You want me to call the doctor?

Ma moves her hand over her face. All I want is some peace and quiet, she says. What's Flossie carrying on about now?

Oh that's nothing, Bernesia says. I sent her outside. She won't bother you.

Ma sighs a big sigh, and I know what she's thinking. I already been bothered, is what she's thinking.

Well, we sold all fifty quarts, Bernesia tells her. You can't beat fresh strawberries, she says. People will drive twenty miles from the city just to get one quart of homegrown berries. My brother was smart when he put those berries in.

Blah blah blah, she goes, about the berries and my father and her father and how hard the farmers have to work nowadays and nobody appreciates their labor, all anybody ever does anymore is complain. And what about those poor dairy farmers? she says. What about all the baloney they have to put up with?

The room's spinning, Ma says.

Then Annie and Mikey start hollering out front, getting louder, and we open the front door and there's Flossie trying to take the jar of money from them.

Give that back to them, Bernesia yells at her.

I'm bringing it in so nobody will steal it, Floss says.

Nobody's stealing it, Annie cries. We're right here watching the stand like Ma told us.

Flossie, Bernesia calls to her.

Then Suse starts crying under the kitchen table, and I go get her and bring her into the parlor, blatting full force.

Now see what you done? I tell Bernesia.

How dare you talk to me like that, Bernesia says.

Then Gramma's car pulls in and Annie and Mikey start screeching at her to make Flossie give them the money back, so Gramma yells at Flossie and Flossie throws the jar and the money goes all over the grass and she runs away crying.

I'm going to have a stroke, Ma says.

Sullivan's trash heap is loaded with junk: rusted-out buckets and coil springs and rubber cow teats from his milking machine and two big tin cans, big as bongo drums. I pull them out and shake the dirt and bugs from them.

The grass is high since the cows don't come out this far. Too lazy, I figure, which is fine with me.

What I got is a big sheet of tin bent in half like a tent. Wires go out in four corners to tin cans upside down on wood stakes. I take off the two smallest cans and put the big ones in their place, hook the wires back up. The station catches the sun, sends signals out. In the night it catches the moon. In a storm it'll catch lightning. And if that spaceship is sending out signals to find me, the signals will land on the tin so they'll know to come check out what's here.

I sit down in the field and watch the sun striking off the sheet of tin. I chew a blade of grass and feel the electricity moving through the air, going out in space, going somewhere.

I wonder what the people out there look like, what kind of clothes they wear, what they do all day, if they got school and cars and bicycles, but I can't remember anything. My real ma? I think. Who is she?

Mikey's the only one really knows about it. When I told him he said, Can I come with you? I told him I didn't know. I tried to tell Ma, but she don't know nothing.

Uncle Jack's just trying to be friendly, she says. What's so terrible about that? What's so terrible about our home?

This ain't my home, I tell her, looking to see if she'll let on what she knows. But she plays dumb.

How I figured it out was easy. I was out in the chicken coop one day after Daddy walloped me for no good reason and Ma stood there watching, crying for the hundredth time, How'd I end up with you? Where'd you come from?

All because Bernesia and Flossie had gone snooping through our house like they always do, looking for old photographs and pillowcases and knickknacks they said belonged to them from way back before Daddy got married and I called them nosy pea-brained old goats and told them to get out of our house and leave us alone.

This isn't your house, Flossie cried. Ma, Ma, get them out.

Crying to her ma, the dead one, not mine.

Then my ma starts crying: I don't have a house. This was never my house. I wish I was dead. Putting her hand to her heart crying, Oh, I don't know how much more I can take.

And Bernesia coming after me with a geography book she picked up from the end table, raising it high in the air to hit me with it, saying, What did you call me? What did you say, you little so-and-so?

And Daddy going Judas Priest God Almighty while he's taking off his belt coming at me.

Till I ran and ran and kicked them damn chickens out of the chicken coop and threw their no-good damn chicken eggs after them and then sat on top of the watering can smelling the heat and straw and chicken shit, thinking, God, what you done to me?

And then it came to me, the dream I had of a spaceship landing in our front yard, all lights and a sharp humming sound that scared me but made me feel good too. I remembered getting up to go to the window and see it. Right there in the chicken coop I realized that wasn't no dream because I remember going to the window awake and seeing it, that part wasn't in the dream. So it all fell together there, with the backs of my legs smarting from Daddy's belt and the chickens clucking and squawking because I'd kicked them out in the yard.

The more I thought about it, the more came back, and everything made sense—all them years of Daddy and Ma saying Where'd you come from, Flossie saying This house ain't yours. But I never could remember enough to get Annie and Mikey and

Suse in the picture. So I don't know if we come from the same place or not. Most likely not. Them telling me, You think you're the boss of everything. You think you can tell everybody what to do.

Why not? I figure. Me, Rex the King.

3.

Gramma's in the kitchen starting supper. She eyeballs me and scowls. I thought I told you to watch the baby, she says.

I *did* watch her, I say. I watched her till you came home.

I'd expect you'd be old enough by now to know how to act, she says, turning to stir the pan full of green peppers.

Is Ma okay? I ask her.

No thanks to any of you, she says.

Ma's laying down on her bed with the shades down and a glass of water and her prescription bottle next to the radio on the stand.

It's me, I tell her.

She squints her eyes open. What? she says.

Nothing, I tell her.

The room is still and quiet. Suse is asleep in the crib. All of a sudden I'm sleepy too. I get up on the bed with Ma, careful not to get too close or touch her, since she's nobody I know.

Stop rocking, she says. Did you find all the money? She's talking up to the ceiling with her eyes closed.

Yep, I tell her, though I ain't seen Annie and Mikey nor been out front where Flossie threw everything.

We should make Flossie go picking through the grass for it, I tell her.

She doesn't answer. I try not to jiggle the bed.

That Sears swimming pool is almost three feet deep, I tell her. I'm gonna swim every day. I'm gonna teach Mikey to swim, I say, trying to make her get the picture that we got to get that pool no matter what, heart spells or no.

Hmm, she says.

I wish we had that pool right now, I tell her. It's hotter than pig shit outside.

I feel her go stiff on the bed.

I don't know where you learned to talk like that, Ma says. Why do you have to be so bad all the time?

I don't know, I tell her. It's in my blood.

She makes a little snorting sound.

I get it from Daddy, I tell her. He swears all the time.

Daddy's a grown man.

Then he should know plenty damn better than me.

I roll off the bed quick, before she has time to hit me.

Hail Mary, she says. Hail Mary, I prayed for a daughter and this is what I got.

I hear Joe Edwards's truck pull alongside the road out front and Daddy slam the door and start crunching gravel down the driveway.

I run out to meet him, but Annie and Mikey already beat me, holding up the money jar while Joe Edwards drives away.

We picked eighty quarts, I holler to Daddy.

Flossie tried to take the jar from us, Annie cries. She threw our money all over the grass.

We can't even find it all, Mikey says.

Can't I come home in peace just once? Daddy says, swinging his lunch pail past us.

Ma's sick, I tell him. She had a heart spell. Gramma had to go get a prescription.

Judas Priest Almighty, he says.

4.

Ma comes out to eat supper with us, but then gets up from the table halfway through to go lay down on her bed again.

Indigestion, she says, rubbing up high on her stomach.

Aunt Bernesia and Daddy and Gramma look at each other.

Daddy shakes his head and swears. Bernesia takes Flossie outside to walk around the yard and look at the daisies and buttercups growing in the weeds near the roses, which is one of the things she does when she's afraid Floss is going to start up.

Gramma holds Suse on her knee and pushes a big red strawberry into her mouth.

Not a day goes by, Daddy says, without something going wrong.

I go get the Sears catalogue.

Look how they got these clips like clothespins to keep the liner on, I tell him, pointing to the swimming pool we're going to buy.

See *that* one, Mikey says, pointing to the biggest one. That's got a slide going into the water.

Someday I'm buying that pool, I say.

Me too, Mikey says.

I want a canopy bed, Annie says, trying to turn the pages to show Daddy.

That's for sissies, I tell her.

You're a tomboy anyway, Annie says. What do you know?

Get away from here, Daddy says. Take that damn Sears catalogue somewhere else and leave me alone.

Never mind the catalogue, Gramma says. The three of you can start doing the dishes.

That's all I got to hear. I leave the catalogue on Daddy's lap and make like I'm looking for something in the parlor. Instead I sneak out the front door.

Aunt Bernesia's got Flossie by the arm, steering her away from the poison ivy growing in the rose bushes while Uncle Jack stands there next to them trying to light his pipe.

Now what the blasted heck is he doing back here? I'm thinking.

There's plenty to eat if you didn't eat supper, Bernesia tells him.

Hell, I'm stuffed, he says. I already ate. What you think, I come around on purpose at suppertime looking for a handout?

You always come when it's time to eat, Flossie tells him.

Stop that, Flossie, Bernesia says. That's not true.

When he sees me his face lights up, but I do a quick turn and start running for the chicken coop.

Don't leave on my account, Jack says.

I scrounge through the straw, the chickens squawking and rustling and moving out of my way, till I find an empty feed sack. I shake it out to make sure it's got no holes, then I go looking for ammunition.

The crab apples are too small, so I head out to the big trees in back. I pull a few green apples off the branches, but they're small too. I start scrounging for rocks till I got a good load of rocks and apples in the bag.

Let that bastard come near me, I think.

When I get to my radio station I lay the sack down and go check the tin can connections. I put a can to my ear and close my eyes, listening to the hollow sound of outer space, listening for what's out there: meteors and asteroids and planets and spaceships a million miles away.

I go touch the big sheet of tin and feel the heat in it. Then I stretch my arms out and look up at the sky. I hold my arms out to feel the electric currents, trying to see if anybody's radioed in and tried to reach me.

The sun is a hard little ball hanging low over Sullivan's cow creek. The sky's got streaks of pink clouds running through it. I stretch my fingers far as they'll go, but don't feel much.

Then I start turning in a circle with my arms up to the sky and my eyes closed tight so I can concentrate.

I send my thoughts out harder than I ever done: *Come get me, I'm here, I'm here in Sullivan's field. Oh Great Mother, Oh Great Father, it's me, your son, Rex the King, shipwrecked in a cow lot, waiting for you every day to come find me and take me back home.*

I done my duty, I tell them. *I stayed with these farmers, I put up with it all. Come for me, come bring me home,* I tell them out loud.

My hands tingle. I can feel something out there. I open my eyes up at the sky, turning, watching, humming. A bird flies overhead in the pink sky and I think, Soon I will be up there too.

Oh Sheeba, let me take you home, Uncle Jack says, and I stop dead in my tracks.

What are you doing here? I say, and while I'm talking I'm thinking two things at the same time: where's that sack of rocks and now I have to move the whole station where he won't find it.

I didn't mean to scare you, he says.

You didn't scare me, I tell him, and I move over near the sheet of tin and look behind to see the feed sack where I left it on the ground. I stand there near the sack.

He moves closer and touches a tin can.

This is some getup, he says.

Don't touch that, I tell him.

My, my, he says.

He looks the station over, real interested. Is this where you play? he says. Is this why I can never find you?

I'll tell Daddy if you don't leave me alone, I tell him.

Why do you have to be so mean to me? he says. Did I ever hurt you?

I just like to be left alone, I tell him.

One of those solitary sorts, he says. Well there's nothing wrong with that. But you got to have a little fun in life too. You got to have people. No man is an island, he says. Didn't you ever hear that?

Big deal, I tell him.

He puts his hands in his pockets and looks around.

So just what the hell is all this crap?

I pick up the feed bag and start walking away.

Hey, there's no need for that, he says.

In a minute I hear him following me.

You better leave me alone, I tell him, and I start running.

Sheeba, you're breaking my heart, he says.

I stop and turn around. He's standing there in the cow field with the grass up to his knees, in his gray work pants and dirty white T-shirt, just like he's ready to bring his cows in.

I reach in the sack for a green apple and fling it right at him, but it misses.

What you go and do that for? he says.

I fling another, and then another. One gets him in the leg, and still he doesn't move, so I let them fly, rocks and apples together.

I deserve this, he says. You're right. Hit me, I deserve this.

I drop the bag and run into the woods.

Once I get a ways in I crouch behind a tree stump and listen. After a long time of hearing nothing I creep through the woods over near the edge where I can see the field. My station's standing, just like before. Then I see Uncle Jack way down, with his hands in his pockets, heading back toward the house.

I wait a long time after he's gone. Then I go out to inspect the station.

Everything looks all right. I think of putting the station in the woods so he won't find it, but I'm afraid it won't pick up any signals in there. But then I'm thinking maybe it's better in the woods. Don't they tell you not to stand under a tree in lightning? Maybe all them trees will draw the electricity in, pick up any little signal that's out there.

I go over to lift a tin can to my ear to listen when I see a daisy laying on top of the can. I look around and see he's put a daisy on top of each can. I rip them apart and throw the pieces into the weeds.

Then I drop down into the grass and sit there thinking. There just ain't no letup. A big hole opens in my stomach. If I had a tent I could run away and live in the woods. Who needs a tent, though, I figure. I can take Daddy's army blanket and run away—walk all night and sleep in the day so they won't find me—till I make it to the Adirondacks. Then go off up into the mountains and build a fort. Fish and pick berries and apples and things and nobody'll ever find me. They won't even miss me. Except when it's time to work: pick strawberries or change Suse's diaper.

I look at the radio station turning fuzzy gray in the dusk. I try to picture what my other home looks like. I try to picture who my real mother and father are and what it's like living with them.

Why'd you leave me here? I ask them. How could you forget that you left me here?

I look up at the sky turning gray, the white moon showing pale and empty up there, and the hole in my stomach just opens bigger.

Far off I hear a siren, and it reminds me of something. When the sound gets louder I stand up to listen where it's coming from, but I can't tell. It sounds like it's all around me. After a while I see flashing lights way off near the road, spinning off the treetops, and it hits me like a shot of lightning: The spaceship. They've finally come.

For a minute I can't even move. I keep my eyes on the turning lights and the eerie siren sound that I remember now from a long time ago.

You came, I say, and I start moving toward the road.

But then I think of Suse and Annie and Mikey, leaving them, never seeing them again, and it feels so bad I can't stand it. And Gramma and Daddy and Ma.

Ma, I think, I'll be so sad to leave you, mean as you are.

I slow down, keeping my eyes on the lights, afraid of going someplace I can't even remember. I'm from royalty, I remind myself. I'm above all this. But I been with these people since I can remember.

Then I get really scared. What if they hear my thoughts and take off again without me?

Ma, I call out, meaning my real ma, the one I don't know. Wait for me.

I start running fast as I can for the red lights, praying I'm not too late.

Ma, I cry, don't leave without me.

Dan Chaon

Fraternity

Cal used to be president of their fraternity. But then he was in a car wreck. Cal and Hap and a group of boys from the fraternity house had been out to the bars, and they were on their way home. Afterward Hap often pictured Cal dipping his hand into a cooler of beer, letting the water run off the can, popping the tab. Cal's head was tilted back, Hap could see him in the rearview mirror, and it was when he looked back to the road that he saw the parked truck. Hap remembered, or thought he remembered, someone screaming, "Mom!"

John wasn't hurt that bad. He was in the hospital for a few weeks, but then he didn't come back to school. He was still at home, working in his father's auto parts store. He didn't drink anymore, he didn't go out. Talking to him, Hap remarked to people, you'd think he was middle-aged.

Alexander wasn't injured at all, but he graduated early, finished up his major, and got out of school and their fraternity as quietly as possible, packing up like a swindler without even saying goodbye.

It was Cal who got the worst part of it. He'd ducked down at the last minute and covered his head, but it was his side of the car that was crushed. They had to cut him out of the wreckage, where he was pinned between the car door and the seat.

Cal was in a coma for nearly a month, and all that time they were expecting him to die. He woke up one morning, but he wasn't the same person. There was brain damage and he had to go to a rehabilitation clinic.

Hap had been driving the car. He wasn't drunk, and in fact he took a breathalizer at the site of the accident. All he could remember were the faces peering out of the slow-moving cars, and the whirlpool of red and blue lights from the police cars. He passed the test. He'd had a beer or two, of course, but he was definitely within the legal limit. It was an accident. And it wouldn't happen again: he didn't drive anymore.

Not that anyone ever blamed him. Still, he sometimes noticed how their eyes darkened sidelong when he reached for another beer. He noticed how their faces suddenly tightened when he was in a good mood and got to laughing. It was as if, he thought, he'd turned for a second into something unclean.

Hap tried to put everything back in order. They held an emergency meeting when they found out Cal wouldn't be returning, and since Hap was vice president at the time, they told him the presidency was his if he felt up to it. And so he stood there, with bandages on his head and hand, talking in nervous circles, saying how life had to go on, how Cal would have wanted it that way.

A few months after the accident Hap began to pass out in unusual places. The first time it happened was for real: he woke in the hallway, with no idea how he got there. Magic Marker was scribbled across his face and belly, as if he'd been trying to write himself a message.

After that first time it became an act. On mornings after parties, his fraternity brothers began to find him in the foyer, curled up among the discarded advertisements and catalogues, or in the shower, fully dressed, with the water running, or outside under a tree, his hands caked with dirt as if he'd been digging. At first they thought it was funny. They joked that Hap ought to have bells tied to his heels before he was allowed to drink a beer. Some of the incidents became amusing anecdotes.

He planned things in advance, considering which place might be most surprising, most ridiculous. One night he'd squeezed onto a shelf on the trophy case, twisted around the gold statuettes of basketball players and wrestlers and the engraved plaques. Even in that precarious position they couldn't tell he was faking. He opened his eyes with a start, and sat straight up. One of the trophies fell clattering onto the living-room floor.

Often he'd wait a long time before anyone found him. He'd get frustrated, sometimes, and decide he was just going to forget it and go on up to bed. But then he'd hear voices and his heart would pound and his mind would begin to whir like a fan. He could feel the shapes of them as they moved closer, slow, hovering, and he'd open his eyes with a start to find them leaning over him like surgeons. Once this pre-med named Belcaster reached down and took his pulse. The pressure of his finger had run through Hap like an electric shock. He jerked straight up, and everyone had laughed, circled around him, shaking their heads.

But the novelty began to wear off. "Oh brother," he heard Charlie Balbo say one morning. "Look who's passed out again." Balbo pulled on Hap's arm. He was in ROTC and always woke up early to do exercises. Hap could hear Balbo sighing through his nose. "Rise and shine, buddy," Balbo said, and when Hap fluttered his eyelids and moaned, none of them were smiling. Hap figured they were all thinking about the accident.

Cal's mother called. Cal was back home, she told Hap, and she hoped some of his fraternity brothers would come for a visit. It had been six months since the accident.

Hap wondered how she'd gotten his number. He hadn't met her, really, just shook hands with her once during parents' weekend when Cal pointed them at each other and said, "Mom this is Hap he's one of my best pals," or something like that, quick and stilted; that was the way he talked. Later, after Cal had gone to the clinic, Hap sent a get-well card to his home. He'd never visited the hospital, though he told people he had: "Cal's doing real good," he said. He'd called the hospital a number of times, and that's what they told him. "Under the circumstances," they said, "he's doing well."

As the visit approached, Hap would feel a wave of panic pass over him, and he was desperate to call Cal's mother and make some excuse. But what? He couldn't think of any excuse that wouldn't provoke disbelief. He would think of it from time to time, when he wasn't expecting to. That Saturday, a week before he was to go, it was like a rushing at his back.

There was a party that night, and Hap had been downstairs long before anyone else, organizing guys to clear the furniture and push it against the wall, directing the football players to lift kegs of beer into ice-filled trash cans, hurrying to get the tap or the strobe light. There were certain things Hap did which he felt no one else could do quite so well. He was the one who liked to put up decorations and make up themes for parties—putting red lights in the windows and taping up orange and yellow poster board in the shape of flames, so the house looked afire; lining the dance floor with old mattresses and balloons; setting up elaborate spreads of dips and vegetables and so on. He played the music, building up to the best dance songs, urging the crowd into a kind of frenzy. He'd stand up on the window ledge and look out over their heads, calling out chants which the crowd would repeat. It was like a fiefdom, for one night at least.

Cal used to shake his head. "Geez," he used to say. "Take a Valium." Hap remembered one night, they'd gone to this place, Elbow's Room, where they didn't card. It was a dim, hazy bar, with country music on the jukebox, and they went there before a party. Hap was anxious to get back, he didn't want to miss anything. But Cal was in no hurry. Hap was telling him that he was going to miss the fraternity when they graduated, that it was one of his main reasons for staying in school, and Cal stared at him. His face was lit by the fireplace glow of neon, made spooky and dark by it. Hap was hoping he'd say, "Me, too," or even, "Yeah, when we go that place is dead." But all he said was, "Christ, I can't wait to get out. You're crazy, Hap." He shrugged, and Hap felt something clench inside him; it was like Cal was abandoning him.

That was one of the things that stuck in his mind that night. The dancing had died down early, and Hap was making his way upstairs to his room. There were four girls on their way to the ladies' room when they saw Hap rubber-legging up the steps. He nearly fell over them, and they caught him, laughing. It was what he did, sometimes, he wasn't sure why. He liked to act more drunk than he was. The girls wrapped their arms around his shoulders and guided him toward his room—someone in the hall directed them. Hap kept his eyes closed, and shortly he felt one of the girls sliding her hand in his back pocket to get his keys. "I can't believe I'm doing this," she said breathlessly, and another whispered, "Is he out?" He wasn't, of course. But when their grip loosened he slumped to the floor, and another girl said, "I guess he's out." They carried him in and put him on the bed, but he didn't sleep. The more he lay there, the more awake he became, listening to the music pulsing through the floor. A couple stood outside his door, thinking they had privacy, and murmured urgently—he couldn't tell if they were arguing or making out. When he was sure the party was over, nearly five in the morning, he went downstairs. He planned to pass out again, this time sprawled on the pool table.

It was a gray morning: It could have been dawn, or dusk again. When he passed the window in the stairwell a heavy bird lifted from the sill and blurred into the fog. It startled him, and he felt suddenly that there was someone watching him. He wondered if the house was all closed up. Often after a party he found the front door hadn't been bolted or one of the fire exits was slightly ajar, or a window on the first floor was open, crepe paper streamers trailing off into the breeze. Sometimes it was hard to feel safe.

Everything seemed to pause, waiting. He peered in on each floor. All the doors were closed, lined up as still as motel rooms. Long shadows stretched in the dim hallways. He felt as if the place had been abandoned.

When he went downstairs the living room seemed thick with haze. No one had cleaned up after the party. The furniture was all cleared out still, and there were cups cluttered on every surface. From across the room he could hear the wind blowing through an open window. He squinted in the pale half-light. For a moment he was certain he saw the shape of someone standing there, a figure by the window, with the curtains fluttering around him.

"Hello," he called, and his voice ran hollowly in the empty room. "Hello? Is someone there?"

And then he turned and ran up the stairs to his room. He bolted the door and put on the radio. He wanted to wake someone up, just to prove he wasn't alone in the house. He kept turning the stereo louder, until at last Doug Cohn in the next room began knocking heavily on the wall between them. Hap turned off the stereo and sat there in the bed until it was light enough to sleep.

There were times, lots of times, when it seemed like everything was back to normal. Hap would go downstairs in the late afternoon to find a group of guys standing around the pool table, tapping balls into the pockets with the palms of their hands, and the talk was all easy jokes and gossip. Mornings, he'd walk into the bathroom, where a line of people from his floor were all at sinks, shaving, and move in beside them without a hitch. Even that next day, when he woke, there was a moment when he imagined himself shrugging to Doug Cohn, he heard himself chuckling, "Hey, thought I saw a ghost last night, Doug. Scared myself shitless."

But later, when he saw Doug Cohn on his way out the front door with his bookbag, it seemed to him that the things he planned to say were frivolous and artificial. He drew back, acting as if he hadn't noticed Doug, and he thought it was probably best not to mention anything at all. After that, the day didn't seem like it would cruise along so easily. There was always some little snag to send him spinning.

The late afternoons were the worst, after everyone had gone off to the library or their girlfriends' rooms. He flipped through channels in the television room, one after the other so the voices and music and yelps of white noise melted together in a collage, an abstract code he could almost recognize. Or he'd end up back in his room, listening for someone to come down the hall, or making lists: party ideas; things he planned to do tomorrow; friends, in ascending order of closeness. He'd number things from one through ten. It was calming to mark things down.

Sometimes he thought he would just give in, that he would let himself spend the whole day brooding about Cal, but he found he couldn't. He tried to remember something specific about Cal, some significant conversation they had, the special things they used to do together. But his mind would go blank. Or rather, he'd remember how once someone spray-painted ELIMINATE GREEKS on the outside of their house. They'd circled the *A* in ELIMINATE, and there was a picture of Cal in the campus newspaper, standing in front of the big red *A* in his Greek letter sweatshirt and grinning. He recalled the time he and Cal came up with a way to combine philanthropy and partying. They planned to get a bunch of organ donor cards from the Department of Motor Vehicles and use them as admission tickets to a huge bash. They were going to have T-shirts that said: Lose Your Liver—donate an organ and have a beer!

It seemed to Hap that all these memories were grotesque, like the old photos he'd found once in his basement at home, pictures half-eaten by silverfish. He wondered if something was wrong with him. He believed that if things were the other way around, Cal would remember him better—that Cal would have fond stories of the night they pledged or the time they were both elected officers of the fraternity; some recollection that would make everyone laugh.

He didn't know what the others were thinking. At the chapter meeting on Monday night, he announced as if effortlessly that "a group of brothers will be visiting Cal Fuller this Sunday," and then went on with the other items on the agenda. When he scanned their faces he couldn't read anything. Even the other three guys who planned to go to Cal's house didn't seem to respond. Eric sat staring at the textbook he'd opened on the table in front of him; Charlie Balbo rocked back in his chair, balancing on two legs; Russ, Cal's freshman year roommate, traced his index finger across his palm.

He didn't know what he expected. But he didn't like it when Balbo patted him on the back, and said, "I guess you made it to bed Saturday night, for once." He didn't like his own reply: "Yeah, your girlfriend showed me the way." He gave a short laugh, and the sound of it made his face feel white and blank.

There was no party that Saturday and the house was unnaturally still. Yet he felt too edgy to go out. In the distance, up and down the fraternity quad, people were calling and laughing, on their way to other parties. Any other Saturday night, Hap would have been out there with them, on his way somewhere to unwind. He'd melt into the heat and flex of crowded rooms, nodding at acquaintances, easing into casual conversations with girls, pressing into the shadows, and just letting the smoke and alcohol work through him. There might even be a moment, late at night, when everything seemed perfect—like the time he and Cal had sung "Papa's Got a Brand New Bag" on their way home, very slowly, and there had been a few bars of clear harmony, echoing against the walls; or the time an enormous raccoon had regarded him from a rain-soaked lawn, standing on its haunches, holding an apple. Heavy clouds of steam were rising from manholes, drifting low to the ground, all the way down the sidewalk.

Hap could see his reflection in the window, staring in at him. The ivy was thick across his window so he couldn't see who was laughing outside. All he could see were twisting vines, the shadows of leaves showing through his reflection like an X-ray of something, he wasn't sure what. This was what it was like for

Cal, he thought—floating as people passed below you, as if you'd levitated out of your own body.

When Russ knocked on the door, Hap was staring out the window and feeling as if he might jump out of his skin. He hoped there wasn't an edge of desperation in his voice when he said, "Come on in, buddy. Have a beer with me."

"I was just stopping by to let you know when we were going to leave in the morning," Russ said. He glanced around as if he were entering a room full of strangers. When Hap handed him a beer, he sat there considering it. For a moment, they sat not saying anything, both moving their heads vaguely to the music that Hap had playing, constantly.

"So anyway," Hap said at last. "It'll be good to see Cal again, huh?"

Russ shrugged. "I guess," he said. He moved his mouth as if to say more, but then took a quick sip of beer instead. He swallowed. "I mean, you know," he said.

"Well, anyway, they say he's doing pretty well," Hap said. "It'll be cool. We'll just sit around, shoot the breeze for a while. No big deal."

They nodded at one another. Russ had never been easy to squeeze conversation out of; some people used to say that if he hadn't been roommates with Cal freshman year, he'd have stayed in the dorms, studying his Saturday nights away.

Yet it seemed that it used to be easier to talk, even to Russ. Hap used to believe he could connect with most any of them, that they would all get together in twenty years and exchange gossip and old stories. He used to imagine that his fraternity brothers would think of him from time to time for the rest of their lives. Some little thing—the back of a head or a face glimpsed as an elevator closed—would startle them, and they'd think suddenly: Hap! What's he up to these days?

Russ lifted the beer to his lips; when he set it down, a droplet of moisture trickled slowly down the side of the can. Russ seemed to be waiting for him to say something. But all he could think of was small talk, trivia: sororities, classes, sports teams. It made him cringe. Outside, the wind came up. Hap could hear the muffled buzz of a motorcycle speeding down a faraway street, someone showing off.

"Anyway," Hap said. "I don't think it'll be so bad tomorrow."

They nodded at one another. "Yeah," Russ said at last. "It should be all right. I mean, I'm sure you'll do fine."

Hap said, "Hey, I'll be sober, at least."

Russ looked down and shook his head. "Yeah," he said softly.

"No big deal," Hap told him. "It won't be any big deal."

Cal's home was in a new development called Stone Lake. It was at the far edge of the suburbs, and some of the streets weren't marked clearly on Russ's map. The trees hadn't grown much yet, they weren't much taller than Hap, so the rows of houses stood bright and unshaded against the clear sky.

The boys were all still as they circled through Stone Lake, so quiet that Hap could hear Eric in the back seat, breathing through his nose. Every time they passed a street sign, Russ slowed and gazed at it uneasily. At last, he pulled into a driveway. "This is the place," he said. Hap saw him cast a quick look at Charlie Balbo. None of them seemed to look at him, though if they had he would have simply smiled firmly.

Cal's mother came to the door, but she didn't open it right away. She peeked through the curtains, and they waved at her uncertainly. Hap could hear the bamboo wind chimes that hung from the porch, the deep hollow tones as they rustled in the breeze. Then he heard the lock being turned, and she stared at them through the half-open door.

"Hi, boys," she said.

"Hi," they echoed. They stood for a moment on the threshold, and she took Russ's hand. He'd stayed over one Thanksgiving, and she spoke lightly: "Good to see you again, Russ," she said. Then she turned expectantly to the rest of them. Eric and Charlie introduced themselves quickly, and she shook their hands,too. "Welcome, Charlie, Eric," she said. Then she smiled at Hap.

"I'm Hap," he said. "We talked on the phone."

"Of course," she said. "I believe I met you once at a reception." She had dark eyes. They seemed wet and glittering as their hands met. Hap thought that maybe she was wishing the same thing on him, wishing him crippled or dead, though she held his hand for a long moment, tightly. She was always angry with Cal, Hap remembered, she always complained that he spent too much time socializing and not enough studying. Hap wondered if she thought it was he who led Cal astray. He wished he could tell her that everything, everything had always been Cal's idea. "You're very lucky," she said softly, and dropped his hand.

She ushered them past several framed photographs of Cal—as a baby; as a long-haired high-school boy; another that Hap recognized as the one Cal had taken for the fraternity composite when he was elected president. They walked into a living room, and it was then that they saw him. He was sitting cross-legged on the floor, watching an old black-and-white movie on television. He didn't move. He had his face turned away from them, and the mother seemed not to notice him.

"Can I get you anything to drink?" she asked, and it sent a shiver through Hap as if it were an accusation. "Coke? Milk? Water?"

As she went toward the kitchen, Cal looked up, and Hap lifted his hand hesitantly, as if to wave, or to shield his face. But Cal let his eyes drift shyly over them, then turned back to the TV. He didn't recognize them, Hap realized. Their stares made him shift bashfully. He leaned toward the television as if to be swallowed up by it and vanish. None of them looked at one another, or spoke. Hap just watched the screen, thinking that all of them were sharing the same images, at least.

The curtains had been drawn, so the TV was brighter. The sleepy dimness of the room reminded Hap of winter, of childhood sicknesses. Everything was muted. In the distance, beyond the tinny, old-movie voices, he could hear ice cubes being cracked into glasses.

Mrs. Fuller came in, carrying their drinks on a tray. Cal continued to watch the television until she said, "Cal, honey," very firmly. Then he looked up at her impatiently. Hap tried not to glance at him. He held tightly to his glass, staring down into it.

"Do you see your friends?" Mrs. Fuller said. "Look who's come to visit you!"

"Hi," Cal sighed, and Hap's hands began to throb. He wasn't the same person, Hap thought. He tried to put on a polite smile, but he knew it looked false. All he could think was that Cal must be in that body somewhere, but sleeping, or maybe only vaguely aware, like someone drugged; he imagined the real Cal was submerged somehow, curled up like a fist, struggling to break out.

"How's it going, Cal?" he said, and Cal gazed up at him. Russ and Eric and Charlie were lined up on the long sofa that faced the television, and Hap was a little apart from them, in a high-backed easy chair, his hands clasped tightly in front of him. Everyone was watching him. "How's it going?" he said again, but Cal didn't answer. He glanced back at the movie.

"Cal," Mrs. Fuller said, in her calm, stern voice. She got up and shut off the TV, and Cal's head turned as she went, noting each movement wistfully. "Look, Cal," she said softly. "Who are those boys?"

He hung his head. "My friends," he whispered.

She was close to him, avid, bright-eyed. She lifted her finger suddenly and pointed at Hap. His heart leapt. "Who's that boy, Cal? Who is that?"

Hap caught his breath, stiffening, but Cal was silent. The quiet stretched out like a long shadow, and Hap felt that all of them were waiting for him to do something. He stood up. For a moment, he just wavered there, awkwardly, as if he'd been asked to give a speech, but at last he began to move forward a bit, smiling at Cal, nodding encouragingly. "Who am I, Cal?" he whispered, so soft he could barely hear himself, and Cal closed his eyes. He slumped down, and for a moment Hap thought he'd fainted. But then his eyes snapped back open. "I don't know," he said.

The room seemed to darken. Hap kept inching forward, holding out his hand, though he could see that Cal didn't quite trust him; he drew back a little, the way a child would when a stranger's friendliness seemed false. "Hey," Hap said. "It's *me,* Cal." He raised his voice. "It's *me.* You know—Hap." Cal sat there on the rug in front of the television, his legs tucked carefully under him, and Hap just hovered there, looking down on him. He thought that maybe he ought to crouch down on the floor, too, so that Cal could see him face to face, but before he could, Cal stood up and walked over to his mother. He sat down next to her, leaving Hap alone in the middle of the room, facing all of them.

Mrs. Fuller put her arms around Cal, and he leaned his head against her shoulder. "When he came out of the coma," she said—Hap stood there helplessly, as if they'd surrounded him—"he didn't even know who *I* was." She smiled ruefully. "He was like a baby again: couldn't dress himself, feed himself, anything. But he's come a long way." She couldn't look up. They all watched her, hypnotized, as she spoke in a slow, sweet voice, as if to Cal. She told them how happy she'd been when he'd drawn a circle on a piece of paper, when he played a game of Chutes and Ladders with a nurse. "Who knows what he remembers?" she whispered, her mouth close to Cal's ear. "He'll look at those pictures from your fraternity for hours. He's just fascinated. And sometimes he'll say something and he'll sound almost like himself."

She sighed. "But you can't think of it that way," she said. "He's a new person now. And we have to love him in a different way than we used to. Not any less," she said. "Just different." She laid her hand on Cal's cheek, and he nuzzled against her. There was a long silence, and at last, the spell broken, Hap edged back to his chair. That was it, he thought. Cal was gone. He imagined a bright flash burning everything clean, leaving only a blurred whiteness, a hiss of static. He saw it so clearly that for a minute he felt as if the chair were tilting underneath him. He put his hands on the arms, tightly.

"Of course, he'll always need to be taken care of," Mrs. Fuller said at last. "Like a little boy." Then she was quiet again, stroking Cal's hair, watching the movement of her hand as if mesmerized.

"You see how his forehead is scarred," she murmured finally. A kind of thrum went over Hap's skin as she brushed Cal's bangs back to reveal rows of reddish, rounded strips. "It's hard to believe, isn't it? That's the pattern of the car seat. And he was pushed forward with so much force that the imprint is still there." She was moving her hand slowly through his hair, as if thinking of something far off, but her eyes were fixed on Hap. He couldn't meet her gaze; he could only look at Cal, who was enjoying the touch of his mother's fingers over his brow. He had his head tilted back, his expression relaxed, staring up as if stargazing. And for a moment, Hap felt as if he himself was up there in the distance, a meteor shrinking into the stratosphere, layers sloughing off him in fiery husks until he was just a tiny speck, plunging into the dark. He and Cal stared up toward some distant point, and for a moment he felt as if he were about to remember something important, something he'd forgotten. But then it was gone.

No more than a few words passed between them as they drove home. They each took a corner of the car, each tilted in different directions like compass points. Russ held the steering wheel in both hands, staring out at the signs, the road. Eric turned his face away from Hap, resting his head against the window, pretending to be asleep.

It almost seemed as if it were late at night, that the world was calm and dark. But it was still daylight, and when Hap closed his eyes, orange flashes beat irregularly against his closed eyelids: the sun, flickering through the trees.

On the very edge of sleep, Hap could feel the shape of a dream. It was a party, and Hap had just joined the fraternity. He could see someone moving toward the dancing crowd, clapping his hands, shouting. Everything began to stop: the music faded, the lights came up. One after another, the dancing couples separated, began to clap in rhythm, and the men from the fraternity emerged out of the dark. Then he felt himself lifted. He was up above their heads, carried on a rippling of dozens of hands. Their chanting echoed beneath him as they poured out into the open air, under the night sky. He was floating, and when he looked down he saw a boy waving at him, at the end of a long tunnel of people. Cal! he thought.

He started up with a laugh.

George Cruys

Cadet Barnes Learns the System

The Stratton Military School for Boys is a quadrangle surrounded by low buildings, surrounded by a stone wall, surrounded by the mountains of north central Pennsylvania. The school is on a hillside above the white clapboard houses of the nearby town. It is a steep slope, the kind where kids might go sledding in winter. But when the school was built the hill was scraped flat where the barracks would be and they bulldozed the quad so the cadets could march.

There are exactly four hundred and eighty cadets at the Stratton School: five companies of two platoons each, each platoon made of four squads of twelve boys. The first two companies form the junior school—kids from sixth through eighth grade. The remaining three companies are the high school. You get into the high school by joining in the sixth grade and working your way up, as I did, or by entering at ninth grade and learning fast. Jim Barnes, who was in ninth grade like me, was new at the Stratton School. But he was not learning fast.

Through the open doorway of our barracks we watched the rain fall, cold puddles collecting in the low places of the macadam. We could hear the rain running down the gutters of the building. And we could hear something else: deep booming with a concussion, like artillery fire.

We were pretty small for soldiers, lined up against the wall of the corridor in over-long raincoats like real people cut off at the knees. They had us at attention in the "brace" position, with the back of our necks flat against the cinder blocks and chins pushed down into wrinkles as far as they would go. You were supposed to have a wrinkle for every year of age, and the experienced kids, like me, had even more than that.

All of us stared straight forward; all of us pressed hard to hold the wrinkles. We stood as rigidly as possible because Lieutenant DiPosti was shouting at us from the opposite side of the narrow corridor, and because the wall behind us was shaking from what they were doing to Barnes.

"Boom!" We could hear it and we could feel it, too, just like artillery. "Boom. Boom."

They were explaining to Barnes the importance of folding the loose end of the raincoat belt precisely at a forty-five degree angle, and the exact tuck required to keep it from dangling. They were explaining with their hands gripping fistfuls of his uniform. They were explaining by banging his back against the cinder-block wall.

Barnes was a fuck-up. He had gotten things explained to him before. They had explained to him about being late for formation. They had explained about walking around with your hands in your pockets. They had explained about not loosening the uniform tie during study hall.

Barnes didn't like the Stratton School. He wrote home to his mother and told her about the explanations. He told her he wanted to go home. The officers knew about this because Barnes wrote during the required letter-writing period on Sunday nights. They knew because they collected the letters at the end of the period and because, in Barnes's case, they opened the envelope and read what he had written. We knew because they lined us up the next morning and read it to us: slowly, and with feeling.

I watched Barnes that morning. He didn't make any faces. He just stood there, even when they got to the "please kiss Gramma and Grampa" part. Sickening. We got a good laugh out of that. We started calling him Gramma Barnes. That night, after study hall, Tom Oxford—my roommate, we call him the Ox—swiped the picture of Barnes's mother from the pocket of his desk blotter

and put it in the urinal. We all took turns pissing on it. By the
time Barnes got to it, the photo was pretty limp. He picked it up
with his bare fingers and washed it in the sink. Disgusting. He
dried it out between a couple of paper towels and put it back in
his wallet. He didn't say anything, he just went to his room and
got in bed. We all looked in on him before lights out, just to say
"nightie night" to his mom. We could see him lying there,
red-faced against the sheets. I was starting to think he had no
self-respect at all, that he was just gonna sit there and take it. But
in the morning, when the lights came back on, he was gone.

Barnes was too much of a fuck-up to be gone for very long.
The Stratton School is backed against the wall of mountains that
cut the northern half of the state off from the south. The
Susquehanna River slices through that wall, and all the roads and
train tracks follow it. That's how they knew where to look for
Barnes and why, less than a day later, they were able to bring
him back.

They didn't like Barnes before he ran away. The night after
he got caught, they took him up to the library and gave him a
general order. A general order is like a court martial. They strip
your rank (Barnes didn't have any), cut off your weekend
passes, give you extra duty, call you a bunch of names, and write
nasty things in your record. It's all very official. After the general
order they turned out the lights in the library and the adult
officers left. In the interest of athletic competition, a few of the
upperclassmen took Barnes to the gym for a workout.

The day after the general order I was in my room, rolling my
laundry, and I saw Barnes limp past the doorway.

What a fuck-up, I thought. When you're on general order,
you're also on room confinement. You don't step out of your
room even to pee without a signed order from an officer. But
there was Barnes, sneaking down the hallway, thinking he
wouldn't get caught. And my first reaction, of course, was that I
should report him myself. They could be testing me. They could
have told him to sneak around out there.

So I was rolling my laundry, minding my own business. It's

not that hard to figure out the system at the school. You've got
the top of your dresser, there's a hairbrush there with no pieces
of hair left in it. That's on the right, an inch and a half from the
dresser edge. Next to that is your comb, clean. Then comes your
plastic soap dish, with the soap dried out by toilet paper after
every use. Then you've got your toothpaste, with the tube rolled
tight, and last is your toothbrush, bristles up. None of this is hard
to do.

In the top drawer of your dresser are your socks, paired and
balled. They're all regulation black, so it's not too tough to make
a match. To the left of them is your underwear, rolled into tight
little sausages. In the second drawer you've got your fatigue
shirts and sports uniform. In the third drawer, more clothes, also
rolled. Each drawer is left open for inspection a bit farther than
the one above, like steps. Then you've got your closet—standing
metal with no door—and your pressed uniforms arranged by
length. The shoes are lined up at the foot of the bed, spit-shined
toes pointed outward.

That's the way they want it. Everything in its place. And the
place for Barnes right then was not to be tiptoeing toward the
head without a pass. I looked in the hallway to see if anyone was
watching. All I saw were empty doorways and Barnes, looking
back at me, scared. I was ready to scream bloody murder, but
then I thought, This guy's a runner. I didn't want to be paired up
with him, even to turn him in. I stabbed my arm in the direction
of his room, looking as furious as I could. I figured that would
cover me if it *was* a test. He looked at me a long minute to see if
I was going to do anything else. Then he went on.

What an asshole, I thought to myself.

A couple of minutes later Barnes came back.

"Thanks," he whispered as he went by my door.

"Get fucked," I told him. We don't like runners. A little pee
gets on his mother's picture so he runs away. What's a guy like
that gonna do when the bullets start flying? The marines at
Tarawa waded seven hundred yards through shoulder-deep
water under constant machine-gun fire. You don't want a runner

covering your flank when that happens.

The next time I even talked to Barnes was a few weeks later during King of the Hill. Every other Friday, C Company meets down at the football field for aggressiveness training. We play games. The field is cut into the mountain slope on one side, leaving an embankment about twenty feet high. Lieutenant DiPosti explained the rules.

"You fucks in First Platoon are at the top of the bank. You fucks in Second Platoon are at the bottom of the bank. You get half an hour. Whichever platoon owns the bank at the end of half an hour gets Saturday off."

I'm in Second Platoon. We all run up the bank, slipping in the dirt and clawing for the top. The first guys up start duking it out with First Platoon. I'm smaller than the upperclassmen, but I can figure this out. The object is to do as much damage as possible without getting damaged yourself. At the top of the bank I grab somebody's leg. He kicks me in the chest. I twist the foot and he goes down, falling backwards over the bank. I have just enough time to stand up when somebody grabs my shirt from behind and sends me after him.

The next ten minutes go like that. I get up, run up the hill, twist a foot or two, and get tossed down myself. I'm too small to just take a swing at somebody. I have to trip them up.

DiPosti is watching the action from below. You have to keep moving. Somebody kicks me in the back. I crawl forward, lunge at another foot, and get kicked in the mouth. I let go and reach up. Not too bad. A little blood is good for you here. DiPosti looks for that kind of thing. I go after another leg, near the edge of the crowd. I grab on and twist, but nothing happens. I look up and see Barnes looking down at me. He's calm—like there aren't a hundred guys fighting around him—and he says, "You're bleeding."

"You're goin' down," I tell him, twisting the foot.

"Come off it," he says, shaking me loose. "We're in the same platoon!"

Barnes is pretty big for a ninth grader and he looms over me while I grab for his ankle again. For a split second he's got a great chance to put a foot in my ribs, but he misses it. I twist the ankle, throw a shoulder behind his knees, and he goes face forward down the bank. I can feel DiPosti watching. I don't care if he is in my platoon, Barnes is on general order. He's worth extra points.

I took it easy on Barnes compared to most of them. That's partly because he was bigger than me, and partly because I knew the system and I didn't do anything that wasn't going to get me something in return. Beating up Barnes in private just didn't do me any good, but there were a lot of people who seemed to find it very worthwhile.

When you're on general order you try to avoid being alone with a group of cadets. Suddenly the system becomes your friend. They can't come in your room after dark because it's a curfew violation. They can't break formation to get you, so you're okay there. If two or more adult officers are present, somebody's going to have an attack of conscience. In class you're okay, in meals you're okay, in chapel you're okay. You've got to watch any time when the rules get suspended. Gym, the locker room, to and from class, nighttime before lights out, mornings in the shower. That's when they got Barnes.

You don't break any bones, you don't leave any unexplained cuts or bruises. A black eye, well, you could explain that. He fell. He bumped into my elbow. It was the same with scratches. You could say he was shaving. Playing football. Some of the things you did didn't leave any marks. Hold his head under water in the toilet. Or pushups—down for fifty, down for a hundred, down for a hundred and fifty thousand.

We had regular activities at the school, but always with a twist. We buried a time capsule like other classes do, but ours was a green ammunition can. The losing side at soccer did twenty laps with rifles held over their heads. If the football team got beat, we got extra duty on Saturday to encourage school spirit. "Health" class, for some reason, included military training. We learned the four food groups and the proper method for throwing hand grenades in the same period.

Winter activities were no different. We threw snowballs by platoons: two squads up the middle, one squad trying the right flank, one held in reserve. During the first big snow of December, First Platoon was defending the slope in front of the library. They had a low wall for a snow fort. I was in the flanking squad of Second Platoon. People were throwing snowballs like they meant it. You got hit and you went down, hard. I saw a guy get it in the open eye, the snow packed into the socket. He zigzagged out of the action. Sharpshooters climbed trees. Logistics groups handed up snowballs to them. Firepower is key to any military engagement. We scooped up snow and threw as quickly as we could. The air was full of flying snowballs.

Our attack on the flank just fell apart and I was trying to get out of there with my skin when three of our guys tackled Barnes and threw him over the wall to the enemy. There was a lot of eager yelling on the other side, and then everything just stopped. The whole slope got quiet and both platoons stood around to see what would happen to Barnes.

This is the only place I've ever been where the snowball fights have executions. They tied Barnes's hands, lined him up against the library wall, and let him have it from a row of eight upperclassmen. It was all very organized. DiPosti went across to call out the positions: "Ready, aim . . ." They all aimed for his face. Barnes lasted three volleys before he started crying. He sank to his knees in the snow. The wall behind him was freckled with white impacts. A couple of the guys walked up and kicked snow on him.

"Fuckin' baby," somebody said.

I don't know. An execution is one thing. But I guess they didn't have to kick snow on him. Standing around after everybody left I was thinking, They didn't tie your feet, asshole. I mean if he's the kind of guy that runs, why didn't he just run? Sure, he's gonna get caught, but you got eight snowballs coming at your eyelids, what are they gonna do to you that's worse than that? I couldn't figure it out. I thought, Well, maybe he's just stupid. And then I realized I'd waited around too long because Barnes looked up at me standing there and said, "Untie me, will you?"

A couple of days after the snowball fight it was the end of fall quarter. I knew already from DiPosti that I got a promotion. Acting sergeant: two dark blue stripes on the sleeve, four inches down from the shoulder. I went down to the bulletin board at the dining room to check out my grades. Barnes was down there looking up at the roster. I stood back and let him move out of the way.

"How'd you do?" he asked me from the side of the board.

I just looked at him. He still had a black eye from the snowball fight.

"I see you got promoted."

"Yeah," I said.

"They're not promoting me these days."

"That's because you're a stupid fuck."

"Yeah, well, maybe."

"Definitely."

"Okay, sure." He had a mean shiner. The left eye was swollen up and bulging like it was going to pop. He looked like half man, half fish.

"Nice eye," I said.

"I had an accident. I bumped into something."

"Yeah? What?"

"First Platoon."

"See, that's your problem. You gotta stay with your squad."

He shut up for a second, then he said, "Listen, does this place ever seem strange to you?"

I knew what he was getting at. I looked straight in his face. I stood right up to him, human to fish.

"No, man," I said. "I think this place is heaven on earth."

"Oh," he said. He sounded disappointed. When the door shut behind him, I breathed out—one long breath—and shook my head. If he couldn't cut it, let him wise up. No way was I getting dragged into his problems. I looked up at the board again. Not bad. I got an A in health. Couple of C's. I ran my finger down the rows of names, looking at the other scores. The type was pretty small and I couldn't see at first. Then I got "Barnes" under my fingernail and squinted up in disbelief.

It said Barnes, first in the class. I stood there with my mouth open. "Shit," I said. "So much for stupid."

Barnes left again at the end of January. We heard about it at calisthenics formation, six A.M. It was still dark. It was really cold. A couple of snow flurries swirled in the air.

"Too cold to snow right," the Ox said as we dressed up the squad. DiPosti was talking to the company commander, his back to us, hands slapping his biceps. We could see the steam from his breath rising over his head. The battalion commander called attention from the platform by the dining hall. They did the roll call: "A Company all present and accounted FOR," shot the first company commander. "B Company all present and accounted FOR," said the next. "C Company, one man missing," said our guy. It sounded strange. Nobody was ever missing and the language didn't ring out when he said it. The final two company commanders finished their reports. A murmur ran down the long rows of the formation.

"At ease," snapped DiPosti to our platoon. We shut up, but you could see everybody looking up and down the columns. We marched into the dining hall after exercise, scanning the blank spot in the formation and then DiPosti's back. Man, was that guy pissed.

We had three good days of rumors before we heard anything new about Barnes. They looked in the town. They sent a couple of squads of seniors down to the river. The adult officers searched the road in their cars. By the afternoon of the first day, they called the police.

"Stupid fuck could have picked a better time to split," said the Ox on the second morning, slapping his gloved hands together.

Barnes had no money and no civilian clothes. The school kept it like that for all of us. I thought about it in a tactical sort of way: Where do you sleep out there at the end of January?

I ran it all over in my mind. He had to sneak past his roommate, out of his room, down the corridor of the dorm, past all the open doors (they keep the doors open at night), out of the building, over the wall, through the town, down the road—something like fifteen miles—to the river, down the highway to Harrisburg, through Harrisburg, and then a long run of seventy miles to New Jersey. That's if he was going home. All the time he had to be freezing his butt off and scared to hitchhike because that's the way the officers usually picked you up.

"He's dead," I told the guys in our group. "No way he could make that."

"He's dead if they catch him," said the Ox.

"He's dead, anyway."

They never actually did catch him. We got it all on the rumor mill. His mother called. He made it all the way home. He told his parents about the general order, about room confinement, and the beatings, and how he missed them, and how he wanted to come home, and then they sent him back. It was his stepfather's idea.

His stepfather drove him up to the administration building at the end of the week. He had a long meeting with the school superintendent while Barnes sat in the hallway in civilian clothes. The cadet officer of the day was DiPosti. He stood over Barnes at parade rest, his leather Sam Browne belt crossing his chest. DiPosti was smiling.

Barnes got a double general order. They lined us all up in the building and we could hear the artillery booming again, the wall shaking with it. DiPosti assigned two cadets to be with Barnes all the time. If he was going to class, two cadets walked him to the building. If he was due at formation, two cadets met him at his door and took him there. If he was going to pee, they went with him right into the latrine.

The escorts knew where Barnes was all the time. So it was easy for DiPosti and the upperclassmen to find Barnes walking past the athletic fields on the way to the barracks. It was easy to get him alone in his room between classes. There was no problem catching him in the latrine with only a few other guys. Usually the escorts held him.

They had the escorts on rotating duty, and when the Ox and I were up we had to walk all over campus with Barnes. We were on our way to the library when he got the urge to talk.

"What's up at four o'clock?" he asked me.

"We're supposed to take you to the soccer field."

"What for?"

"Soccer practice."

"In February?"

"Maybe they're starting early," said the Ox.

Barnes reached over and put his hand in the middle of my chest. I stopped. I looked at his hand and then at his face. He took the hand away.

"You know what they're going to do to me down there."

"That's not my problem."

"Keep moving, asshole," said the Ox.

We took him to the library. His hands were shaking while he looked something up. We could see the individual pages vibrating. I wanted to just hold his hands for a minute to stop the shaking. Just so he could read better. But then I looked at Ox standing over him, hands on his hips, and I thought to myself, How could a guy like this be number one in his class? I looked over to see what he was reading. We had to watch him because he wasn't allowed to see any maps. He had some book about the Civil War. They had a lot of good war books in there.

"You like the Civil War?" he asked me as I fingered the page.

"It's okay."

"You know why they fought it?"

"South shelled Fort Sumpter."

"They fought it because of slavery."

"So?"

"You know what slavery is?"

"Do I care?"

"It's when somebody else controls every minute of your life

and they make you do things you don't want to do and they keep you away from your family."

"Fuck you."

"Think about it."

That bastard. We took him to soccer practice. DiPosti was the winter coach.

I guess Barnes never liked soccer because he made another break for it a couple of mornings later. He never had a chance. We were standing around on the macadam just before six. It was still dark outside. People were coming out of the dorms, rubbing their eyes. I was talking to the Ox when one of the fire doors of our building flew open. It was Barnes, with no coat, his shirttail flapping behind him. He jumped out of the fire door, slammed it shut, and ran over the parking lot away from formation.

In a couple of seconds, the fire door banged open again. Four guys ran out. DiPosti was with them.

"Shit!" I said.

Almost everybody was out for calisthenics. They all got quiet and watched Barnes. He ran past the gym toward the tennis courts. He had about a fifty-yard lead.

"No way," somebody said.

"He's fucked," I told the Ox.

Barnes jumped onto the fence around the tennis courts. DiPosti's group was gaining fast. Barnes's feet slipped on the chain links, then he got a toehold and pulled himself up. DiPosti was already past the gym. Barnes got stuck at the top. His shirt ripped, and he fell over onto the court. DiPosti was already at the other side of the fence.

"Stupid asshole," said the Ox. "DiPosti's gonna kill him."

Barnes got up and ran across the tennis court. It was icy and he slipped. He got up. He slipped and fell. DiPosti cleared the fence. Barnes was crawling across the ice. DiPosti stepped carefully. He knew we were all watching. Barnes got to his feet again. There was no fence on the mountain side of the courts. He ran over a patch of snow and up into the woods. DiPosti was right after him. The rest of the group was only a few steps behind. About a dozen guys from formation ran after them, too.

"Why don't they send the whole battalion?" I said.

Ox looked at me. "Say what?"

"I said they don't need to send the whole damn battalion after one guy, that's all."

Ox stepped back a little and turned his head.

It only took five minutes to catch him, but they used about half an hour to bring him down from the mountain. He didn't look good. He "fell" again up in the woods. They took him to the administration building. He was coughing, and they carried him part of the way.

The Stratton School doesn't have a triple general order. You get two chances. They waited a couple of days till he looked better, then called his parents. The school made a big point of throwing him out. They put notices all over the place, but hell, everybody knew he was trying to *get* out all along.

Barnes's stepfather picked him up over the weekend. A couple of us watched from the quad. Barnes came out in a red jacket and pants. They wouldn't let him wear his uniform. He walked down to the car, the engine started, and they drove right out the front gate and down the hill toward town.

"He got what he wanted," I said to the Ox.

"He got his ass kicked."

"Yeah," I said, "but he got what he wanted." Ox rubbed his head from the scratchy wool of the overseas cap, but I kept looking out the driveway where it passed through the stone wall. It was cold that morning and it took a long time for the exhaust from Barnes's car to rise in the winter air.

Andre Dubus

Woman on a Plane

for Marie

She was in her thirties, a poet, and she was afraid to fly. Her brother was dying in another city. She did not have a husband or children, but she had a job that held her in the city where she lived. Until her brother went home to die, her job was work she gave her time to. But now it was taking time from her. She could feel it.

She read poems that students wrote; she read poems in books and in the evenings she lived with them, thought of what she would say about them next day in the classroom. She knew that she could not plan everything she would say; she could only plan how she would begin. It was a matter of letting go in front of the students, and waiting for the light to come. The light would come with images and words she must not hold before class. Her holding them could take away the life they drew from revelation, turn them into dead objects she possessed and carried with her to show the students. She knew that teaching a poem was like writing a poem: she could only begin, and reach, and wait. If she tried to impose a design to save herself from failure, there would be no revelation on the page, or with her students. Before each class she was afraid, but it was muted, and she knew it kept her from being dull and removed. She loved all of this until her brother was dying, and drawing her to him. Then she felt separated from her work, and had to will herself into her voice, into her very flesh.

Grief held her. Always: while she was talking with students, eating with friends, its arms encircled her. Alone, she gave in to it, allowed it to hold her while she fed and cleaned her body, and breathed. It held her when she sat at her desk to do the work that was only for herself; it pressed her biceps to her ribs, her back and breast to her heart, and she could not make a poem grow. She sat with paper and pen, and wrote words, but she felt as she did when she drank coffee and ate toast, that she was only doing this because she was alive, and awake. On weekends she flew to her brother.

As she drove to the airport on Fridays and rode to it with her father on Sundays, fear scattered her grief: it lay beside her, hovered behind her. Shards of it stayed in her body; she could touch the places they pierced in her brain and heart. But fear was in her blood, her muscles, her breath. She heard herself speak to airline clerks. She did not make up anything: she did not look at the eyes, the posture, of other passengers, to find the one whose number was up and visible, or the one who wanted to die by explosion in a crowded plane. She did not imagine the plane's sudden fall, her back to the stars, her face to the earth, the seat belt squeezing her double, as she waited for words to utter before the earth she loved tore her apart. She only breathed, and moved onto the plane, always to an aisle seat.

The width and height of the aisle held breath and light, and she gazed at it. On her other side were shadow and two people filling two seats, a bulkhead with a dark glass window, an overhead whose curve sealed her. For two hours she flew to the city where her brother was dying. She drank wine, and looked at the aisle.

Her brother was dying from love. At first she had watched her parents' eyes for shame, but she saw only the lights of grief. Mortality had raised him from his secrets; there was nothing to hide, and he lay whole between clean sheets. It was she who left parts of her behind when she entered the house. Her brother was two years older than she, and he was thin and weak in his bed. She did not see fear in his eyes anymore. For a long time it had been there, a wet brightness she wanted to consume with her body. He looked at her as though death were a face between

them, staring back at him. Sitting on the bed, she bent through
death and held her thin brother. Her breasts felt strong and vital,
and she wanted to absorb his fear and give him life. She held
him as if this were possible. She did not know when fear left
him, but it had. Now wit and mischief were in his eyes again,
and a new and brighter depth. She did not know what it was.
She only knew it was good to see. Sometimes she believed it was
simply that: goodness itself, as though death were stripping him
of all that was dark and base, mean and vain, not only in him but
in the world, too, in its parts that touched his life.

So she felt she could tell him now: She was afraid to fly. She
was holding his hand. He smiled at her. He said: Fear is a ghost;
embrace your fear, and all you'll see in your arms is yourself.
They could have been sitting at her kitchen table, drinking wine.
He could have been saying: Read Tolstoy; lie in the sun; make
love only with one you love. He had told her that, drinking wine
at her table, years ago. She looked at his face on the pillow,
wanting to see him as he had seen himself, holding his fear in his
arms. She saw her brother dying.

On the plane going home, she folded her arms beneath her
breasts. Then she closed her eyes, and hugged. She saw herself
buckled into the seat, under the tight arc of the plane's body. She
saw the plane in the immense sky, then her brother in bed,
poised as she was between the gravity of earth and infinity. She
had tried with a poem to know his fear, months ago, when she
could still write. But the poem changed, became one about love,
and the only fear in it was hers, of loving again, of her heart
swelling to be pierced and emptied.

Lightly embracing herself, she saw that, too: the words of the
poem coming from her pen, the notebook and her forearms and
hands resting on the oak desk her grandmother had used,
writing letters. She saw her grandmother, long dead now, writing
with a fountain pen. She saw herself sitting in the classroom, at
the desk where some afternoons chalk dust lay, and she brushed
it off with notepaper so it would not mark the sleeves of her
sweater. A trace of someone who had taught before her, who

nervously handled chalk. Traces of herself were scattered in the world. She saw the book she had published, held open by hands she would never know. She saw herself holding her last lover, under blankets on a cold night, waking with him to start a day.

She liked starting: a poem, a class, a meal for friends who crowded her kitchen while she cooked. But not starting a day, now that she was alone. She woke from night and dreams to the beginning of nothing. For minutes she lay in bed, gathering her scattered self. Then she rose to work, to be with friends. She liked the touch of leather boots on her calves, soft wool on her arms, snow on her face.

She wondered what her brother saw, now that fear had left his eyes. Her grandmother's eyes were like his, when she was old but not visibly dying: she seemed to watch from a mirthful distance. Perhaps connected to wherever she was going, she still took pleasure in the sport of mortality. Maybe it was a gift, for those who had lived long, and those who were slowly dying. She wanted it while her body was strong, while she was vibrant and pretty. Hugging herself, her eyes closed, she wanted it now as she breathed in this shuddering plane, speeding through darkness under the stars. She was afraid until the plane stopped on the runway.

Stuart Dybek

A Confluence of Doors

After days of drifting, the man arrives at a confluence of doors. Had he been adrift on a river, instead of the ocean, it would seem as if he has encountered a logjam from some long removed past when the virgin forests were being dismantled. Had he been adrift on city streets, he might have come upon these doors hammered up into a makeshift barrier, a dead end walling off the wrecking site of a condemned neighborhood.

From afar, their surfaces shimmer like an ice floe. As he floats closer they appear like a sargasso of wood instead of weed, a gigantic deck without a ship, a floating graveyard where doors come to rest, undulating with the gentle roll of the sea.

The man rises unsteadily, shading his eyes, balancing his weight in the gently rocking life raft. From where he stands, the doors appear tightly butted against one another like pieces of a gigantic puzzle. He can see doors of all designs—plain and ornate, hardwood and pine, some varnished, others painted, all of them weathered. Some have peepholes, some have mail slots, some have numbers, foot plates, knockers, locks, doorknobs of brass, wrought iron, glass, and some have only puttied holes where the doorknobs are missing. He can't see any hinges. The doors are all floating with their outsides up, facing the sky, and their insides face down in salt water.

He paddles the raft along what seems the shore of a strange, uncharted island, and moors it, carefully securing the line to the knocker of what must once have been the stately door of a mansion. He bellies from the raft and stands accustoming his legs to bearing his weight again and to the slight roll. With each undulation of the sea a clear film of water washes across the surface of the doors, glossing them like a fresh coat of shellac. As he walks he can hear the slosh of his cuffs and the creak of his footsteps on the warped wood. It's too quiet. He'd hoped for the bustle of nesting seabirds, sunning turtles, fish leaping up and plopping back at the edge where the water laps. He'd hoped, at least, for the company of his shadow. After so many days at sea, he was looking forward to having a shadow again, a real shadow, with its long legs striding in time to his own. When he can't detect one, he is suddenly, inordinately disappointed. All that keeps him from weeping is his realization that, in isolation, his emotions have grown childish. He has begun each new day of drifting by promising himself that, whatever happens, he will not panic, and that promise now restores his composure.

He walks farther inland, a single figure on a wooden plain, then whirls as if he's heard someone following him. For a moment he could swear that he's heard footfalls other than his own. Of course, there's no one there; just isolation playing its tricks. But, standing quietly, he hears a sound that can't be ascribed either to his own footfalls or to the rhythmic slap of water along the shoreline. He hears it again—a steady, nearly imperceptible knocking.

He proceeds inland and now not only can he hear the sound, but he can feel its vibrations through the soles of his bare feet. Each door he steps upon knocks back from the other side. From the elegant doors there comes a polite rap, from the ornate, stately doors, a firmer, more commanding knock, and from the nicked, peeling doors comes a battering of knuckles that threatens to build into an abusive pounding.

The farther he walks, the more insistent the knocking becomes. It is no longer restricted to the doors he steps on. The doors all around him have picked up the sound—each door with its own particular rap, its own pitch and rhythm, its own demand or plea, though he can't tell if he is hearing the blows of someone desperately trying to enter, or of someone locked in and trying to escape.

The barrage of fists and feet against wood is becoming deafening. The flat landscape of doors trembles as if straining at hinges he can't see. He seizes the knob of a plain pine door and tries to yank it open, but it's locked. He tries a charred-looking black door on which the darkened paint has been buckled by intense heat, a door that sounds ready to split under a rain of blows, but it is locked as firmly as if it has been nailed shut.

"Hello!" he yells. "Who's there?"

There's no answer except for the knocking, which becomes still more furious.

All the doors are locked. He knows that without trying them one by one. They are shut tight, as if the weight of fathoms, the pressure of a deep ocean trench, is holding them closed. And even amidst the pounding he has an odd flash of memory: how, as a child, he would tease his younger brother mercilessly, until his brother, who had a terrible temper, lost all control and came at him with a baseball bat or a hammer or a knife. He would run from his brother through the house, into the basement, and slam himself behind a shed door, holding it shut while his brother pulled furiously from the other side, shouting, "I'll kill you!" When he couldn't force it open, his brother would expend his anger by hammering at the door, kicking it, hacking it, beating it with the bat, but they both knew that he would never get it open, and that they were both safe from the sum of his rage, and safe from facing each other. What would have happened, he wonders now, if just once he had opened the door his brother thought would never give?

He remembers other doors he's hid behind, and doors that he's pounded on that remained closed. Perhaps it's doors like those that have drifted until they've gathered here: doors never opened, doors that remained mute and anonymous, doors slammed in faces, doors locked on secrets, and violated doors, doors stripped of their privacy—pried, jimmied, axed. If not for the crescendo of knocking, he might lean his ear to each door and hear its story, listen to the voices muffled behind it, the singing or laughter or cursing or weeping, and perhaps he would recognize the voices he heard so that it would seem as if he were walking down a long corridor lined with all the doors of his life.

But by now the pounding has become too terrible for him to even consider listening for voices. It is a racket beyond control, rage or panic desperately unleashed, like someone beating at the lid of a coffin. He covers his ears. It seems impossible that the doors can continue to withstand such a battering. And if one of them should give—split by the fury of blows—would all the pressure from beneath come gushing through that single doorway, spouting like a monstrous wave into the sky, then storming down, crushing, drowning, sucking the surface under, leaving only the bobbing flotsam of shattered doors behind?

The vision terrifies him. He begins to run back across the doors, his footfalls drumming as he retraces his steps to the edge of the sea. Now it is as if all the various knocks have been reduced to a single, massive fist pounding as steady as a heartbeat against a single, massive door. Each concussion knocks him off his feet and sends him sprawling across the wooden surface. As he dreaded, he can hear the wood begin to splinter and a network of cracks spread as if it is ice rather than wood that he flees across.

At the edge of the doors, surf pounds in, in time to the pounding of the fist. The surge of breakers buckles his legs. He's rolled back across the doors, then, caught in the backwash, sucked out towards the sea until the next wave sweeps him back again. He manages to catch hold of the knocker and he clings to it while waves slam over his body. With his free hand and his teeth, he works to untie the knot to the line of the raft, while, at the other end of the line, the raft jerks and strains like a terrified dog at a leash. Finally the knot comes loose, and he times the backwash so that its momentum sweeps him into the raft. He's thrown in on his face, water piling onto his back, while the raft bucks wildly in the surf, spinning away from shore. At any moment he expects it to capsize.

He is on the sea, drifting once more toward the horizon,

staring out into a monochromic blue, and not a bird in the sky.
He paddles aimlessly, waiting for a current to seize the raft.
Behind him, the doors gleam like a beach in the sun. They have
fallen silent again. Whatever was awakened must be sinking
back unanswered into dark fathoms. When he turns the raft for a
final look, ripples slap the bow like the last reverberations of
those desperate blows.

Paul Griner

Grass

Poa compressa, Canadian bluegrass, grows well in both damp and dry climates, blooms the entire season, won't brown even with a late frost, and is a real royal blue; in the right sunlight it looks painted. The first crop on my brother Nelson's grave has come in thickly, almost plush, and kneeling on it, sliding the outside edge of the grass shears' blade flush with the polished granite headstone, I hear the swift double knock of a woodpecker in a tree and remember Nelson in his youth as sharply as if he stood before me now: a tank top, shorts, dusty shoes. His skin is tanned and cut from falls, from fights, from accidents. His shoulders are muscular, his slicked hair glistens in the sun. Mother stands above him, shaking a lemon over his bent brown head as if to baptize him, scolding him for his latest mischief, and when she drops the lemon, Nelson picks it up, runs his thumbnail over its skin, and raises it to his face to smell. Then he hands the lemon back. Mother straightens, turns away, smiling, rubbing the lemon as she walks. The incident has already vanished from her mind. Nelson pulls a book from under his shirt and sits against a tree to read, the book's red leather binding propped on his knees. The book is a tale of pirates and their deaths, which he has stolen from the library. Hours later, near dusk, the mosquitoes swarming, swallows rising through the heavy blue air, Father finds Nelson still sitting against the tree with the book. He takes the book from Nelson's hands, marks the page, lays it aside on the grass, and slaps Nelson across the face, twice. The slaps echo off the garage, like twinned distant shots. Nelson has been dismissed from yet another school, gambling again, on golf. He is twelve years old.

I sit back on my heels and take a small leather notebook from my pocket to write down this memory, which is one of the many things I hope to tell Sandra, my great niece. The brown notebook is old but unused, and I hear its spine crack as I smooth open its pages. A few days ago, Sandra called and asked how I was feeling, if I were still following baseball, how my garden was coming. I'd taken her to a few games as a child, collected autographs for her, but that was years ago, and I knew that the real subject of her call was yet to surface. I believe she is interested in asking some questions about her relatives, especially my brother, her grandfather, and his wife. At least, this is what I am hoping.

Nelson is not buried next to my parents. He has a plot he paid for years ago, between his wife's and a tilting box elder. The neat green rectangle their graves make leaves no room for other graves, not even for those of their daughters. For years, I thought I would never tend Nelson's grave, though I admired how he withstood those slaps, his imperious refusal to acknowledge them even when the red print of my father's hand lingered on his face for hours because of his fair skin. After Father hit him that time, Nelson picked up the book and began reading again, or pretended to. The light was fading so fast I doubted he could see the page. The swallows, still tumbling and turning like a school of fish, I perceived as a sense of movement in the dark sky, a darting shadow.

Father never hit me, or any of the rest of us. Nelson seemed marked off, as if he and Father had agreed early on that the hitting was in some secret way necessary, though the hitting never seemed to change anything: Nelson was suspended or dismissed from four other schools before finally graduating from St. Martin's in the Field and going on to Yale. Father died years before I thought of asking him why he had hit Nelson, and Nelson, even at twelve, seemed distant from the family, as if he were watching us all, himself included, from some private remove. Had I asked him, I believe he would have ignored me. That aloofness first attracted and then repelled me; I wanted to be like Nelson, I wanted nothing to do with him. Now, passing my hand over the thick blue grass above his grave, letting the blades tickle my palm, feeling them bend beneath the weight of my slight touch, I am simply happy he was my brother.

Finished with Nelson's grave, I move on to his wife's. The grass is thicker here, powdery soft. Its roots grow many feet in a season, binding the soil, keeping wind and rain from blowing everything away. Like most grass it has a peculiar, earthy smell, which to me is the smell of death, I've encountered it on so many graves. Their stones are the same clay-colored granite, though Delia's requires more work to keep clean. A few steps closer to the cemetery road it collects that much more dust in its carved letters. Rubbing dirt from the letters, I see her name written across my reflection on the polished stone.

I met Nelson's wife a year before he did, at the Chatter Box Club's Christmas ball. Delia is a pretty name, but for some reason Nelson always called her Pete, even putting that name on her stone. I was standing by the punch bowl when she entered, and saw the smooth whiteness of her neck and shoulders when a chaperone took her stole, her soft curving profile as she turned away. Her neck reminded me of a swan's and I had never seen lips so red. I walked by her seat three times, the second and third times waving to an imaginary friend at the far end of the floor to give myself a reason to pass, but I hadn't the nerve to talk to her or even to come close enough to smell her perfume. She sat on the edge of the chair, looking out over that sea of dancers expectantly, her tulle dress spread out at her feet, and I found her beauty unapproachable. She and Nelson were a good match. The notebook I am using was hers, her initials stamped in gold leaf in the upper right-hand corner. I found it in one of Nelson's drawers.

I was an usher at their wedding. For most of it, I stood on the edges of the crowd and stared. They seemed to me like people you might read about, otherworldly. Their guest list numbered close to six hundred, the social editor at the *Democrat and Chronicle* devoted a full page to their reception. I think that's why I asked first Gwen and then Abigail to marry me that next year; I wanted in some way, in many ways, to be like them.

Done for the day, I stand and take a few steps back to inspect my work, the straps of my gardener's kneepads pinching the skin behind my knees. My back is sore and my fingers ache but Nelson and Delia's graves look splendid. Green and trim, they stand out from those around them like islands in this sea of ragged stones, as the two did in life.

Tomorrow, I will work on Abigail's grave, and Mother's and Father's, and then, if the weather holds, earlier generations later in the week. Abigail, who was once my fiancée, and whose grave is the only one I tend that is not a member of our family.

Driving back through the cemetery, slowly, so as not to raise dust from the rutted dirt track, the trees' shadows moving up over the hood, I remember Nelson and Delia's first child, stillborn, and never buried. I think that was the only moment of their lives I wouldn't have lived.

Home again, I place the spade, trowel, gardener's fork, and grass shears on the rubber mat by the door and lean their pitted wooden handles against the wainscoting. Above them I see a framed picture of Nelson and remember the heat of the day when the picture was taken as if the memory existed in my body and not my mind. I feel drained and heavy, submerged in a bath of too-hot water.

The yellowed picture, with decorative, scalloped edges, is not a very good one—you can just make out Nelson's face, and mine in profile, looking at him, both of us nearly overwhelmed by the jungle growth surrounding us. But I've hung the picture by the door on purpose. I see it whenever I leave or enter the house and it reminds me of Nelson's better qualities. I will have to show it to Sandra.

I was a sergeant in the Chemical Warfare Service of the Army in World War II. Nelson joined the Navy and was named skipper of his own ship, a mine sweeper, though before the war he had never served. In fact, his only experience with boats was on transatlantic crossings. He rose to the rank of Lt. Commander. I was stationed in Hollandia, Dutch New Guinea, for ten months, and I never quite understood what my assignment was. It's called Sukarnapura, Indonesia, now. Mostly I dug ditches, which other people later came along and filled. Once, in the middle of a hot day, a day like a blowtorch—and it is the sapping weight of this heat I remember—I was digging ditches with Fletcher, who was from MIT and weighed 118 pounds, and Stevens, from some California school. He stood six and a half feet tall and his Adam's apple looked like a partially swallowed brick. Working, we'd stripped to our shorts and T-shirts, the same color green as the swarming, buzzing flies and the watery mud sucking at our ankles, and I'd just lowered my head onto my crossed wrists for a rest when I heard someone whistle at us, as if we were pretty women.

I looked up and saw Nelson on the berm, all in white, his brass buttons shining in the sun, behind him the razor grass waving like wheat in the hot wind. Stevens and Fletcher, seeing the uniform, straightened and saluted, their dog tags tinkling, but I couldn't move. "Nelson's dead," I thought, and this was his ghost. My body pulsed like a single giant nerve. I felt the hailstone-sized welts the fly bites left on my shoulders and the warm mud eating at my rotten feet and my swollen hands squeezing the wooden pickaxe handle so hard I thought they'd burst. Somehow he'd come to tell me and I didn't blink when sweat stung my eyes, afraid he'd disappear.

"Good thing they've got you three here," Nelson said, smiling. "If they put you anywhere else you might lose the war all by yourselves." He returned the salute and told us to knock off work for a while, having arranged it with our CO.

He had wangled leave to come and see me. He'd had a chance to go home and see Delia and his daughters—I found this out later, from one of his friends and superiors—but had come west instead, farther into the combat zone. I believe he thought I was in much greater danger than I ever found myself (though Stevens was killed by a sniper's bullet as he wandered along a beach) and wanted to talk with me again in case something happened.

I have always relished that memory—it overlaid some earlier, painful ones—and I take the picture from the wall and study it, searching Nelson's face for clues to what motivated him, then and always. His inscription—*To Francis, Nitz* (the name his friends always called him)—is faded to a rust color but still legible, and I trace the letters with one dirty fingernail before rehanging the picture and climbing the narrow stairs for a bath. On the upper landing the sun through the window is still hot and I pause in it, warming myself like a cat, one of the true pleasures of age.

Before bathing I lay out my clothes, and opening the squeaky sock drawer I smell the faint scent of cedar. This is Nelson's bureau, which I took after he died. On the back, scratched in rickety handwriting seventy-five years ago, is my own name. I doubt Nelson ever saw it. Mother always kept bags of cedar chips in our drawers, lavender in hers, and it was that lavender scent which first attracted me to Gwen. She was a brief interlude in my life, but she marks a change for me, the time when Nelson first began to show an almost casual cruelty towards me. This story may pain Sandra, but I believe she should know it, and so, like my other memories, I record it.

I had asked Gwen to marry me. Though far wealthier, she was a pale imitation of Delia, skin neither as smooth nor as soft, her neck a bit too short, retiring where Delia was anything but. We had dated for several months. Dances, picnics in brown October fields, skating on our summer house's frozen lake, a chaperoned trip to New York. In a horse-drawn cab there, holding my hand, momentarily free of the chaperone, she had given me reason to hope. Outside, I remember, it was bitter cold; the horses leaned into the drilling wind, mufflers and a turned-up collar hid the cabbie's face. A string of gaslights circled the park like a necklace and every few seconds gusts of snow blew across them, spreading their light in the air like a stain. Gwen's fur-framed face shone in the gaslight, lending her small, uneven features a transitory beauty, and the lavender scent of her perfume filled the cab; when I bent to kiss her I thought I had sealed our future.

A month later, standing outside our house on a cold sunny day in early spring, I asked Nelson if he knew why she had turned me down. The lake ice was pewter-colored in the sun, charcoal in the shade. Ribbons of fine snow lay across it, like blown sand.

"Don't you know?" he said, lighting a cigarette and narrowing his eyes against the smoke that curled around him.

I shook my head. A blast of wind made us lean closer. I could see that his hair had frozen in tufts.

He looked down the long, narrow expanse of the lake toward the tree-covered hills on the far end, the afternoon sky above them a pale watery blue. "It's because of the way you are."

He glanced at me briefly, as if awaiting my response, but I didn't have one. I didn't know what he meant. He looked away again over the lake and inhaled deeply on the cigarette, the end of it brightening, blew smoke slowly out his nose.

"You live your life an inch at a time," he said, flicking the cigarette away. We both watched the wind pick it up, send its glowing red end skittering over the bumpy pewter-colored ice. When the glow died out, he said, "She's not like that, and she said it would drive her crazy." He turned to face me, his back to the wind. "Frankly, it would me, too."

Even as a child I had always suspected Nelson disapproved the care I took with things, but he had never been so obvious.

Father traveled: Rome, Prague, Paris, Madrid, then later Bangkok and Peking. From every city he brought me coins. Nelson wasn't interested. Once, he accompanied me on the downtown trolley to Sibley's and waited patiently while I chose among several display cases, settling finally on a mahogany frame with etched glass and gold corner seals. When I thanked Nelson he dismissed the notion, saying he'd done it only because Father had said he would give him an extra two dollars for the trip, and planned to buy cigars and a new shirt with the money, which he did. But he carried the case home for me, and a year later, when he ran into my room to tell me one of the cooks had started a fire in the kitchen that threatened the house, he grabbed the case and carried it out onto the lawn.

The fire never spread, but in gratitude I spent the next morning cleaning all the coins with a silver polish that smelled like ink, memorizing their locations and descriptions so I could impress Nelson with my knowledge. He accepted the collection, ran off with it tucked carelessly under his arm, and traded it for two peppermint ice cream sodas, neither of which was for me. Still, these things were hard to read; for every seemingly cruel or thoughtless act there was another equally generous one. After Gwen, Nelson's actions became more sharply defined.

Less than a year after Gwen, I was engaged. Abigail was a sweet girl. My friends all envied me, though Nelson didn't seem to approve. He told me he and Pete wouldn't make it back from their Brazilian trip for the wedding, but that both of them knew it would be a fine affair. Two months before the wedding, there was an accident. I was driving. Abigail was only twenty-four when she died. All these years later, I still tend her grave.

Sitting by my open window and watching the blue sky turn violet, I hear children shouting in the street and the burring sound of mowers as a few late-working fathers cut their lawns. The phone has not rung tonight, as I hoped it would, which has left me feeling the slight, dry scratch of disappointment. Looking at my desk I see Delia's open brown notebook, and the disappointment turns into the sudden burn of shame. I often felt that way around Nelson, times he denied me. But then I tell myself to have faith, to wait, that Sandra will call, that I have not misjudged her.

I have taken a hot bath and completed my regimen of stretching and rubbing eucalyptus liniment into my shoulders, arms, and legs. Never especially limber—and therefore, never much of an athlete—if I fail to do this nights after working on the graves I sleep fitfully and awake the next day stiff and barely able to move. Now and then a breeze blows through my curtains and cools my damp chest, bringing with it the smell of the cut grass, and when the breeze is still, the eucalyptus liniment clears my sinuses. A sort of cosmic breathing in and out, the smells of age and death.

At the end of his life, I kept much the same regimen for Nelson. He could not bend enough to reach his feet and care for them. Each night I rubbed a Dixie cup of ice over his heels to relieve his swelling, and in the mornings, after he bathed, I worked the eucalyptus liniment into his heels and ankles to loosen them. His feet were dry, rough, very light—almost as light as the feet of a child—but the oranged, horned skin gave them away. In places, it bubbled away from the muscle like the skin of a grilled chicken. I worked fifteen minutes on each foot. I would wake him with a phone call and by the time I arrived he'd have finished bathing; at night, I would stop by about nine and find him dressed for bed. We rarely spoke but I believe he appreciated my care. I moved his bed closer to the window, as he said he liked to watch the night sky.

It is an unusually warm night, in the seventies though it is now ten o'clock, but you still know it's spring. Even with the windows open, the night air is quiet. A month from now, it will be filled with the songs of crickets. I remember watching Nelson shimmy down the drainpipe from these same third-floor windows summer nights, on his way to meet girls or friends or just to find adventure. I would hang out the window, the sill cutting into my stomach, and he would call to me standing a white blur in the dark, dusting his hands on his trousers, urging me to come along. The scent of manure from Mother's garden and the chirping of cicadas filled the night air, and though I wanted to, I could never bring myself to join him.

One summer—my tenth, Nelson's thirteenth—I finally joined in on some of Nelson's mischief. It started as a way to save money: on weekends, we would walk the seven miles from our house to the farm instead of taking the morning trolley, saying we had caught a later one. Soon the walks came to be about more than money, they were about pleasure, a mutual pleasure in the physical world. The wheat and corn fields lining the road crackled in the summer heat or rustled in the wind with a sound like rain, and the sun reflecting off the pavement baked our cheekbones. Dust covered the ground, so thick sometimes it was choking, rising to turn our black shoes white, and we walked through it quietly for long hours, only our footsteps on the macadam making noise. We would both look up at the sudden shadow of a passing cloud or the silent flight of distant birds, and when we heard cars coming from a long way off we stood on the roadside and tried to guess what make and model they would be from the pitch of their engines. Nelson suggested we wager on our guesses. Most times he won my carfare. Towards the end of that summer, I had started to call him Nitz.

All this we both liked without ever having to say so. I liked being with Nelson, equals for once, just the two of us on the road, searching for snakes and frogs and dropped treasures from cars. Occasionally, when we tired or saw storms moving towards us over the hills, we hitched a ride, but more often we walked through the rain, enjoying the steam rising from the pavement when the first drops hit and our clinging clothes and the streams beneath the bridges swelling and foaming in the sudden downpours.

Our walks came to an abrupt end in August when Father found out what we were up to. I'm still not quite sure how. One humid morning Father pulled me into his office by my ear. Heavy curtains shut out the light and in the darkness I stumbled over an ottoman, but even as I fell Father didn't release his grip, so that for a few seconds I seemed to be swinging in space by my ear. I gasped at the pain.

Father let go and stood looking down at me where I'd fallen on the rug. "Your brother made you do this."

"No," I said, rubbing my ear. I knew what he was talking about but for a moment I couldn't say anything, rocking on my knees to quiet the pain. Father never liked us to show we felt things. "It wasn't like that at all. It was his idea, but I wanted to. I'll repay all the money. We didn't do it for that." I stood, cupping my ear. It was circled by a ring of pain, like fire, and the ring was pulsing. "I wanted to."

"How much money?" he said, looking at me.

"I don't know. I haven't kept track. Fares out to the farm every week. It's really not that much. I can repay you in a month."

He didn't answer. He moved to his desk and pushed a glass ink bottle in and out of the desk lamp's circle of light, slowly, the blue liquid sloshing up the bottle sides and leaving pale blue stains as it receded. This was his way when he was lost in thought, occupying his hands and ignoring whoever else was in the room.

Later, I sat on the curb, marking it with a hunk of chalk. Nelson came out, his face red and glowing. The skin looked as if it had been exposed to the sun for too long and then had four strips peeled off. Those were the marks from Father's hand. I had heard some of the slaps over the lawn.

"Nitz," I said, reaching for his arm. He pulled away and I chased after him.

"Nitz! What happened?"

Suddenly I was face down on the ground and Nelson was astride my back, pushing my face in the dirt.

"You know what happened, you bastard. You told him." He kicked my legs with his heels.

Arching my neck to get my mouth out of the dirt, I said, "I didn't. I swear."

"Did you tell him about the money?"

"Yes, but he knew."

He slammed my head down again. "Father said you told him everything." Nelson punched me once and got off. The red on his face had intensified. Though I ran beside him, the chalk still gripped in my hand, he refused to listen to anything I said. He had learned that trait well from Father.

Lying in bed, my ear still sore, I realized there was the slightest chance that Nelson was right, that Father had pulled me in to his office to talk about something else—swimming in the lake with no adult supervision, which he had strictly forbidden and which we had begun to do the week before—and that I'd blurted out news of our walks prematurely. I didn't think anyone had seen us but I would never know, of course, because if I asked Father I might get us in trouble for something else and he would ignore the question, anyway. As for Nelson, he would always be sure of my betrayal.

Those roads we walked are gone now. Widened, abandoned, developed: I couldn't walk them if I chose to, they exist only in my memory. Once, after Nelson died, I started to drive out to find them. On the way, after passing the first familiar building—a partially collapsed but still recognizable barn—I realized that too much had changed and if I drove the roads I would be driving them through my memories, changing them forever, and losing them as I had lost Nelson. I turned back without regrets.

For the rest of that tenth summer, and for all the summers until we learned to drive, Father had us driven out to the farm. He made us repay a summer's worth of trolley fares and it wiped out my savings. Nelson had none, but getting money was easy for him; he played three rounds of golf with older men and won twice what he needed.

And sure that I'd turned on him, Nelson removed himself from me every chance he got. Soon enough he was off on other schemes with older friends, stealing grapes from Wylie's vineyard, swimming in the nearby abandoned quarries and canals, watching the servant girls take tub baths in their quarters, but I still wish those walks had never ended. Losing them was bitter then, and seems so even now.

On some of those nights I went to Nelson, one of his feet cupped in my palm, I was tempted to tell him, "Nelson, you were wrong about me, I never betrayed us. Father already knew." But I didn't. Nelson should never have said the things he said to me, because he was my brother, and because he was my brother I did not tell him he had been wrong. It would have served only to bring regret into his life at a time when he could do little to assuage it. For so long, he had been the protagonist in my life and I his shadow, and now it was my turn to shoulder some of the burden. So I held my tongue and worked on his painful feet until it was almost dark, and he was asleep or resting.

The sweet scent of vanilla grass, *Hierochloe odorata*, fills the air. The cemetery is quiet this morning—some birds, a squirrel chattering at my presence, the distant rumble of a jet. The early yellow sunlight slants onto the gravestones through the trees, shifting over them with the wind. I sit in the car a few moments, the door open, my shoes on the brick roadbed, and let the smell of the vanilla grass fill my lungs.

Sandra will like this smell, I believe; it's sweeter than perfume.

Nine months of the year I keep a small portable mower in my trunk; Novembers I bring it into my basement, wash the housing, drain the fluids, and disassemble the engine parts, soaking them in oil to loosen the grime and dirt before drying and reassembling them. I discard the spark plug and oil filter and wrap the motor in a sheet to keep it dust-free, then reverse the process in the middle of each March. One year I catalogued forty-three different types of grasses in the grit, including a seed of the inaptly named meadow oat grass, *Arrhenatherum elatius,* which flourishes along the edges of deserts in the Southwest. I thought perhaps it had come this far north caught in the feathers of a migrating goose. Like all meadow oat seeds it had a twisted awn protruding from its back, which untwists and drives the seed beneath the soil when it rains. I moistened my palm and watched the seed try to bury itself in my skin.

Though the mower weighs only thirty-seven pounds I can feel it growing heavier each year. I have perhaps two or three more summers where I can use it, and now, before assembling the handle, I look over Abigail's grave. Last week, what had been a cold spring gave way to ninety degree heat in mid-May, and the magnolia blossoms have come and gone. They are so thick on the ground I have the momentarily disconcerting impression that it has snowed on Abigail's grave, and hers alone, or that her grave has been covered in lime. Cholera victims used to be marked off that way. At nighttime in this cemetery, I have read, ranks of their graves fairly glowed.

I walk to her grave and scoop up a handful of the silky magnolia petals, rub them between my fingers. Graves have their own lives. A bright birth attended with great fanfare, a long stretch of slowly decreasing attention, spans of forgetfulness, finally abandonment. Abigail's grave, like her life, moved through these phases more quickly than most.

She was her parents' youngest child, and their favorite. They were not from here, and they bought a creekside plot—not an especially advantageous site—in a small dell in the cemetery. It isn't easily reached, and wasn't then. I think they wanted to forget that she had died, not to forget her, but the practical results were the same. They stopped visiting before too long, and, as Abigail died before she was an aunt to nieces and nephews, none of them looked after her grave as they grew older.

It is not a particularly prepossessing place even now. Her parents planted the magnolia too near it, and it has never grown to any great height, so its low branches give too much shade and the covering vanilla grass is thin, even patchy. Still, I like it here. This grass blooms far earlier than other grasses and almost no one ever sees it flower, which is somehow fitting. The grass has other qualities, as well, though I admit I didn't recognize them at first myself. It grows in swampy places and in wet meadows, and is the sweetest smelling of all grasses. In the South, Creoles make fans from it and Western Indians burned it ceremoniously. Nearer to home the local Indians used to weave the whole plant into screens, then dampen the screens and place them in a breeze to perfume the air. Even now, in northern European farming villages, villagers scatter vanilla grass before the churches on Saints days and holy festivals to make the pathways leading to saints' shrines fragrant. There, they call it holy grass.

I have a busy morning, clearing vines from Abigail's stone and applying a fertilizer mix to the yellowed grass, phosphates to thicken it, nitrogen to make it green. A year after Abigail died, I was sitting at the end of our dock at night. The noise and smoke of Nelson and Delia's house party had made me claustrophobic, so I'd wandered outside to get some fresh air. After a few minutes, when I'd begun to forget the noise coming from the house and could hear behind it the quiet voice of the summer night—waves and crickets and rubbing branches on the shore—I heard footsteps thumping down the long dock towards me. Drunken, I guessed, from the way they hurried and stopped, wobbled, then went on, and soon enough Nelson called out to me, and when I turned he was waving a bottle and grinning.

"Morose," he shouted.

I didn't answer, and he waited until he was right beside me and said, "Why are you always so morose these days?"

I looked back over the water. A car was making its slow way down West Lake Road, and I watched its lights funneling through the darkness. Nelson fell into one of the Adirondack chairs beside me.

"Is it that damn Abigail thing?" He leaned closer to me, his white teeth flashing, and I could smell the gin on his breath. "Don't be stupid." He held out the bottle and I shook my head, so he swigged from the bottle, emptying it, and threw it on the water, in front of where I sat. "You're better off the way you are, you know. I mean, she was all right, if what you wanted was a life without much pleasure and a lot of boredom."

He was still punishing me for something that hadn't ever happened, all those years earlier, but because I still had that little sliver of doubt about my own complicity in what he saw as my betrayal, I sat there and took it. I watched the bottle bob away, ghostly white on the dark water, and wished he would leave. Nelson tapped his foot on the dock, keeping time with an up-tempo song the band had begun to play, and let his head loll back against the chair. I could feel his tapping reverberate up my spine. "Lots of stars," he said, looking up at the sky, and it was true, there were. The Milky Way arched above us like a vast dust cloud. "Thousands of them. Might make you believe in God."

He leaned towards me again. "You do believe, don't you? I mean, I know I've had my doubts. In fact, I never believed in God until you had that accident." He sat back. "It was the best thing that ever happened to you. She was a . . ." I dumped him into the lake, chair and all, before he could finish, one of the few times in my life I've acted precipitously, and I have never regretted it. It was years before that comment ceased to burn, and even now, when I'm at the club and hear someone drunk in the summer or the smell of spilled gin at the bar tickles my nose, I find it hasn't completely healed.

Before gathering my tools, I look at the leather notebook, open in my palm, two creamy yellowed pages untouched as yet by ink, and decide not to write down this story; it is perhaps better left unknown.

For lunch I sit against a tree with a cheese sandwich and a thermos of iced coffee, Mother's favorite meal. High white cumulus drift across the blue sky, and reeds rattle over the stream in a warm breeze, shaking their flat seeds on the water. They will float downstream and embed themselves in banks. My fingers take a few minutes to uncurl, habituated as they are to the hafts of tools, and I spread open the Kodak newsletter to read while I wait, anchoring the corners with shears and the sweating thermos.

The company is turning a profit once again, always a good

sign. I worked there as an engineer for thirty years. I discovered ways to make faster film—film that developed images with little light. Nelson was a banker, an investor, what they call in the papers now an entrepreneur. He made a lot of money. He was also an Olympic swimmer; twice, he set world records. He would get letters from other men offering to have sex. Nothing made him madder but it meant he was noticed, somebody, a face, a name people remembered. I never once received a letter from a stranger and few enough from friends. Even at Kodak my work went unheralded.

I first realized we were headed for different futures at Yale. Both Skull and Bones, I was probably the least likely member they ever had and he one of the likeliest. I know why they let me in. A year after Nelson graduated he came back for a dance. Standing in a smoky back hallway, fumbling with my cuffs before entering the crowded room, I overheard Nelson talking with a few of the upperclassmen, who told him they'd inducted me only because of him. He laughed, adjusting his tie, and said he wasn't surprised; he'd never thought me Skull and Bones material. I wondered even then if I wasn't meant to overhear them, and about what I should do. If the situation had been reversed I knew Nelson would have resigned.

Nelson must have seen from my face that I'd heard. He was still adjusting his tie in the mirror, jutting his chin out to be sure the collar rested just so, and he said to his reflection words which were obviously intended for me. "Haven't you learned to lie yet?" It seemed a point of honor with him that he had.

I wasn't quite sure what he meant, but I took it to be comforting and let him lead me by the shoulder into the dance, and, though often burning with shame, stuck out three years in that club, an inch at a time.

Done with lunch I fold up the wax paper for reuse, bag it, then push up off the tree. I see myself for a moment walking towards the rest of our family stones as if I were a stranger crossing the dirt roads and meadows: crickets buzzing, the sun beating down, a white shirt almost glowing in the light, dust rising to cover my shoes. Thousands have walked these paths before me, I can almost see their footsteps worn into the green grass. Early on, Nelson found the care I took with graves morbid, a long attending on death. Nearer the end, studying stones, he seemed to think differently. He walked the cemetery's rutted roads with me, evidently recalling his own childhood memories, asked questions about our more distant relatives, stopped often at the empty plot beside Delia's. He was ready, I think.

I liked those walks, and that he came to rely on me. I helped plan his estate, the sale of his house and the distribution of those possessions he worried his daughters would fight over, made the arrangements for his funeral. He seemed to want me near him in the end, and no one else. Sandra came to see him twice, but he wouldn't let her in. Those last months, I was the only one allowed to see him without his dentures.

The stones are brilliant white in the afternoon sun, scrubbed weekly with bleach and water. The chlorine smell reminds me of summer mornings outside our kitchen, the maids on their knees scouring the floor with the sudsy water, ranks of purple impatiens spilling over the walk. Nelson would take his bicycle from the garage and leave without saying goodbye. I keep up all the family graves—cousins, aunts, uncles, parents, nephews. Most of our family's graves had fallen into disrepair when I started—it had been years since many had been cared for, decades for some. Toppled stones, chipped names and dates, stones grassed over completely. I started after Abigail's death, researching where many of the people were buried, digging through aunts' and uncles' attics for family letters. I asked Nelson if he had any. He hadn't.

There are Millards and Wentworths and Farleys. I know about Gwyneth, who wanted to marry at thirteen, bowed to her parents' objections, and married at fourteen. Twelve children later, aged twenty-six, she was dead. I had to buy her a new stone, the old one was illegible. Her parents built the largest mausoleum in the city. Nearby are other relatives' graves. One,

Porter Farley, left town for sixty years, living as a tramp, and was returned only after death. He appeared one evening at an inn near Woldoboro, Maine, gave a gold pocket watch as security against his lodging expenses, then declined supper and went upstairs to bed. The next morning, when food was brought to him, he refused it, saying that as he had no money he could not expect to eat. Six days later he died, probably from starvation. The innkeepers sold the watch and shipped him home. His sister, Mindwell, is buried nearby. She had a brief span of glory, three weeks as skipper of her husband's ship. Two days out of Rio he died of yellow fever, as did the first mate, and she pickled his body in an unused beef barrel and took command of the ship, having learned navigation from her husband on their many voyages. His grave is at one remove from her, displaced by her second husband.

This knowledge is not morbidity. If it weren't for me, no one would keep up the graves. And each of them, in some way, calls up memories. Now, when my knees are sore from kneeling, or the sun climbs high enough to make the day too hot, I sometimes pause in my rounds and try to remember not only my own but what I imagine to have been Nelson's memories, as well.

It is a beautiful cool June Sunday and I am sitting in church. The men smell of talc and cologne, the women of lavender and roses. Sunlight streams through the stained-glass windows and looking up I feel like I am inside a jeweled box. When the breeze blows through the open church doors, it rattles the thin pages of my hymnal.

Singing the hymns, the minister's high voice sends me into reverie. Aside from the war I traveled only twice, once to the Holy Land, once to Italy, taking both trips in the middle of winter so as to escape our dreadful weather. In Italy, in a small walled town in the Perugian hills, I stumbled across a museum dedicated to grasses. At first I thought I was imagining things. Except for the Latin terminology I couldn't read the exhibits—I spoke no Italian—and the white-haired old woman in a black dress who took my money was either deaf or pretending to be, but I photographed each display case and the plaques saying what they held, then had the photographs enlarged and translated when I returned home.

The day was warm and sunny when I entered the museum. I came out to a violet dusk, the stone buildings blue, water glimmering in the gutters after a shower, iron gratings rumbling as they closed. There was a fresh chill wind. I couldn't believe my good fortune. I still have the pictures: a smoky vial of vernal grass perfume, clear glass made from melted wheat straw, topaz-yellow glass made from barley, illustrations of how on all grasses the sheaths lap successively left and right, just as the leaves are borne alternately on opposite sides of the stem. Technically, this is called two-ranked growth. One of the plaques discoursed on grass's ubiquity and anonymity; many things we don't think of as grasses are—corn, wheat, oats, reeds, hay, moss-like grasses in cold countries, bamboo and sugarcane in hot. I don't know who had built the museum, or why, but really it didn't matter. Some kindred spirit, I supposed, interested in what much of the world found uninteresting. It is odd connections such as that on which I am counting.

I haven't spent any of the money Father and Mother left me. I thought of setting up a fund to insure the upkeep of our graves, investing the principal and using the interest to pay a man to weed and trim the various graves a few times each year, but I am gambling on Sandra to take up where I will at some point leave off.

This is the way I've come to see it. Family is a loop you can't escape, and though at first I resisted that idea—almost resented it—I've come to find comfort in it: the constancy even of things that make you raw. After Nelson's funeral Sandra began asking questions. About him, about us, about our lives as children. She has Delia's long-necked beauty. I remember the first stirrings of my own interest after a funeral in this same church years ago. The minister had just snuffed the altar candles and their smoke

curled slowly towards the vaulted ceiling where the echoes of
the minister's voice and the mourners' song and the organ's bass
notes still lingered like a presence, and I realized, seeing that
transformation from flame to rising smoke, that the service
imitated the soul's birth and passage and ascension. It was as if a
single string had suddenly vibrated with sound deep inside my
chest. I always feel that same note now at the end of a good
service, during the few seconds where everything echoes—sights
and sounds and memories—before people begin moving and
talking, set loose again into the material world.

I had asked questions then, too. A few days ago, Sandra
called again, asking if she could accompany me to see the
graves, so this morning I am not surprised to see her here, her
tanned face demurely hidden beneath a straw hat, her white
teeth showing when she sings. In my jacket, I feel the notebook's
comforting solidity against my breast. This is not Sandra's church,
nor do I know if she is especially religious or even religious at
all. I am gambling that her interest is genuine. Not gambling,
really; I have thought about it for a long time. Yes, I tell myself
here in the church, listening to the Psalms—songs of captivity
and return—Nelson was my brother and Sandra is my
great-niece and Nelson was her grandfather, but those are just
words and do little to unravel the mystery.

Susan Hubbard

An Introduction to Philosophy

Jamey promised to lend me a copy of *Nausea*. He had borrowed the book from Mr. Loden, the only English teacher at our school who wasn't a nun. Mr. Loden was a Quaker, and he liked to loan us books that weren't in the school library. He owned seven copies of *Catcher in the Rye*. At one time he owned eight, but he had loaned one to my sister Edna. Then my father found it and tore it into pieces. Luckily he never knew who it belonged to. None of us would say a word. You'd have thought the book grew up on its own, like a fungus, in the corner of the living room.

I first saw the *Nausea* book when Jamey and I were at a school basketball game. We both hated basketball, but this was the city-wide final, and attendance was compulsory. They held it one afternoon in the school gym. Jamey sat on the topmost bleacher, ignoring the cheerleaders, reading *Nausea*. I sat next to him, my skirt folded carefully to cover my knees. I had a good view of the book's cover—a pale man with black hair, naked from the waist up, scratching himself, a look of disgust on his face. I wondered if the man was Jean-Paul Sartre.

The game went on and on, and we never cheered. One of the cheerleaders—a big blond girl, whose chest and thighs shook when she jumped—kept looking up at us, anger and horror mingled in her face. I had been thinking that Jamey and I were a good-looking pair—both of us lightly built, with pale skin and dark hair and big dark eyes. But from the way this cheerleader looked at us, you might have thought that we were gargoyles, or the Antichrist himself, sitting in the upper bleachers of Assumption High.

When the game ended, we ran down the bleachers and walked home. As we walked Jamey told me about *Nausea*. "It's existentialism," he said.

"What's that?"

Jamey smiled. "Somebody once asked Sartre to define existentialism. Sartre pointed to an empty blackboard. 'That's existentialism,' he said.

"You can't define it," Jamey went on. "It just *is*."

I could think of nothing more to say. We crossed the street. Jamey's younger brother Tim was standing around with five or six other boys, smoking cigarettes in front of Ryan's grocery. They met there every day, to smoke and talk.

"Hey, Jamey, you seen Clancy?" Tim shouted.

"No," Jamey said.

"Was he in Latin today?"

"Probably," Jamey said. We kept walking. I thought about all the afternoons I had seen Jamey standing there with the other boys as I walked home from school. I had never thought, then, that he and I would become friends.

Friends was the word I used for it. I wasn't sure what else to call it.

I wondered if Jamey ever missed those long afternoons of smoking and fighting and talking—but then I thought of one afternoon when my friend Mary Beth and I had been standing inside the grocery, selling tickets for a church raffle and listening to the conversation of the boys outside. They were talking about knees. Girls' knees.

John Clancy said that you could tell a Protestant girl from a Catholic girl by the shape of her knees. Protestant knees were round and sometimes "lopsided," he said, while Catholic knees were "lovely and square." "It's all the kneeling in the church that makes them square," he said.

Mary Beth and I had exchanged glances.

Pat Muldoon challenged Clancy's theory. "What about scrubwomen?" he said. "They spend half their life kneeling, but

I've never seen one with your lovely square knees. They're all bumpy, sort of."

Clancy said that scrubwomen kneel on a different part of the knee. Their weight was thrown forward as they scrubbed, he said. Whereas Catholic girls knelt in an upright position, which distributed their weight evenly across their kneecaps.

Mary Beth and I laughed about it later, but at the time we were stealing looks at each other's knees.

I decided now that Jamey must have outgrown that sort of conversation.

"How do you live, if you believe in existentialism?" I asked him.

"You don't believe in it, exactly," Jamey said. "It's more like all of a sudden you're different. You see things differently, you act differently." He pushed back his hair from his forehead.

"Like, Sartre is in a café and he sees a glass of beer," he went on. "Perfectly normal glass of beer, nothing odd about it. Except that suddenly he *sees* it, like for the first time. He can't take it for granted, the way other people do. It's *out* there. It scares him."

I didn't know what to make of that. "A man scared of a glass of beer?" I said. It reminded me of something my mother said: "The French make everything into a problem." Of course, she was thinking of the Delacroix family over on Water Street.

"Wait." Jamey stopped walking. He pulled the book from his jacket pocket, and began to flip through its pages. When he found what he wanted, he read it aloud to me.

It was exactly as he had described it. A man scared sick by a glass of beer. But there was a bit at the end that made sense to me. "Read that part again," I said.

He read: "'I am alone in the midst of these happy reasonable voices. All these creatures spend their time explaining, realizing happily that they agree with each other. In Heaven's name, why is it so important to think the same things all together.'"

"*That* I understand," I said.

Jamey looked up from the book. His face was serious, his hair was in his eyes. I thought for a second that he might try to kiss me right there in the middle of Butler Avenue.

But I looked away and shifted the books in my arms. We walked on.

After a while, I asked, "What kind of teacher is Loden?"

"He's all right," Jamey said. He looked over at me. "All the girls seem to think they're in love with him."

"Really?" Of course I already knew that, thanks to my sister Edna. Mr. Loden had long brown hair—long enough to touch his shirt collar—and he wore gold-rimmed glasses and tweedy suits. I had passed him in the hallway many times, and after he went by, I could still smell his after-shave. Mr. Loden was the only person in the school who smelled like that. Edna said it was English Leather. Good stuff, she said, a cut above the Jade East and Brut that some of the seniors wore.

Jamey was still looking at me. "I'm not in love with him," I said.

"I didn't think you were," he said.

We reached my house and stood for a moment on the front porch. "Let me borrow that book when you're through," I said.

"Sure," he said. He was watching me intently. I liked the way he looked, standing there in the shade of the porch, his hair falling into his eyes as usual, and I liked the way he was interested in me. He never took girls for granted, he seemed to think them mysterious. And he seemed to find me more mysterious than anyone. I assumed it was because he didn't have any sisters.

"See you later," I said, and went through the front door.

"Hey, Kathleen?" he called. I turned around. "I'll talk to you later," he said.

I smiled and shut the door. Cryptic, be cryptic, I told myself. Keep him guessing. Inside, I set my books on the stairs. The house smelled like corned beef. I held my breath as I walked toward the kitchen.

My mother was paring potatoes at the sink. She said I could do the carrots. Then she asked about school. The smell of corned beef was everywhere. I didn't want to talk much. I didn't want to open my mouth and let the smell of corned beef get inside.

"What about those tests?" my mother asked. She took a peeler from the kitchen drawer and handed it to me.

"Tests?" I said, thinking of the corned beef. "Tests?"

"Those tests you were telling me about," she said. "L.Q. tests."

"I.Q.," I said, picking up a carrot. I began to scrape away the grayish skin. "Sister says they'll have the results next week."

"And?"

"And the guidance counselor will call each of us in," I said. "But she won't tell us the number, the actual I.Q. Sister said she'll tell us we did poorly, or average, or good, or very good, or excellent. She said two years ago they had someone who was *very* excellent. Someone like Einstein, I guess."

My mother thought for a minute. "It might have been the eldest Clancy boy."

"Roger Clancy?" I was skeptical. I remembered him as a fat boy with pimples. Now he was studying to be a priest.

"He had a photographic memory, everyone said." My mother didn't understand these things, but I wasn't about to correct her. "These numbers," she went on, "these I.Q.'s, what do they mean?"

"Sister said they are a measure of intelligence," I said. "They measure your ability to think in certain kinds of ways."

"But they use them to award the scholarships?"

"I'm not sure," I said. "Sister said that I.Q. is very important. But she didn't say exactly why."

I finished paring the last carrot and went to put the peelings into the garbage can. Then I came back to the table to cut the carrots. My father liked them cut lengthwise, then in chunks. The home economics teacher at school said it was more nutritious to cut them only in chunks, leaving the cores intact. I had told my father this, and he said, "Baloney."

"This way all the vitamins escape into the water," I said to myself, as I cut the things lengthwise.

"What?" my mother asked.

"Nothing. How was your day?"

"Well. Bridget was a fussy one," she began.

My sister Edna came in. "He's home, and he's into the scotch whiskey," she said.

My mother kept on peeling potatoes, but her mouth twitched.

"And he's tired tonight," Edna said. "He's painting that house at the corner of Leicester Avenue, that high red one, so he's bound to be tired."

"Well, stay out of his way," my mother said. She looked worried, but she almost always looked worried. Her mouth turned down, and her eyes had a vague look to them. Edna said our mother had a rough childhood. Her parents were dead, and she never talked about them.

I put the pan of carrots on the stove. "What are your plans for tonight?" my mother asked Edna. I left the kitchen.

The upstairs bathroom reeked of mineral spirits. He used the stuff to clean his hands. Slime clung to the bathroom sink, with flecks of red paint in it. "He's worse than a child," I whispered, cleaning most of it away with toilet paper.

Supper started badly. Bridget grabbed a potato from the dish, then shrieked and dropped it. My father shouted at her.

"The potato was hot," my mother protested.

"That child will not throw good food on the floor," my father said, ignoring my mother. "She will learn that I won't tolerate it."

The rest of us ate rapidly. We waited for him to finish, but my father wasn't very hungry that night. He left a large piece of meat on his plate. "Too much fat," he said.

"Usually he likes the fat," I heard Edna say as she and Michael went to scrape plates in the kitchen.

I went upstairs to do homework. I felt a little guilty, leaving my mother and Bridget alone with him.

It was turning dark, and the sky was streaked with red. My lamp made a yellow circle on the table that I used as a desk. I did all of the math, then the science. When I began the English I turned on the radio. The top-forty station was playing requests. I stopped writing to listen between the songs, in case anyone dedicated a song to Kathleen.

Soon after nine, the telephone rang. The noise was faint, muffled by the rooms below me. But I heard it, and stopped writing. My brother, Michael, came to the foot of the stairs and shouted, "Kathleen!" I jumped from the chair and ran down.

It was Jamey. He said he couldn't talk long because he was going to help his father work on their car.

"Did you do your homework?" I asked.

"No."

"I'm still doing mine," I said.

"I've been reading *Nausea*," Jamey said. "Also I went to see Clancy. We're going to buy a guitar."

"What kind of guitar?"

"An electric bass. A Gibson. I'll take you to see it if you'd like to."

"I would like to," I said. "I didn't know that you played guitar."

"I don't yet," he said.

We seemed to have run out of things to say.

After a while, Jamey said, "How was your day?"

I tried to think of something I hadn't told him earlier. "We didn't have history," I said. "We had a movie instead."

"Any good?"

"No. It was about modern industry. It had cartoon characters in a factory. Like, Donald Duck makes steel. Daisy Duck worked in the cafeteria, and gave him a hard time. Larry Baker got sent to the office for mocking it."

"They make those movies for little rich kids who don't have a foundry down the street," Jamey said.

"Probably. Mr. Logan came into study hall later and told us that he thought it was a dumb movie, too."

Jamey was silent.

I pretended to kiss the receiver, making no sound. "Tell me more about existentialism," I said.

"Hold on," he said. "I'll get the book."

I heard laughter coming from the television set in the living room. But no one was laughing in our house. Probably a rerun, I thought.

"Okay." Jamey came back on the line. "Okay, listen: 'Nothing happens while you live. The scenery changes, people come in and go out, that's all. There are no beginnings. Days are tacked on to days without rhyme or reason, an interminable, monotonous addition.'"

I disagreed. But I kept quiet. I listened.

"'There are moments—rarely—when you make a landmark, you realize that you're going with a woman, in some messy business. The time of a flash. After that, the procession starts again.'"

His voice was a monotone. I tuned it out, briefly, then began to listen again. "'But everything changes when you tell about life; it's a change no one notices: the proof is that people talk about true stories. As if there could possibly be true stories; things happen one way and we tell about them in the opposite sense.'"

I was about to comment on this when a voice said, "Will you look at that." My father had come up behind me. "I thought that you were upstairs, doing your homework." He stood in the hallway, his hand on the wall. I could smell the whiskey.

I put my hand over the telephone's mouthpiece. "Daddy, I was. I've only been talking for a few minutes."

"Give me that," he said. He grabbed the receiver from my hand.

"Look, you," he said into the telephone. "Kathleen has better things to do than waste time listening to your nonsense. Do you hear me? You children have schoolwork to do." He hung up the receiver.

I stared at him. "You had no right to do that."

"No right? In my own home?" He kept his eyes on the telephone. "It's you that has no right, as long as you're living under my roof. Now you remember that."

He brushed past me, headed for the kitchen. Then he turned back. "Get yourself upstairs and finish your homework. Your mother keeps telling me you're a smart girl. Don't you be silly and throw that away. Talking to boys at night at your age." He shook his head. He would become maudlin next, I thought.

I shook my head back at him. "I hate you," I said, my voice low.

"Ah, she hates me." He grinned, and turned back toward the kitchen. "Go on now," he said over his shoulder. "Upstairs with you."

I didn't move. "Coward," I said.

He stopped walking.

"You don't face up to yourself," I said. "Instead you bully us."

He whirled around and took three quick steps toward me, raising his hand. I ducked to the right, to spare my face.

But he didn't hit me. When I looked up, he was on his way to the kitchen again. He slammed shut the door behind him, and I heard his voice bellowing for my mother.

I ran up the stairs and into my room. I sat at my desk, vowing that I wouldn't cry. Crying, I knew, was what he wanted. I pulled a piece of paper from my notebook and drew a line on it. The line was my life. I penciled jagged upswings and downturns. I labeled some of them: "Bridget born," and "Began seventh grade," and "Met Jamey." Then I made the line turn upward and climb steeply, without fluctuating. I labeled the turning point: "Eighteenth birthday—left home."

I left the paper on my desk, but I kept looking at it as I got ready for bed.

After I switched out the light, my mind turned over and over again. Eventually it settled to thinking about my father. For some reason I thought of the night three years before, when President John Kennedy died. We watched the television all evening, and later, when I was unable to sleep, I went downstairs again. My parents were still sitting on the couch. The room was dark but for the television's blue flicker. My father was lying in my mother's arms and he was weeping. I never saw him cry before or since. He was saying, "I loved that man. I loved that man."

At the time, the words had moved me. But now they made me feel nothing. The scene was unfamiliar, unlikely, as if I'd dreamed it. I tried to sleep. But the image remained in my head like a photograph.

Long after midnight, I heard the foundry whistle signal the changing shifts. Later I heard the train, gathering speed as it pulled away from the city. I lay in bed with my eyes open until the room began to grow light again. I heard my mother walk downstairs to make coffee and my father cough as he ran water in the bathroom. I listened without any anger to the noises they made. I couldn't find it in me to hate them.

When it was time for me to get up, my body felt stiff and cold. I pushed my arms into the shirt that was part of the school uniform. As I buttoned it, I caught sight of the paper on my desk, with the map of my life on it. It seemed childish, silly, to me now. I tore the paper into bits. Then, to amuse myself, I pulled up my bedroom storm window a few inches and pushed the pieces through the gap. They fell as lightly as dust or dandelion fluff. A moment later I saw my father walk over them, as he left the house to go to work again.

Robert Olmstead

Kennedy's Head

I read in *The New York Times* where Luis Alvarez, professor of physics at Berkeley, did this experiment wherein he thought Kennedy's head was much like a melon. Now this Luis Alvarez did win the Nobel Prize and he did invent detonators for the atomic bomb and he did watch same bomb, nickname: Little Boy, dust off Hiroshima, so you'd think he'd've called it quits. You'd think he'd've had enough science on his hands for one lifetime, but I guess not. He had to go and think of Kennedy's head being much like a melon.

It seems Professor Alvarez thought the high-velocity bullet impacting on a soft target would not give up much energy, but would pierce the target and propel material forward along its path. He and some students set up an experiment in which rifle bullets were fired at melons wrapped in filament tape to see what the laws of physics require.

The result was that the melons recoiled in the direction of the rifle. The explanation was that the bullet energized a fast jet of fluid and solid matter in the bullet's direction producing the backward recoil, the rocket-jet recoil of Newton's law of action and reaction. This forward jet effect is clearly visible in frame 314 of the Zapruder film and in the Alvarez melon photographs.

There'd been much ado about Kennedy's head going in a direction one would not expect and this gave credence to conspiracy theories that involve a second gunman.

I thought, Shit, I can do that. I got rifles. I got bullets. I can get melons, all kinds of rifles, bullets, and melons. Now, I'm not fond of melon. Cantaloupes tend to repeat on me much like cucumbers. I'm not fond of watermelons either. My last memory of watermelons goes back to 1979. I was working in the nation of Texas, building a power line. In that part of Texas there were miles and miles of watermelons we'd drive through. The crew would jump off the truck and steal those melons. They'd eat them and then as we'd pass by another crew they'd all wing the rinds at each other, breaking mirrors, windshields, and opening up heads. Let me tell you, a watermelon rind at forty miles an hour can do some damage. They'd yell insults, too, insults at each other's mothers who weren't even around. Then things would really get hot. These were the great watermelon wars of south Texas. You might've read about them. I was there. I ate some of that pink flesh. It was our idea of fun at the time. I ate so much watermelon, I don't care if I ever see one again.

While we're on the subject, I don't like physics, either. When I was a kid, my grandmother's cure for all maladies was a physic. She'd say, That boy needs a physic. She'd smile when she said it and head for the kitchen like that's where everyone keeps their medicine. Like that's where everyone deals with matter, energy, motion, and force. I did one time, though, have a substitute science teacher who spoke lovingly of the fourth and fifth dimensions. That was beautiful to hear, but then she never came back.

It's funny how memory can follow you like that, it changing your mind before you've made it up. I think it's the way memory lingers quietly in there next door to a lot of low-rent facts long after cause, long after experience or inception.

My memory made the idea of shooting watermelons and calling it physics quite appealing. You might say I'd be killing two birds with one stone.

I called my friend Wood. He's a good shot, able to raise much hell with quail, pheasants, and sporting clay. His name is Wood Gill. I like having Wood Gill for a friend. When I introduce him, I say, This Wood Gill. I say it in a way so as most people mishear it to be This Would Kill and it always gets the meeting off on the wrong foot.

I told him Luis Alvarez wrapped a melon in filament tape and fired rifle bullets at it.

He asked if Luis Alvarez didn't have anything better to do, apparently mistaking him for another Luis Alvarez we both knew and mistrusted.

I said, "He did already invent the atomic bomb, drop it on Hiroshima, and win the Nobel Prize."

Wood said, "Well, why didn't he name it the Alvarez Bomb if he invented it?"

"I don't know," I said, "but this thing with the melon. It proves why Kennedy's head went in the direction of the rifle as opposed to the direction of the path of the bullet."

Me and Wood had talked about seeing the Oliver Stone movie, *JFK*, that was getting so much play on the television, but it costs over six bucks a head and that buys a lot of bullets and melons.

He said, "Is this something you want to do or just talk about it?"

"Don't play with me," I said. "Come along."

I go easy with Wood. He's just coming back into the world. In 1980 he went inside his house because he'd shot another man and he didn't come out until 1989. He'd seen the video *In Country* and thought going to the Vietnam memorial was the thing to do, a way to come back, but he didn't feel anything the way they did in the movie. He didn't feel anything. He felt nothing.

He told me afterwards there was this woman sitting on the steps of the Lincoln Memorial. He could see up her dress. He'd come to the Capitol to see the sights, but he didn't reckon on seeing that. He told me she didn't look to be a loose woman, but she did have on these red shoes and a short red skirt, so he thought she could be either way. He told me she was so beautiful he wanted to stay there forever. He hoped he wasn't menacing. He prayed she wouldn't catch him looking at her, because between her tan thighs it was so dark and he wanted time for his eyes to adjust.

The man Wood killed was a black man named Lloyd Kuntz. It had nothing to do with him being black and all. It was that he was a salesman and somehow he'd crossed Wood's threshold without calling out. Wood shot him. Some say Wood shot him on the front step. Some even say he shot him in the yard and then dragged him inside. That's just being smart. If you have shot someone you should drag him inside your house and say that's where he was shot. It makes things a lot more simple. That's about all for history and advice.

I met up with Wood at The Three Pines in Mount Holly. It's where I met him for the first time, late at night, long after last call. The bartender was a young guy I knew of who carried a spring-loaded nightstick that'd leap to extension at the push of a button. In his hands, it surely was a stick of night. I'd seen him drop a few drunks, a few of the obstreperous. Wood wanted a beer and the young guy said no. I'd taken an immediate liking to Wood when he walked in the door, so I clued him in and gave him my emergency six-pack I keep in the trunk next to the spare and the flares.

Wood pulled in beside me, our vehicles aiming in opposite directions so we could talk out our windows.

He said, "So no school today?"

"No. Not today."

"That's right," he said. "You teach at the college. How many hours is it you teach?"

He likes to hear how many hours I teach. I tell him eight or nine a week. I tell him I meet with students, too, and I write a lot.

Wood plucked at the bill of his cap and tromped on the gas. His engine had been racing and now it stopped.

"You don't write dick," he said. "You call me up on the phone, talk a little and then you make up shit. You're not a writer. You're a tape recorder."

Little did Wood know that he'd just stumbled across the latest in literary critical theory. At least I think it's the latest. Things in that field are happening as fast as the printers can go. I myself have trouble keeping a straight face about a machine called a laptop. One time, though, I did go to the Modern Language Association Conference. It was in Washington, D.C. The Maharishi Yogi was holding a press conference in the basement. I hung out for a while hoping to see what he looked like, but his gunmen chased me away.

"Come on," I said. "Let us go out to the range. I have melons and duct tape and bullets and guns."

"Sounds like a party," Wood said.

Wood doesn't work much, either. He got hit in the head. He's certified crazy. So he, too, was free for the day.

He followed me to Dillsburg, ghosting along behind. I watched him in the rearview mirror. He'd pull at his cap and sip from a Styrofoam cup. He drove with one hand. I was glad he was coming, otherwise I wouldn't've had the courage to go.

It was a weekday morning in January and nobody was at the range to ask us questions. We took out the melons, cantaloupes, and wrapped them in duct tape. I should say here we used duct tape because I didn't know what filament tape was and as I write this I still don't know, and don't care.

They were small melons. That's to say they weren't very big melons. They were the size of a smaller man's head, say like your Japanese-type man. I'd brought a watermelon, too, but I had that hid. I was saving it for a kind of surprise.

I'm reminded by myself here that there was another time I had with a watermelon. I was a senior in high school. We took out a plug and spiked it with vodka. We took it into English class for an end-of-the-year occasion. The teacher's name was Mr. Butler. He's still in the world someplace but where, I'm not sure. Could still be teaching high school English. He loved literature. He had a small head, too. I remember I studied hard for his final exam and I got an A on it. He was very appreciative, like I'd done it for him and I guess I did. It was rough sledding, though, too rough to turn into a habit. It's how I got through school. I scuffed along, trying to turn it into something of my own. Even now, as I teach people who want to learn to write, I should tell them to fail more often. It will be good practice for life, for the work. It's something they should get used to. Even though I should, I don't, because failure is easier to learn when you're alone, when no one is around to bring it to your attention.

We set the melons out fifty yards. We stacked shot bags on the bench to make a gun rest.

"Do you want to be the scientist," Wood said, "or do you want me to?"

"Oh, you go ahead. You're a better shot than I am."

It's right here where I should stop and get something off my chest. One time me and Wood were hunting cockbird and one came running out of the sorghum into a grass alley I was walking. I wasn't thinking and I shot that bird on the ground. Wood was real quiet and in his quietude let me know what he thought of my conduct. It wasn't a tasty bird but I made myself eat it. No, that's not true. It was a tasty bird, but I didn't let myself enjoy it. Actually, that's half true.

Wood shot the first melon and I wanted to ask him if he felt more like Lee Oswald or Luis Alvarez. But he wouldn't understand, because he always feels like himself.

"What'd you see," I said. Wood can see a bullet hit, much in the same way Ted Williams could see the bat hit the ball. Myself, I used to carpenter and when you were firing on all cylinders, say in August, say late in the day's heat, you could see the shank of the spike shiver its way into the lumber. This would've been artistic and all Zen-like if it hadn't been New Hampshire.

"Nothing," Wood said. "I didn't see nothing."

I know what you're thinking, and you should watch those thoughts if you're prone to them, because people who use double negatives simply mean it twice. Wood meant he didn't see nothing.

"Shoot another," I said. "Try the aught-six."

I watched those melons go down one after another. I kept asking him what he'd seen and he kept telling me nothing, nothing at all. I'd push him, but it was like pulling teeth, like getting blood out of a stone.

It just comes down to the fact that the truth is the truth.
There's a lot of difference between a melon and Kennedy's head.
For instance, nobody remembers where they were the day Luis
Alvarez shot the melons. Plus Kennedy had that beautiful wife.
The melon doesn't leave behind a beautiful, grieving widow
who goes on to become a book editor and comes to know my
name because of a book review I write one time. Of course, I've
always known of her and always felt much sympathy and
compassion for her. When I was in Texas, by the way, I did see
John Connally. He came into the bar I was in and I'll be damned
if he didn't order milk. John Connally doesn't know me from a
bag of assholes.

"What I get a kick out of," Wood said, "is how the guy who
invented dynamite gave a prize to the guy who invented the
bomb."

"It's not like that," I said. "Nobel is dead so he couldn't give
the prize himself and Luis Alvarez didn't invent the bomb. He
invented a detonator. What he got the prize for, I don't know."

"Oh well, by Jesus. Their hands are clean then, aren't they?"

"There's a lot of responsibility to go around. There's a lot of
evil in the world."

"You lied to me," he said.

"Yes, I did. Think of it like the government. I did it for your
own good."

"What good?"

"I haven't figured that out yet, but when I do, you can be
assured I'll tell you."

"No matter. We'd best sashay on out of here before some of
those save-the-melons folks show up. I'd hate for there to be a
confrontation."

I collected my guns and loaded them into the trunk alongside
the watermelon. I'd spent an hour out there and now I was
leaving the shot melons to rot. I'd spent an hour out there with
Wood, a guy I had made up. I'd made him up for purposes of
shooting melons and didn't like the idea of bringing him back to
where I lived.

Later, as I drove the rolling hills, piloted my car parallel to the creek, I considered how Luis Alvarez thought Kennedy's head was much similar to a melon. Now I'd agree we've had presidents where one could assume as much, but it was never my impression of Kennedy. How could he think Kennedy's head was like a melon, and while we're at it, back in '45, if Luis Alvarez was so goddamn smart, couldn't he hear the earth sigh when they dropped that atomic bomb? Didn't he get to see the birds ignite in the air, the people's internal organs boil away, the schoolgirls struck blind, riddled with glass, and burned to char? Couldn't he feel some of the fifty thousand degrees, see at least one of the seventy-eight thousand souls?

War drove those scientists, but all along it was truth they were looking for. Can we ever be so fond of truth again? Would we take our killed into our house for any reason?

Wood punched me in the arm, called me Hoss, said he didn't look forward to my moody company.

"This is something we shouldn't ought've done," he said. "It's disrespectful."

"I know," I said and it was then I confessed I know who it was shot Kennedy. I know where he is, but I'm not telling nothing.

Susan Power

Moonwalk

Margaret Many Wounds was dying. Three years earlier she had been diagnosed as diabetic, and now, although she felt her health rapidly declining, she refused to go to the hospital.

"I am old anyway," she told her relatives. "Leave me be."

Early one morning she called to her daughter: "Let me have a mirror." Lydia fetched her mother a compact mirror, removing the powder puff before she placed it in her hands. Margaret thanked Lydia and fluttered her fingers to wave her daughter away.

Margaret peered at her reflection, moving the compact in a circle so she could see her entire face. She thought she looked transparent as baby crayfish in the Little Heart River. Margaret had never been a vain woman, one to consult each mirror she passed or smooth her hair as she caught her reflection in a storefront window. She simply wanted to make certain she was still there, still flesh and sweet blood and silver hair. There were days she was so light, she couldn't be sure. She felt herself floating beneath the covers, held down by sweat and three-star quilts. She couldn't eat anymore. Tender meat was like gristle, dinner rolls like gravel and the sunflower seeds Margaret had once craved hard as cherry pits. But she requested a bowl of *waštúnkala,* Sioux corn soup. It had been a staple on the Standing Rock Sioux Reservation where Margaret lived, but was now a delicacy as it required extensive preparation. Margaret's twin daughters were busy in the kitchen, fixing what might prove to be their mother's last supper. Evie soaked dried corn in water while Lydia cut venison into strips.

Evie poked her head into her mother's bedroom. "Will you be able to eat it once it's made?" she asked.

"The broth will slide down my gullet just easy," Margaret said, stroking her throat with emaciated fingers as if to demonstrate.

"It'll be a while," Evie told her, for the corn would have to soak overnight, and the broth simmer for most of the next day.

"I know," said Margaret.

Evie was impatient. She wanted to serve it now and see her mother's dark brown eyes shine, flash once again with amber sparks. *This is just typical,* Evie thought. She believed reservation life was out of balance, a place where everything that was trivial took an inordinate amount of time while the momentous things occurred with obscene rapidity. *It's why I left all those years ago,* she told herself. *And why I never came back. Until now.*

"What?" Margaret asked. She snapped the compact shut and placed it on her bedside table.

"Nothing." Evie returned to the kitchen, the central area of Margaret's small cabin.

"And don't you let that Father Zimmer near me!" Margaret called after her daughter. "All he wants to do is have the last word over my body, and go fishing for my soul."

Margaret had spent many years as one of Father Zimmer's faithful. But in past weeks, bedridden and preoccupied with mortality, she had withdrawn from him.

"I'm not a sheep," she'd ranted late at night when everyone else was asleep. "There's still time to go back." Margaret had recovered an old faith from her youth, from the days when there was magic, before the concept of sin had washed over Sioux people as the Oahe Dam had flooded their reservation with stagnant water.

I have been defeated by guilt, Margaret decided. That is when she had her grandson, Harley, bury her cedar rosary in the dirt yard. "Maybe something useful will grow," she told him. She took to praying to *Wákan Tánka,* the Great Spirit of her childhood who had not been a jealous God, she thought, but had waited patiently for her to honor Him again.

"Mama's sure down on the old padre," Evie said. Lydia nodded, cleaning the serrated knife she'd used to carve venison. "You'd think at a time like this she'd want to hold onto him for comfort," Evie continued. Lydia shrugged her shoulders.

"Well, *I* won't let him in." Evie wouldn't push Catholicism on her mother. She didn't like what she considered the powerlessness of faith, preferring the safety of a world she could see with her own eyes.

"I wonder where Philbert's taken off to," Evie said. Her husband, Philbert, had left early that morning in their dented Chevy.

"I'm off to rediscover warrior country," he'd told her, blowing Evie a kiss as he backed out of the cabin.

"He's probably discovered a six-pack and some no-good buddies," Evie said.

Moments later she heard a car door slam in the yard, and her missing husband, chewing Spearmint gum to mask his beery breath, burst into the kitchen and caught Evie around the waist in a powerful hug, as if he'd been magically conjured by her thoughts.

Evie hadn't looked back after leaving Standing Rock and moving to Minneapolis seven years earlier. "You look back, you never get off the res," she told Philbert when he complained of being homesick. But Lydia's short note—*Please come, Mama's dying*—roused her.

Philbert and Evie drove from Minneapolis to Fort Yates, North Dakota, in a day, their trunk full of groceries they bought in Bismark. It was July 17, 1969, and all the way from Minneapolis they listened to news programs covering the Apollo 11 mission to the moon. Astronauts Neil Armstrong and Edwin Aldrin were due to land on the moon in three days.

"It's gonna be a miracle," Philbert had said at the conclusion of each special report. Upon hearing it for the umpteenth time,

Evie glared at him. He was oblivious. He steered the car with his elbows, leaving his hands free to mop sweat from his forehead and upper lip.

"Wish we had some of that air conditioning," he complained. He stuck his head out of the window to catch a breeze but was whipped by sandy grit.

Evie thought Philbert looked like a bug. More like a bug each year with his long skinny arms and legs, loose as tentacles, and stunted round torso. His head was shaved in a buzz cut because he was lazy and didn't like to comb his hair. Philbert was thirty years old, five years older than Evie, and currently retired. At the peak of his rodeo career as a champion bull rider he'd been stepped on. The bull's hoof left a small V-shaped scar directly over his heart, and even though several doctors had declared him healthy, he said his heart couldn't take it. "It won't let me do this anymore," he told Evie when she urged him to ride again.

Evie had no patience with Philbert's heart but she didn't argue. She worked full time as a secretary for a lawyer in Minneapolis and cooked dinner for Philbert when she returned home at night. She supposed there were women in America who would chide her for such slavish devotion, but she knew something they didn't; she had never loved him. She had been drawn to him because he was a successful bull rider, because he was bowlegged and uncomfortable without his dusty cowboy hat jammed tightly on his head. In short, she was attracted to him because he matched perfectly the image of her father she'd developed in a cloud of ignorance. Spoiling Philbert was Evie's way of apologizing for her lack of sentiment.

During the tedious drive from Minneapolis, Evie had time to anticipate her reunion with Lydia. The endless comparisons she'd once made between them had tapered off in the years they were apart, but Evie found herself resurrecting the habit as her husband fiddled with the car radio.

Lydia had always been the good daughter, sweet-tempered and incurious, never dreaming of taking flight. And Evie wasn't beautiful like Lydia. Her nose was too thin and her upper lip so narrow it almost disappeared when she smiled. Her hair was dry and frizzy from too many perms and she wore black-framed glasses attached to a beaded daisy chain around her neck, removing them in order to read. But she had won Philbert because she inherited what he called her mother's magnetism, a term Evie hated.

All her life Evie had envied her sister's beauty and placid nature. Right up until Lydia's husband and son were killed in a car accident. Lydia was pregnant with Harley at the time, and Evie believed his existence was what kept Lydia alive. As it was, she had seen her sister give up pieces of herself, including her voice. Lydia hadn't spoken a word since the accident, although she did sing at powwows.

People said she had the voice of a ghost. When Lydia sang, women would carry their tape recorders to the drum to record her, and men would soften their voices to let Lydia's rise, above the dancers' heads, above the smoke of cigarettes and burning sage, some thought beyond the atmosphere to that dark place where the air is thin and *Wanâǧi Taćánku,* the Spirit Road, begins.

When Evie and Philbert finally pulled up in front of Margaret's cabin, five-year-old Harley was playing in the dirt yard, arranging pebbles and abandoned keys in elaborate patterns. He watched solemnly as his aunt and uncle stepped out of the car.

"Grandma is dying," he said in a voice surprisingly deep and hoarse.

"I know," Evie said, moving past him to enter the house. Philbert remained behind to meet the nephew he'd seen only in photographs.

Margaret's cabin was whitewashed and clean, but bare. There had been a dirt floor when Evie and Lydia were growing up, but now there were planks covered with red-speckled linoleum. There were two large rooms and an outhouse in back. Lydia had placed cornflowers on the kitchen table and was cooking *wóžapi,* a berry pudding, when her sister entered.

Evie thought that perhaps Lydia would finally speak after five years of silence to greet her, but instead she calmly set aside her mixing spoon and gave Evie a quick hug.

"Good to see you," Evie whispered. Lydia nodded and retrieved her spoon.

Evie looked in on her mother, who was so pale she was almost white. *She isn't dying, she's fading,* thought Evie.

When Margaret saw Evie, she said, "My girl," and waved a creamy hand.

Mama looks like a white woman, Evie thought as she sat down on the edge of Margaret's bed.

"You were always my favorite," Margaret whispered to her daughter.

"No, Mama, this is Evelyn," Evie said in a loud voice.

"That's right. I know it."

Mama is confused, Evie decided.

"My girl, I've missed you." Margaret held Evie's hand. "I have just a few things to give away so let me tell you what to do."

Margaret told Evie that a set of books including the complete works of Jane Austen should be given to Harley in ten years, on his fifteenth birthday. Lydia was to have her mother's wedding moccasins, which had only been worn the one time. They were exquisitely beaded: a background of white cut beads framing beaded crimson roses. Evie was to have a gold locket she never knew her mother owned. Margaret pulled it from beneath her nightgown. The gold case was big as her thumb, with the monogram *MMM.* Evie wondered what was inside but didn't ask.

For the next couple of days the sisters looked after their mother together and spent hours at the kitchen table playing gin rummy. Evie no longer enjoyed the game. When she was little all she wanted to do was beat Lydia, even if it meant cheating, hiding unmatched cards beneath sets she spread like a fan and set down with a flourish. Lydia never seemed to suspect Evie's string of wins, but played round after round with dogged enthusiasm, as if she expected to win at any moment.

Evie no longer cheated but found herself winning just as regularly. It was too easy. Lydia gave up the cards Evie needed time and again, and even when she passed them up to help Lydia win, inevitably the card she drew from the deck was equally valuable. She couldn't lose. But Evie continued to play because the game made Lydia's silence less oppressive. As children they had played quietly. Each knew where the other wanted to go, what she wanted to do, with one glance. Evie realized that the present suspension of speech was different, uninformed, but she found it comforting, anyway. It was the way they had always played cards.

Two days after her prodigal daughter returned, Margaret had requested the last bowl of corn soup. It was good to hear the girls moving together in the kitchen. The soup wouldn't be ready until the next day, but already Margaret could taste it, could feel the warm broth in her stomach.

Later that night Lydia and Harley returned to their own little house a half mile down the gravel road. Evie and Philbert made pallets on the kitchen floor, and Margaret could hear them whispering in the dark for a while.

Margaret tried to sleep, but she heard scuffling feet and smothered giggles at the foot of her bed. She saw people crowding her bedroom. They were sitting on little wooden chairs, facing her bed, waiting like an audience. She started to ask them who they were but caught herself just in time. It would be rude. Sioux hospitality required that she welcome all visitors.

"Do you want me to tell you the story?" Margaret asked the dark figures. "It's been in my head for so many days now." They all nodded. Margaret closed her eyes and pressed her hands together. She began to speak:

"Charles Bad-Holy MacLeod returned to the reservation in

1912 when I was seventeen. He came back from the Indian School in Carlisle, Pennsylvania, wearing a white man's suit with a high starched collar. He came back with twenty books and a head full of education. He came back lonely and ignorant. He looked like a full-blood despite the way he'd parted his short hair straight down the middle, but he didn't remember one story about Fort Yates or his own tribe. He didn't remember one honor song.

"We worked a trade to educate one another. He read to me until eventually I learned to make out the words. Our favorite book was *Pride and Prejudice*. I liked that little white girl, Elizabeth Bennet, because she had wit and a backbone. I thought she would have made a good Sioux. In return I told him all the stories and legends about where he came from. I taught him many songs. We liked the warrior ones best because they were so conceited. We would laugh when we sang the chorus: *I have arrived, the battle will soon be over.* I even took him to the Grand River one night so he could hear a ghost. It was the ghost of a chief's son who was a *winkté*—a man who loves other men—mourning the loss of a lover killed fighting the Arikara. You could still hear him singing where his people had camped along the river.

"I wanted to reclaim Charles Bad-Holy MacLeod for the tribe and for myself. I pitied him because the reservation agent had taken him away at age four and let Pennsylvania keep him until he was twenty-one. I was grateful my parents had kept me so well-hidden in the brush of Angry Butte, guarded by *Šúnka Sápa,* Black Dog, each time the agent came around. *Šúnka Sápa* would have eaten the agent's scrawny throat before letting him take me. But we always had the last laugh because those Indians taken away to Carlisle would return to the reservation and make up for lost time. They would become the most fanatical traditionals. Even Charles would have given up his white man's suit and learned to dance again if he'd been with me long enough.

"As it was, I made him learn my crooked ways. I shocked

him. On our wedding night I undressed in the lamplight, folding each garment as it was removed, placing it on the back of a chair. I unbraided my hair and used it to wash my breasts. My mother would have been disgusted because I was so immodest. But I did it because the part in my husband's hair looked like a straight white road, the kind I would never travel. His body was brown and I was relieved. I thought the tight clothes might have pinched him white, leeched the color right out of his cells. I had to undo all those buttons and release him because he couldn't move.

"I had the two best years of my life then. Charles did the accounting for a shopkeeper who didn't mind admitting he couldn't figure numbers and an Indian could. We were delighted with one another. My mother thought we were too delighted. She wanted to know when she could expect a grandchild. It's funny I didn't become pregnant in the two years we were together. Maybe if I'd had the son or daughter of Charles Bad-Holy MacLeod I would have managed better when he died of tuberculosis. I wouldn't have left so much of myself in his coffin."

Margaret's voice had awakened Evie and Philbert. They listened, transfixed, to a story they had never heard.

"Why is she doing this? Who's she talking to?" Evie asked.

"She's telling her life," Philbert explained. "Probably just trying to let it go."

"It isn't fair," Evie whispered angrily. "I begged her to tell me things when I was little, family history, all kinds of stuff. And she would just laugh. Tell me I had to find my own answers in the world."

Evie was crying. Philbert had never known Evie to cry before and he didn't know what to do. He wrapped an arm around her and pulled her close, but she held her body stiff as a statue, unyielding as the hard floor beneath them.

"I guess people change when they see death coming," Philbert told his wife. She was suddenly quiet, her weeping

ended. Philbert believed she had fallen asleep when he heard
her sigh.

"I wonder what those astronauts are doing," she said.

In the morning Margaret waited for the sun to light her room,
expecting to see the faces of her audience. But the figures and
chairs were gone. Margaret heard a cough and looked towards
the window. There they were, clustered around her cabin and
peering in, whole families with children perched on their fathers'
shoulders. She couldn't make out who they were.

"It's pretty hot for so early in the morning," Margaret said.
The crowd nodded and she saw a flash of white hankies drawn
across moist faces.

I will finish the story, Margaret thought.

"In seventy-four years I had just two men. One was big
passion and one was understanding. But that's lucky, don't you
think? To have passion and understanding?

"I was forty-nine years old in 1944 when I came to be
working in Bismark. They called me a nurse, but I'd had no
training, just a willingness to work with prisoners of war. About a
thousand of them were in the Bismark camp.

"I worked with Dr. Sei-ichi Sakuma, a surgeon from San
Francisco. He'd volunteered to work at the camp after his wife
died of food poisoning in Manzanar. Dr. Sakuma had brought his
own surgical instruments with him and they were superior to any
in the camp. I thought those instruments were beautiful and
terrible. They fit nicely in my hand; the weight of them was just
right. I handled them efficiently in assisting the doctor. He would
tell me about his wife as he worked. How she wrote limericks
and how she loved to jitterbug. Her name was Evelyn. I
remember her as someone I knew, although we never met. Dr.
Sakuma said I looked a little like her, and he watched me closely.
'I never knew Indians before,' he said.

"In our loneliness we became lovers. 'I thought I would
never want anyone again. It has been thirty years,' I told him. But
we didn't talk about it much. There wasn't time. There wasn't

space, either, so we had to use the medical supply room to have
any privacy. Dr. Sakuma had thin hair and wore wire-rimmed
spectacles that pinched his nose. He was strong, but the bones in
his face looked delicate. When I kissed him I was gentle.

"My mother never told me you could do it standing up. We
had no choice because the medical supply room was so small.
Three feet by three feet, but most of the shelves were bare, so
we could spread our hands across the wood, pressing for
balance. We smelled like rubbing alcohol and had to swallow
sounds to keep our secret. It became a test of will to see how
quiet we could be; violent, reckless, but horribly silent.

"It sounds vulgar, but there wasn't a vulgar thing about it.
Mostly we needed someone to hold onto, reassurance that we
were alive and warm under the skin. For me, it was a thaw.

"I didn't worry about getting pregnant. I guess I thought I was
an old lady. Then I dreamt one night that I had swallowed two
marbles and could feel them in the pit of my stomach. They were
talking inside me like little chatterboxes. 'Quiet, be still,' I
scolded. Later I realized they were my twin girls talking to me in
a dream.

"From the day I discovered I was pregnant I avoided the
camp. I called the medical director to resign and never returned.
This is a sin I haven't wanted to admit. I left Dr. Sakuma with no
explanations, knowing he couldn't leave the camp to find me.
When the war ended I thought maybe he might try, but if he did
I never knew about it.

"You know, I've asked myself so many times why I did this.
Maybe I was worried my girls would be teased because their
mother went to bed with The Enemy. Maybe I was afraid people
would call them 'breeds.' Maybe I was afraid Dr. Sakuma would
reject me once he found out.

"After Lydia and Evelyn were born I returned to Fort Yates
with a big lie about marrying a Canadian Indian who left me.
That lie made me a member of the church and my daughters
full-blood Indians. But it has never tasted right, and maybe that's
why I can't eat the food my daughters bring me. Maybe the

higher powers are scolding me, telling me to let the lie nourish me as I have nourished it. But it's time for the lies to perish, don't you think?"

Evie was stunned and too angry to cry. She was glad she alone had overheard Margaret's confession. Lydia and Harley hadn't arrived yet, and Philbert had gone for a walk, followed by a flock of wild turkeys. Evie couldn't bear to look at her mother. She imagined she would see the words strung out across the room, suspended above her mother's bed.

Margaret had told her daughters their father was a Blood Indian from Calgary. A champion rodeo rider who had won the All-Around title in North Dakota the year Margaret was forty-nine and starting to get an itch. He had been ten years younger but crazy in love, taking Margaret back to Canada when he returned, where they married. Eventually he'd left her, and she made her way back to Fort Yates to have Evie and Lydia.

That was the legend. That was Evie's understanding of her own history. Margaret had kept his name secret, ostensibly to prevent the girls from trying to trace their father. The family name they used was Many Wounds, Margaret's maiden name. But Evie had come up with her father's name. In a dream she had seen her father riding a Brahma bull, his left hand raised triumphantly in the air. She couldn't see him clearly because the bull leapt and twisted, but she heard his name called by the emcee. "The best ride of the day! Let's hear it for Sonny Porter!"

All her life Evie had been the daughter of Sonny Porter. She'd married Philbert because he rode the Brahma bulls so much the way her father had. Evie had even called the Calgary operator once, asking if there was a listing for Sonny Porter. She'd had no luck but imagined he could be anywhere.

At eight years old she'd drawn a picture of him with the silver All-Around trophy in his hand. His face was empty of features except for a great crescent smile traced above his chin.

She believed her father was passionate and adventurous.

I take after him, she had told herself over the years, and the idea pleased her.

A hot breeze moved through the kitchen, and Evie held onto the kitchen table, half expecting she would drift out of the open window.

She had composed herself by the time Philbert returned from his walk. She focused her attention on the simmering corn soup and a stream of radio reports on the moon landing.

Philbert had brought the television set from Lydia's place to Margaret's cabin. He placed it on her low bureau so she could watch it from the bed.

"What's he doing?" Margaret asked Evie.

"The astronauts are landing on the moon today. We thought you'd like to watch it, Mama."

"I've been there," she told Evie. She watched Philbert struggle to reach the outlet behind her dresser.

"What do you mean?" Evie asked, irritated by her mother's remark.

"When I was little, my *Tunkášila,* my grandfather, woke me up in the middle of the night. I was about your age," she told Harley, who stood directly behind Philbert.

"He carried me on his shoulders to a field of prairie grass as high as his waist. He showed me the moon, told me I could go there if I wanted to bad enough. And for just one second I really was there, looking back at the spinning earth, bright as a blue eye."

"Oh," Evie said. Years ago she would have treasured this anecdote, but it had come too late for her to enjoy or believe.

Philbert brought in kitchen chairs for Evie and Lydia to sit on while they waited for the astronauts to emerge from their lunar module.

Margaret paid no attention to the broadcast.

"Takója, come sit with me." Harley sat on the bed with his grandmother. She stroked the back of his head.

"Someday when you're grown up you should liberate my

grandmother's dress," she told him.

"Mama, we can tell him about the dress later. Don't you want to see the men *walking* on the *moon*?"

Margaret waved her hand at Evie. "Are they going to dance? Are they going to put on a show?"

"Yes," said Evie, and Philbert stared at her. "Never mind," she told him.

"My grandmother's dress was the most beautiful and unusual dress people had ever seen. It took her years to finish beading the top of it, from the collar, over the sleeves, down to the waist. The background was blue beads, and she beaded buffalo and Sioux warriors on horseback running through the sky; pictures of their spirits because so many of them were dead. She only wore it to the most sacred ceremonies, and when she danced at the edge of the dancers' circle, she said she was dancing them back to life."

Harley could imagine a buffalo hunt in the sky. He pulled back his right arm and aimed an invisible arrow at the space module settled in lunar dust.

"Okay, it's any minute now. Look, Mama, the astronauts are getting ready to go out." Evie felt it was important for her mother to see. She looked to Lydia for support but her sister stared straight ahead at the television.

"Someone got hold of that dress after Grandma died, and now it's in the Field Museum in Chicago. The Plains Indian section. I was in Chicago just once, years ago, and that was the only thing I wanted to see. I stood there all day practically, trying to figure out how I could get that dress back."

Harley took his grandmother's hand and gave her the rusty skeleton key he'd found in the yard. "I'll get it for you someday," he told her, slipping out of bed to stand beside his mother's chair.

Evie was desperate for the astronauts to leave their vehicle and walk on the moon. She wanted to see it happen and know it was real; a scientific miracle worked out with equations. "It will be history," she said aloud.

"It's all history," Margaret told her, working the skeleton key in her palm like she was trying to find a way out of her skin.

Evie and Lydia were making fry bread, waiting for the corn soup to cool enough to serve their mother. Philbert sat at the kitchen table eating the bread as quickly as it was made.

"Save some for Mama," Evie scolded.

She was in a sour mood. Her mother had been totally unimpressed by the shots of men walking on the moon. Evie had left the bedroom disappointed, convinced that Margaret was so ill she couldn't understand the significance of what had just occurred.

Even Lydia seemed unaffected, kneading the dough as efficiently as ever. *She's getting more like Mama all the time,* Evie thought.

Harley alone remained behind to entertain his grandmother. He saw there were two moons in the world: one on television and one in the sky outside his grandmother's window.

"Two moons," he told Margaret, curling his thumb and forefinger into a telescope he peeked through.

"More than that," Margaret told him, "many, many more. For every person who can see it, there's another one."

Harley ducked his head. The idea filled all the skies he could imagine, and all the rooms, and the spaces between trees, until moons like opaque marbles tumbled out of heaven to roll in a spectacular avalanche down the buttes.

"That way everyone has a moon of their own."

Harley extended his arm so his hand neatly blotted the moon outside the window. He was bending his fingers to encircle its white image, wanting to cup it in his left palm.

"Mine will be a yo-yo," he told Margaret as he tried to pluck it out of the sky.

"*Takója,* come here. I will show you the moon."

Harley turned away from the window and stood beside Margaret's bed. She told him to close his eyes and pretend. She would pretend right along with him. He felt the moon enter the back of his head. It merged with bone and popped his ears. He felt an expansion, then an adjustment. Harley stood before his grandmother with the moon in his skull, eyes pouring cool light onto her quilt-covered body. Stellar wind rushed through the passages of his ears, wave upon wave like the undulating roar of a conch shell.

Harley could read his grandmother's lips but couldn't hear her. She was saying, "That is the moon. That is the way into the moon."

He shook his head because he didn't understand. So she pointed to the television screen where the men walked in a floating manner that was both heavy and light.

"They can only walk on the surface," Margaret mouthed.

Harley couldn't think. His mind was squeezed, crushed close behind his eyes. The moon left him so suddenly, he fell onto the bed. His small arms slammed across Margaret's legs, making them twitch and shudder. Harley began to cry.

"It's all right," Margaret told him. "It'll be all right. But remember that feeling. Remember what it's like to be the moon, and you, and the darkness and the light." Her hand moved in a circle.

Margaret Many Wounds decided to die early; before a last taste of *waštúnkala,* before kissing her family goodbye, before Father Zimmer performed the Last Rites to purify her Everlasting Soul. She needed the extra time to work her own magic.

Do you have faith? she asked herself. She nodded and slipped into the water. It had been coursing around her bed for two days, parting at Evie's feet, lapping against Harley's sneakers, and splashing hot spray onto Margaret's face. But the water was cool now. She didn't need to breathe, and she was conscious of movement. *I am moving,* she thought, but she couldn't say in which direction. *I am I,* she thought with relief.

After the water, there was no water. Margaret stood in a light without color. She was alone. She couldn't feel her body, but it was still there, she could see it from the outside.

She was wearing her grandmother's dress with matching leggings and moccasins. The beads were brighter than she remembered; each bead sparkled, dazzling as a sun. *I remember the sun,* she thought. A single eagle feather was pinned to the back of her head, tilted at an angle to the right. Her belt was silver conches on black leather with a trailer falling to her ankles, silver at its tip. Three sets of dentalium shell earrings dangled from her ears, set in holes an inch apart moving up her earlobes. Her hair was plaited in two thick braids, weighted at the ends with hair ties made of bullets and bones. She tried to guess her own age but it was useless. *I am beautiful,* she thought.

She looked out from her body. A figure stood before her. It was Charles Bad-Holy MacLeod, still wearing his white man's suit.

"I've been waiting for you," he told her.

"I'm glad to see you again," she answered, confused because her joy was so calm. "They let you dress like that?" Margaret had immediately noticed that his high collar, now a burning, blue-hot white, still bit into his throat.

"I was accustomed to it," he explained.

"I left Fort Yates early," Margaret told him, and Charles nodded. "I have one last thing I want to do."

"That's acceptable to us," he said, and for a moment Margaret thought she heard the others. "Do what you have to and then join us at the council fire."

"How will I find the council fire?" Margaret wished she could go there directly, eager to learn what the ancestors already knew.

"Follow *Wanáǧi Tačánku* to its very end. It won't take long. When you come to the edge of the universe you will see us by the fire. Push across the border. Five steps will bring you to us."

"Mama, your soup is ready." Evie brought the *waštúnkala* into her mother's room.

"She's not there," Harley said. He was sitting at the foot of his grandmother's bed, watching the television screen.

"Of course she's there," Evie snapped. The soup spilled a

little and burned her hand. "Shoot." Evie placed the bowl on the bedside table, cooling her hand with her tongue. "Wake up, Mama, it's what you've been waiting for."

Margaret's body was warm, but Evie knew when she clutched her mother's shoulder that she was dead. Evie felt naked and afraid. "Can you see me?" she asked. "I can't see you. Maybe I'll never see you again." Evie sat beside her mother, holding her soft hand. She reached for her mother's white braid and brought it to her nose. The scent was baby shampoo Lydia used to wash Margaret's hair. She kissed her mother's lips.

Evie didn't cry until she fished Margaret's locket from beneath her nightgown. It opened with a snap, and Evie had to clean the tiny photographs with her pinkie finger to remove the lint. Charles Bad-Holy MacLeod was on one side, his black hair parted severely down the middle and slicked back on either side. A high collar choked him, and his eyes burned with intelligence. The other photo was of a balding, middle-aged Japanese gentleman. His smile was nothing but pain, his teeth hidden behind stretched lips. Evie recognized the smile and the gentle eyes. The expression was Lydia's.

Everyone had forgotten Harley. He dragged the cane-bottom chair in front of the television set and knelt on its seat. His hands rested on the bureau as he watched the black-mirrored surface of Neil Armstrong's face mask.

Behind him Evie and Lydia were washing their mother. They used the mildest soap and gentlest strokes. They washed her hair and spread it on the pillow to dry. It ran over the edges like a spill of white ribbons. Lydia painted Margaret's face the old way; she dabbed crimson lipstick on her forefinger and ran it down the part of her mother's hair. She drew a large circle above each cheekbone, then filled them in. Lydia removed the old nail polish and put on a fresh clear coat. Then she and Evie dressed Margaret in the silky buckskin dress she had worn to powwows, wrapping her in a dance shawl quilted with a thunderbird design on the back.

You will fly with powerful wings, Lydia was thinking.

You will never dance again, Evie thought.

They dressed Margaret in the wedding moccasins she had willed to Lydia. The soles were still clean on the bottom, and the sisters were startled when the slippers were in place because it looked like roses grew from the arch of each foot.

Father Zimmer sat in the kitchen over a cup of black coffee. He was inconsolable. Philbert stood across from him, hands plunged deep in his pockets, jingling change. Philbert thought the priest was going to cry.

"I should have been here to ease the passage," Father Zimmer said, stirring his coffee with a spoon, though he'd added nothing to it. The rising steam was like the vapor of souls. He cried to think that Margaret's soul would hang over the buttes like fog because she had died without his blessing. He didn't want her to be caught between Here and There.

"I will say a mass for her," he said, and Philbert bowed his head.

Harley's knees were beginning to ache, but he continued to kneel on the chair. As he listened, the voices of Walter Cronkite, the astronauts, and Ground Control at Cape Canaveral were sucked away. He heard the Sioux Flag Song pounding from the black vent on the television set, but when Harley checked over his shoulder, he saw that no one else seemed to notice.

Neil Armstrong and Edwin Aldrin were facing the camera, and Harley smiled because they reminded him of two white turtles standing upright. Armstrong was using an aluminum scoop fitted into an extension handle to collect samples of rock without bending over. Aldrin was using a set of tongs to pick up larger pieces.

Somewhere inside the music, Harley heard a familiar voice calling, *"Takója."*

Harley was no longer lonely or invisible on the chair. He saw his grandmother's figure emerging on the screen, dancing towards him from the far horizon behind the astronauts. He recognized her weaving dance as Sioux powwow steps, but her beautiful blue-beaded dress was unfamiliar to him.

At first he thought, *Grandma is young.* But then she smiled at him, and the smile was old. Her hair was black, and her hair was white. Her progress was steady, and he noticed she didn't bounce like the men in space suits.

He waited for Armstrong and Aldrin to see her, but they must have seen only the ground. Finally she came upon them, and Harley caught his breath because Margaret danced through Neil Armstrong. The astronaut never ceased digging at the ground, leaving footprints like heavy tank treads, but his oxygen system quivered a little as she passed.

Margaret Many Wounds was dancing on the moon. *Look at the crooked tracks I make like a snake,* she thought. At first it seemed the circuit she was making would take a long time. *Am I dancing or flying?* she wondered when instead it happened very quickly.

Names came to her, though she had never learned them. *That is the Sea of Crises,* she knew, *and that is the Sea of Serenity.* She crossed the Sea of Fertility and then backtracked to the Sea of Tranquility. That was where she felt Harley's presence.

Takója, she called with her spirit. *Look at me, look at the magic. There is still magic in the world.*

Margaret danced beyond the astronauts and their stiff metal flag. She kept moving forward until she came to the beginning of her trail in the gritty Lake of Dreams. She raised a foot and found *Wanáği Taćánku,* the Spirit Road, rippling beneath her feet. She set off, no longer dancing, walking towards the council fire five steps beyond the edge of the universe.

Mona Simpson

Van Castle

When I was a boy, my grandmother clutched my chin and said, "Promise me one thing. That you'll never let that mother of yours buy a Mercedes." I promised. It was easy. There was no chance of our buying anything. We filled out sweepstakes for an hour every night that we sent away with stamps that should have been our rent money. "You're Jewish. Don't you ever forget it," she said.

My grandmother never considered that I might someday own a car. I was a seven-year-old Noah in a wheelchair with osteogenesis imperfecta, short and wrong and big-headed. I'd already had thirty-one fractures. She was sure as she was of everything that I would never drive.

And here I was buying German, not a car but a van, and one custom-made. It was Kempf, not Mercedes, but if she were alive, she'd raise her eyebrows and want to know what Kempf was doing during the War. Still, I hadn't paid. I wondered if that made a difference. I could have explained, I suppose, to Owens, but Owens was thick about religion. He was dumb with ethnicity, too, except his own. He was adopted, and all he knew was one of his parents was Arab. He could seem vaguely charmed if a young guy he was thinking of hiring or a woman he wanted a date with was Lebanese, but nothing much. If the guy wasn't that good or the woman wasn't that pretty, it was Lebanese schmebanese. When I told him I was Jewish, he said, "Really? Does that make a big difference to you? You know me, I don't notice those things." I always ascribed that to his being

adopted. Maybe it was, maybe it wasn't. With him you never
knew.

I was the one to find the child curled up asleep in his garden,
because I went looking for someone to show my new prize to.

The van that Owens bought me had just come in. I'd gotten
the call that morning from his secretary, Ileene, green-eyed
Ileene. I asked if he wanted to go see it or inspect it or anything,
and without him ever getting on the line, Ileene told me no, it's
your truck, just enjoy it.

This was so new. Genesis had gone public three years ago, and
Owens had had a party then, but until today when the van came to
me out of thin air, I hadn't really registered that Owens was rich.

The mom-mom had to take me to pick it up. My sister,
Michelle, and I called her the mom-mom whenever she did
something motherly. When we were growing up, she was
always telling us she wasn't like all the rest of these mom-moms,
she didn't have free time and free money. It was an hour drive to
the lot in San Jose, but then we saw the van and it was
everything. She loved it, too, I could tell. She ran her fingers over
the smooth door. We'd never had a car that nice. My
grandmother didn't have to worry. We were rich twice, from
boyfriends, but never long enough.

I had to ask the mom-mom, after a few minutes, if I could be
alone with it.

"Do you want me to go and come back? You don't want to
have a sandwich or something?" When I was young, each time
she bought me a new chair, it was a big deal, and something we
did alone, without Michelle. And each chair, the day I first used
it, felt wonderful and strong, as if there'd be no more long
afternoons roaming Telegraph Avenue on a loaner while we
waited for the shop to repair it. After we picked the chair up, she
wouldn't take me back to school right away. She gave me the
day to get used to it first, and the two of us always went and
celebrated with a crab sandwich. I still have all three of my old
chairs, in a friend's basement. But I was twenty-two now, with
an administrative job.

"I think I better get going," I said.

It was sleek, fully automatic. Deep navy blue. It was male. It had cost fifty thousand dollars, and it had that shine and technology. At the press of a button on the key, a ramp drew down from the driver's floor, with handlebars on both sides. I leveraged myself up, pushed the chair to the back. There was a way to make the ramp lift automatically, but I was going to discipline myself. I wouldn't use more help than what I needed. Little eases were the first treats on the long slide down to the bed.

The brake and gears, everything was manned on top, with switch bars. I didn't have to use my feet. I'd learned to drive on our old Pontiac, with the metal extension bars you can buy, which was twice as hard, like driving while you're working string puppets. The last few years I'd been using BART and the buses.

Owens had ordered the car complete. It even had a phone. I had to stop thinking *even*. I would get used to having things now. I'd hoped it would have a phone, but I didn't ask. I still didn't touch it. I'd heard that the bills for car phones were outrageous, and I didn't know when the charges started. Maybe if you just picked it up. I had an underdeveloped sense of money. I thought a phone call from a car could cost a hundred dollars or a thousand.

My dead grandmother's prohibition made the leather richer, the roof grand, the luxury more . . . voluptuous.

When the mom-mom drove away in our old Pontiac and I was alone, high up in all that space, I clapped. I got something good for once. Top of the line. I said to myself, out loud, *I lucked out*. I had the best van anywhere, and it was just pure chance, like a lottery. Or maybe because of me. This seemed like the first time ever.

The dealer walked back and gave me my license and my one other ID, and that was all. I never knew how easy it was to buy things.

"I can go now?" I said.

"She's all yours," he said, tapping my roof.

I wanted to do something that was the way I felt, and so I started driving. The van came with a full tank of gas. I knew everybody at work was going crazy today—a group from Belgium was there, visiting—and I didn't want to just park the van and have to forget it. I went up Skyline towards Santa Cruz. I found myself in the hills, parking in a blue space in front of a stucco church, across from the Ice Cream Ballroom. I pressed open the ramp, rolled down, and crossed the street for an ice cream cone. I'd never done that before alone, without someone else's patience and scrutiny. Whims are different if you're watched. And I was unwatched. Independent. Next door was a record place and I bought two CDs. The van had a CD player. I was cooking. It was two-thirty. I decided to blow off work until tomorrow. Nobody'd care. I took 280, just because. Why not? I was in no hurry now and it's a beautiful road and then, all of a sudden, I couldn't contain myself alone anymore. I had to show someone. Olivia was still living at Owens's place then, so I took the exit into the woods and headed up there.

It occurred to me after I rounded the first bend, driving on rich people's land, that this van was my first charity. I should have done it a lot sooner. I felt big. Not like I'd thought. I'd thought it humbled you. We'd gotten money from the government for me, and that made us all feel bad. It was never enough to make much difference. The way my mother was, when a neighbor or someone she knew from work gave her old clothes for my sister and me, she never said no. She never thought we could afford to turn down anything. But the van was new and clean. I was higher than other people on the road and controlling motion from above. I was masterful, and it felt due me, even overdue me, this power.

But elation on this planet cannot last. The best part of the day was that first driving. At Owens's place, I remembered, getting in and getting out was still hard. I went from on high to being a man in a frame. I had to leverage myself down slowly, so as not to skid. I'd build up muscles, I decided. In my arms, which were my two favorite parts of myself. I was weak now from four years in my powered chair.

Owens's place was always beautiful and still, like a cemetery. The gates creaked and banged, loose on their old hinges. He'd bought it from the estate of the Copper King, who had acquired the land to build a weekend house. All over the yard he'd planted outscale copper beeches. But the architecture was a joke. The King had lived hard and died quietly in San Francisco. No one had ever lived in this house before Owens. It was not built to be lived in. It was a party house.

And Owens was anything but a party. He hosted events, but never here. All his celebration tied to business and was held in office buildings or rented ballrooms. Once, he told me, he'd had nine Japanese businessmen here for dinner, and when they'd arrived the people who cook for him had the places set, but there was one setting without a chair. They'd checked everywhere in the house, and there were only nine chairs. Owens even ran down the road to the closest neighbors, whom he'd never met, to knock on their door and ask to borrow a chair. They had parrots in cages outside their front door, huge foreign-squawking parrots. But no one answered. So the nine Japanese men sat around the table, and Owens stood. Even so, before the meal was out, one of the nine chairs broke, and a businessman fell with a dull noise to the tile floor. So now, there were twelve wooden chairs around the dining-room table, ordered the next day.

Wind went through the leaves, and the huge trees swayed like ferns, making sounds you only hear in an abandoned place.

Sometimes gardeners worked the yard, but I didn't see anyone today. For around the house, Owens always found the worst people. It's odd, because he must have known how to hire for work. The whole place seemed dug up and scarred. They were supposed to be putting in an orchard. He was big on that. He wanted to plant his own garden with every kind of bearing tree, he planned to walk out in the evening and pick his fruit. But you just knew it was going to be a long time before he bit into his own apple, and when it all happened, a million dollars from now, the apples would be better from the A&P.

Trees, their roots still bundled in burlap sacks, leaned slant, waiting to be set in. Expensive trees. Everything here looked like a mess of process. Nothing was ever done.

I opened the front door. They didn't lock. He had millions of dollars of art he couldn't insure because he wouldn't get security devices or even lock his own front door. Olivia'd told me that. He didn't talk about money. Once he showed me his storage room. It was like an archive of himself: posters, marquees, magazine articles, boxes and boxes of mementos of the early days at Genesis. A plaque from when they first went public. It was all just lying around with old skis and a motorcycle he rode sometimes in the empty room off the entry hall. I told him he should file the stuff, take care of it. He looked at me, he'd been showing me, digging the pictures out of piles and boxes for more than an hour, and said, "It's probably better if all this gets destroyed in a fire or something. I think you shouldn't live with all this stuff." He could be wise about himself. He understood what in his life was a danger.

"Hello!" I yelled. It was cold in the house because it was dark. No one answered, but that didn't mean Olivia wasn't home. The place was so big you couldn't hear. I wheeled through the dim living room—how not to build a house—they were alone here, on top of a hill, and still, almost no light came into the dining room, the falling-down kitchen they'd never fixed. A piece of ceiling was rotted through. They kind of lived around the mess. About a thousand cherry tomatoes, yellow and red, spilled out over the counter. I popped one; it tasted warm like sun.

I went to the steps that ran up to their bedroom and shouted, "Olivia." Nothing.

O.K. She was either in town or asleep and hungover, tangled in white sheets on the futon. But if she couldn't hear me, there was nothing I could do. The only way up in this place was the stairs or the old dumbwaiter. She was probably in town. Normally you could trace her from her car. She had a white vintage Thunderbird, her one luxury. But it was in the shop again so it not being here meant nothing. Olivia was one of those people who was everywhere when you weren't looking for her, you'd run into her twice a day, but when you needed her she was hard to find. She didn't exactly have a job. She worked free-lance, and so could be anywhere.

I rode over the dirt of the courtyard instead of through the house again. Big overgrown runners for squash scored the ground, the flowers browned and limp. Bees accumulated free around the berry bushes. And in the dip where the garden fell to a carrot patch, in among the overgrown lacy tops, was a kid curled up in the dirt. It was a girl, asleep. I nudged her with my rubber wheel.

"Hello," she said, coming awake. She sat up, most of her weight in her butt, like a top, settling to rest. She rubbed her eyes. "Are you a midget?

"Who are you, little girl?"

"I'm Jane," she said.

"And how old are you?"

"Nine."

"You're nine. Do you know the difference between a midget and a dwarf and a regular man?"

"There is no difference. I mean a midget or a dwarf are both a man."

"So why ask if I'm a midget if I'm a man?"

"I'm sorry. Do you live here?"

"What would you do if I said yes?"

"My father's supposed to live here, but I don't think you're my father because I've seen my father before and my mom has a picture of him. I guess he could have moved." She sighed. "I'm hungry."

I looked over the garden.

"Sick of fruit. I've been eating this stuff already. It's not very good. And there's snails."

"What's your father's name?"

"Tom Owens."

That stopped me good. I'd known him for four years and he'd never said a word about any child. In fact, he talked a lot about wanting to get married and have a baby. I wondered if he knew she existed. Olivia sure didn't.

"My name is Noah Jacobs. How do you do. Where did you come from?"

"I came from, do you know Brownsfield? It's on the other side of the mountains. I lived there with my mom."

"And where's your mother now?"

"She's there still."

"She's still there. Then how did you get here?"

"I drove. But that's kind of a secret."

"O.K. I won't tell. But, tell you what, your father's at work now. Why don't I take you home where I live and you can clean up and we can go get you some new clothes, you got a little dirty sleeping here, I'll take you to get something to eat and we'll call your dad and he can come get you when he's ready."

"Great," she said, fast. "I mean, I have some clothes already in the car. In the back seat. 'Course I love to get new clothes. Probably my favorite thing."

"Well, we can take your stuff and maybe get you one new thing besides. A dress or something." So I guess this is it, I was thinking. This is what happens when you fall into an adventure. She got up and walked with a hand light on my shoulder. With me in the chair and her standing, she was a few inches taller. She led me to her truck, behind the eucalyptus. It was an incredible thing: an old, perfectly shaped Ford truck, browned and weathered and patched, full of rust. Originally it must have been cream-colored with the wide spaced four letters still maroon. I was dying to see inside, it was such a relic, but she just opened her door, used her hands to pull herself up on the seat, and climbed in the way I would have to, and came back out with a brown grocery bag folded down at the top, like a huge lunch.

I showed her my van. "Oh neat," she said, when the ramp came down. "Like a drawbridge to a castle." I told her it was my first day in it. I didn't say that her alleged father bought the van for me. I just didn't want to. That day, the two of us named it the Van Castle. "And that makes you the Count Van Castle," she said.

I asked her if she wanted to go home and call her father first or if she'd rather get something to eat.

"Eat," she said.

I took her to a place I never went. Now I didn't want to go anywhere Olivia could be. I wanted to keep my discovery to myself for a while. There was a time when I'd been half in love with Olivia. Some days that seemed unbearable to me, the humiliation, and I thought we should never speak to each other again. Other days it seemed almost natural and inconsequential, silly, a mutual laugh. Right now it felt perfectly all right. Many men, perhaps a hundred, had been in my position with Olivia. What did it matter? They all went on to live decent lives.

There was an old-fashioned soda shop no one I knew would go to because the food was full of grease. Olivia, Owens, my sister, Michelle, they were all health people. Except when it came to ethnicity. They'd eat Mexican food fat but they wouldn't touch a french fry. Except Owens. You had to grant him consistency but that made him even more of a pain in the ass. It gave me true pleasure to buy Owens's daughter a cheeseburger and watch her eat it with relish, pressing the thing flat in her hands.

Then I took her to the mall. It is a wonderful world. I'd never bought a girl clothing before. I'd been on the boys' floor of department stores and there I shopped for men's clothes in miniature. But these dresses and ribbons and shoes were not just ladies' in small sizes. They had a whimsy all their own. I had a credit card, I'd just got it a few months ago. I could do this. Be an adult.

She was nine years old, and hopping around from outfit to outfit. Given the poor quality of what she had on now (her yellow stretch pants, muddy from washing, a ragged hole in one knee, and her slippers scuffed), she obviously had no money. I had to wonder about the mother, wherever she was. She had to be someplace. The kid couldn't have driven alone. Not over mountains. I still couldn't really fathom how she'd arrived there.

The mother must be hiding. Jane was looking at the skirt of a dress and then up to me. She expected me to pay.

Just that assumption, that I was an adult she could look to, that melted me. I could have bought her the whole store and I would still be paying it off month by month, if I hadn't discovered the extraordinary thing about this child. Even dirty, recently hungry, obviously poor, she was clairvoyant in her renunciation.

I told her to fetch what she wanted. I watched her brush the sleeve of a velvet coat, then relinquish it. She picked out a cotton dress and socks and new sneakers. "Is it too much?" she said.

"Not at all," I answered. "I was thinking, you need a headband." I showed her an orange one with crenelations. "Go try it on." I motioned to the salesgirl to include that velvet coat while Jane ran back to look at herself in the mirror. The woman wrapped it on the bottom of the bag.

We decided to go home. We were both withering. I'd wanted to stop and get her a book to read in case I didn't have enough to amuse her with and at the grocery store to buy cookies, but we still had to climb in Van Castle and out again at home.

"Van Castle," she said. "And we're the Von Castles. Jane Von Castle, how *do* you do."

An hour later she was murmuring in my bathtub, and I called her father from the kitchen. It was my second conversation of the day with Ileene. She told me kindly but firmly that he was in a meeting at the plant if he hadn't left already, and that then he'd be seeing architects for the new office building most of the afternoon.

"Ileene, I have something important. For him. It's about his life," I said. I wanted to tell Ileene, she was a good woman, near forty but a runner, vastly underemployed, so much that I'd always wondered what he paid her. She could be trusted with more than he could, but he was such an odd man, with privacies.

"I'll tell him, Noah."

"And say it's urgent, would you, Ileene?"

"I sure will. There's nothing I can do for you in the meantime? Is the van running all right?"

"Oh yeah, it's perfect. Nothing like that."

I got off the phone because the girl was yelling from the bathroom—did I have any bubble bath?—which I didn't.

"How about dish soap?" she yelled back. That I had and delivered, and with it she conjured a spa of bubbles off the end of a spoon. I didn't know you could do that out of dish soap.

Back in the kitchen, I sat in the middle of the floor listening to her small, uncertain, rising hum. I remembered being a child and being washed, sitting in the high, old, deep kitchen sink. People probably don't do that anymore. Or was that because of me? The way I was. But no, I remembered my sister, too, sitting up in there by the light window, her legs crossed at the knees. My sister has red hair, and her legs, when she was growing up, were covered with freckles and pink scars.

I'd left all the towels I had clean on the toilet seat, and a half hour later she emerged, combing out her hair.

"You didn't know that, Noah, that detergent is like bubble bath? Sure, Noah, it's just suds," she said.

"Do you drink tea?" I really didn't know what children ate.

"Sure."

We sat at my table and ate a box of graham crackers with tea. That was most of what I had.

"Did you call my dad?"

I told her I'd asked his secretary to have him call me. "But I didn't mention that you were here. I didn't know if I should. Is he expecting you? Or is your visit a surprise?"

"Surprise. Definitely a surprise." She giggled, then sighed, a private syntax.

I was ready for a nap, but she wanted to know if I had games. Games, something a person should probably have. Monopoly, chess, even Chinese checkers. I'd get them. I had a lot of movies, though. I showed her the library of movies I'd taped from television. She picked out *Peter Pan*. And we sat and watched. I made a batch of Jiffy Pop. Outside the sky was dark and then it was raining. I gave her one of my sweatshirts and a pair of my wool socks for over her clothes. She lay on my bed and I sat in my chair watching.

Before *Peter Pan* was over, she fell asleep. I covered her with the soft wool plaid blanket, slipped the tape out, and went into the kitchen to read. I wondered what I'd do for dinner. He wouldn't necessarily call before then. It was an evening not to go out. I thought of Van Castle in the rain. I had eggs in the refrigerator and a health food pancake mix from Olivia, maple syrup. That would be enough. We didn't have milk, but we had tea. She seemed to like the tea.

"What if he doesn't call?" she said, in a normal voice from the other room. I rolled into the doorjamb.

"You'll stay here," I said. "Are you hungry for some dinner yet?"

"In a little while," she said.

Late that night, when she was asleep on my bed and I was on the couch with the extra blanket, Owens called. "Hey, have you seen Olivia?"

I told him no, I hadn't seen Olivia all day. I tried to keep my voice down.

"Really? 'Cause I thought she might be with you. You know, I'm a little worried, Noah. She's not here, she wasn't at Barbara's. I called her mom. I thought she was probably over there or out somewhere with you. I'm really a little worried. And I guess I'm pretty disappointed in her, too. We had a fight last night, and we were gonna meet for dinner after work today at our sushi place, you know, to talk about it and just to have dinner and I got there and I was fifteen minutes late and she'd left."

I didn't say anything. He made no mention that I'd called him. I knew Ileene gave him the message.

"She just left. I couldn't believe it. So, I have no idea where she is."

"Well, Owens, I wasn't calling you about Olivia."

I heard the light tap of computer keys near him.

"I called because I went looking for her today at your place and I found a kid who says you're her father. She was waiting for you."

"What's her name?"

"She says Jane."

"Oh, no, that kid. She was at Hillsborough? What was she doing there? Did you see her mother? Woman about thirty, kind of crazy."

"No woman. There's a truck at your place, but no mother."

"Yeah, they've got a truck. That's her. I know her mom. And she's not my kid. Listen, I'll have to deal with her, I'm sure I'll hear from her mom soon and we'll see what she wants, but I can't tonight, I've got to find Olivia, would you mind just keeping her for me there a day or so and I'll come get her and straighten it all out when I get a chance."

"Sure, Owens. I guess so. But why does she think she's your daughter?"

"Well, it's a long story," he said. "And not that good of one. But her mom was with a lot of guys at one point and then when she had the kid, they all kinda split and so she decided that I was the dad. And I'm pretty sure she's not my kid but I had to decide, if I didn't agree to be her father, she wouldn't have a father. So I kind of help them out some. I see her sometimes."

"So she knows you as her father?"

"Did she say that?"

"Yes."

"You think she looks like me?"

"I don't know. No, not really."

"I know. I don't either. Noah?"

"Yeah."

"Do you have *any* idea where Olivia might be? You're telling me the truth?"

"No, but if I hear from her, I'll tell her you're looking for her."

"Tell her I love her. Tell her I love her a lot."

When I got off the phone, the child was standing behind me in the dark. Her hand was on the back of my chair.

"Was that him?"

"Yes."

"What did he say?"

"He said to tell you he loved you a lot." She was a foot in front of me then and dense in the dark. I sensed a change in her when she heard that. She seemed to become an inch or two shorter. Her tension fell. She was loose, and I smarted for the lie.

"Is he coming to see me?"

"Not tonight. Maybe not for a couple days. He asked if I would take care of you until he can come. Is that all right with you?"

She had one foot on the other knee, perplexed. "I guess. Sure. I just don't know why he doesn't come over."

"I don't know, either," I said. I probably should have done better than that, the truth. "But we'll have fun. You watch and see. We'll have a good day tomorrow."

And for three days I dropped out of life, and we did everything I knew that could amuse her. I called in sick to my job. I let my messages pile up. I worked hard: it wasn't like me to remember the names and addresses of fun. But we visited the Mechanical Museum, we put quarters in the telescopes at the Cliff House to see communal seals on rocks. We watched Golden Gate Park's last buffalos move infinitesimally slowly, we went through the aquarium and the museum, and then we collapsed at the Japanese garden and ordered four portions at once of cookies and tea. I got into the habit of planning our meals in advance. I worried about money, in moments of darkness, at night or in the movies. I was spending more than I ever did. But we laughed at the movies and cried, our spoons scraped the bottom glass of our sundaes at Sweet Dreams afterwards. I understood for the first time how people spent their money. Money was worth this. She was not demanding, she hardly asked. I had to guess what she might need and offer.

I didn't know how long I was budgeting for. You never knew with Owens. I was trying to figure out if we could go on forever. I thought we could. Because I'd go back to work and get her in

school. We wouldn't be out celebrating every day. This was just
for now when we didn't know anything. And by the third day we
were wearing out from fun. We missed our normal lives. I did,
even though I hated my job and planned to quit as soon as I got
something better. I planned to be out of there for sure by fall. I
had applications in to schools all across the country, in New
York City, even. She missed her life, too, whatever it was. She
didn't say anything but I could tell. Excitement wasn't meant for
every day and she was tired. When we drove out of the park, full
with warm tea, we passed a Catholic School on Eighteenth
Avenue, and students poured out in uniforms, underdressed,
energetic, shouting. She turned away from the window so they
couldn't see her.

"Do you miss school?" I said.

"I miss my friends."

"What grade are you in?"

"I was in third. And I miss my mother." The left side of her
face went lopsided.

"Well, tonight we have to call her." It was the opening I'd
been waiting for, but she just turned back towards the window
now and shook her head.

By that evening I was worried about her studies. We went to
the campus bookstore and I bought a math book, a science
book, and what seemed to me two decent children's novels. I
made us spaghetti at home, and after, we cleared the table and
she worked on her books for an hour.

While she read, I got out a clean notebook and began to
think with a pencil about our lives. I'd called Owens again today.
At the tea garden, I'd said I had to go to the bathroom. Ileene
told me she'd given him my messages. But whatever Owens
did, he wasn't going to take Jane. He couldn't have a kid. He'd
never be home. The cooks would have to raise her. His cooks
were nice enough people, but she would be lonely in that cold
house. He only allowed about five types of vegetables and
fruit in the kitchen. They didn't have milk, he didn't believe in

flour, he forbade meat and most of the things you need for a regular life.

Still, there was the mother. Of course she'd want to go back to her mother. I asked her, lifting my head from the circle of lamplight on my page, if she'd like to call her mother.

"No."

"Did you have a fight?"

"No," she said.

"Well, you can use the phone to call her whenever you want. And if you need privacy, just tell me."

Then I began to think about us and whether I could keep her. She could go to school, there was a school down the street that was supposed to be good. If I only got into a college somewhere here. But who would pick her up at three o'clock? Before, I'd thought if I didn't get in here, maybe I'd move to New York City. I'd thought I just might do that. But now I wouldn't. There were a thousand reasons to stay here, and this was the last, the one that mattered. Berkeley was the place I'd first been happy. I didn't want to leave. It would be O.K. for me. It would be harder to stay here and make a career, but it could be done and now I had a reason. I'd shop Saturday mornings and cook every night. We had to have food in the house. On what I got from my job now we could do it. And if I got a scholarship or job at school, that would help, and my savings would be over and above.

Pretty soon we'd need a bigger apartment, so she could have friends come, maybe a birthday party. But for now, we could make it work here.

I was scribbling numbers, and when I looked up, she was staring, rubbing her eyes.

"I'm pretty tired. I guess I should go to sleep."

I looked at my watch. It was ten o'clock. No wonder.

"Jane, I'm thinking I should take you and get you registered in school tomorrow. Your dad's pretty busy, I guess, and I'm wondering, whatever you two decide you might want to do about seeing each other, you could always stay here."

"Thank you," she said.

"Would you mind that?"

"No," she said. "Can I go brush my teeth now?"

Registering a child in school isn't easy. They want proof, they want papers. You'd have thought I'd kidnapped her. They needed her birth certificate, which we retrieved from an envelope she'd come with, safety-pinned to the inside of her original blouse. The piece of paper said Jane Mary Hudson, born to her mother, Mary di Natale. Two inked whorls of baby feet marked the page. But when we returned to the principal's office with this document, they said I still needed proof of guardianship.

Through all this I tried to get her to call her mother. She just shook her head and said there was no telephone.

When we returned home, there were two envelopes for me in the mail. One was from the school in San Francisco, the other was New York. Before this, I'd only had jobs where you called them back to see if they'd hire you. I'd never had letters in the mail. I didn't even let myself look. I put them in a drawer before she noticed, and then I called Owens again. Now I was mad. I left another message saying URGENT with Ileene. And he came over that night, unannounced, in jeans and hiking boots, loping in his stride over the lawn.

"Hello-o?" he called, reaching a hand in through our open window. Her head was up in a shot from the table where she was drawing, but all she said was, "Hi, Owens," as if he were the most average thing in her world. This was not what Owens liked to hear. You could see his physical agitation. He was a man accustomed to people fussing.

"Hey, bud," I said, knocking his shoulder. "Want tea?"

"Do you have any fresh fruit juice?"

"Nope. I have tea and milk. And water."

"Oh, no thanks," he said, "So, kid, you want to get your stuff together and I'll take you home with me. I'm really tired. I had a really rough day. I talked to your mom, and she's gonna take a plane here tomorrow."

"You talked to my mom!"

"I talked to your mom and she'll come in at around four o'clock or four-thirty and tomorrow night we can all sit down and figure out where you two want to live and where you'll go to school. I think it's probably a pretty good idea if we find you and your mom an apartment somewhere around here. So tonight I'll take you home and you can have a little vacation there tomorrow while I'm at work. Vanessa and Terry are these people who help me out around the house and they'll be there and they'll make sure you get something to eat and you can just read and relax in the garden and watch movies. Maybe we'll even watch a movie tonight."

"O.K. Cool," she said.

In five minutes they were gone, her strapped into the low seat of his sports car, her few belongings in the narrow back. I still hadn't given her the velvet coat, I'd been waiting, so when I packed her things I slipped it in the bottom of the bag. His car fired up and then sped off into the night.

And then, the depression came on again, in a way it had before but I'd forgotten and only now remembered. I sat outside in my chair in the cool night, the two envelopes from the drawer in my lap. One envelope was thick, one thinner. Because why should Owens have everything, just because he already did? People in the world who had too much got more, and those with nothing lost and lost until sometimes they didn't even have themselves. And Owens didn't deserve her, he wouldn't know how to cherish a child. I'd often envied him his women, but now it seemed I would not be up for that, anyway. Sex was too high for me. For now, anyway. I was tired. The fog soothed my forehead, I could feel my curls tightening against my neck. But I could have taken care of a child. I could. I had begun to learn, and I had things to teach.

And what would Owens give?

He had slept with a woman and then tried to get her to go away. And that was what made men fathers and men in this world.

I sat there for a long time that night, looking at the various stars in the sky, the bright points, the dimmer, the ones that seemed spent, leaving trails like flecks of chalk. Now I was free to go where I needed. I rubbed the paper of my envelopes, sealed and secret. Out at the end of the lawn, the van was still there, and it was mine.

Sharon Solwitz

OBST VW

Next year, writing his personal experience essay to convince admissions at Penn he's Ivy League material despite uneven grades, he'll describe in amusing detail the one baseball game his father took him to, and get in on a scholarship despite his father's explicit pessimism. And he'll do well, though he's not as brilliant as his father, just a pretty smart kid who's used to working hard. But now on Rachel's bed, unraveling a hole in the knee of her jeans while her parents yell at each other downstairs, he cannot join in her raillery. "Let's go," he says.

"Wait. This is the part about who was the first unfaithful one!"

"Let's go!" he says. He has a curfew, a job to get up for tomorrow. Then there's the air outside the house, the smell of new grass mixing with the smell of Rachel when she lets him touch her under her T-shirt.

"Dame, please. It's funny, really. It's high comedy."

But she doesn't protest as he takes her hand and leads her down and outside.

Rachel is seventeen, a year older than Demian, though in the same grade. She lost a year when she went, as she says, loony, and spent several months in the bin getting her spirit broken to the point where she'd attend school and respond, numbly, to teacher and test questions. Still, her grades are better than his. Sometimes it seems to him he can't stand her, half an inch taller than he is, the way when she's not thinking about it she arcs down into herself like a long-necked bird, the way tall girls aren't supposed to. He used to love to play baseball, it was all he wanted to do—if not on the field then in a symbolic version with cards and dice in his room—and when this feeling of loathing comes over him, it brings on a desire for baseball, for playing shortstop, to be specific, standing between second and third with his knees bent, whispering in the direction of the batter—hit it to me, I dare you. He remembers his two best friends from then, brothers a year apart, Tom and John Frank, the clean, sharp edge of the way they bad-mouthed each other after the game. And then the queasiness comes, because something he has done with Rachel or is about to do has rendered him unfit for baseball.

He walks quickly now, a step ahead of her, over to the playground behind the local preschool, where they've gone the past months to talk and kiss and perform all but the final technical act of sexual intercourse. The ground is laid in gravel through which sharp, hard weeds poke up, but the chain-link fence is low enough to climb over, the large wooden sandbox lies half in the shadow of the building, the sand is cool and dry and molds after a while to one or the other's back.

Tonight, though, they do not embrace. Rachel sits down on the dark side of the sandbox. At first she seems to have disappeared. Then he sees in the dark the lesser darkness of her face, the pale stretch of her shoulders, too wide for a girl. She smells sour and sweet like strawberries. He is moved by something in Rachel, her craziness, her cynicism, facets of personality he dimly perceives he may have to own some day. He remembers a school assembly where she danced on center stage with the other dancers weaving around her, her turns and leaps bolder than theirs, more complete. "Rachel," he says, "I really like you."

She doesn't respond, but the prickle of the skin of his arms tells him he has said the wrong thing. He tries again. "You're a really good dancer." He elaborates on the performance he saw, comparing her dancing to the way he used to feel about baseball. Still feels sometimes. She doesn't help him out. Her silence is a hole he walks around and around.

"Rachel," he says in despair, "I feel bad for you." He doesn't mention her parents. Really, he doesn't want to talk about them. Their dads by some fluke knew each other in college, and Rachel's sometimes asks him how his father's doing, a show of interest or courtesy his father doesn't return. Demian himself can barely manage to speak to her father, who makes more money than his father and calls him the Old Hippie. "Ask him about Woodstock," Mr. Geller once said, and Demian said, "Why don't you ask him yourself," knowing his father hadn't gone to Woodstock, as Mr. Geller also knew. Mr. Geller is soft-looking and bottom-heavy like an old pear. Demian can't stand Mr. Geller, has only broached the subject as a gift for Rachel.

She says, "They're not my real parents."

He laughs, though she has said that before.

"I'm going to divorce them," she says. "There's a new law, in Vermont."

"In Massachusetts, I think."

She shrugs, irritated with his quibble. He talks quickly to assuage her. "Then you can marry *my* parents."

"Who wants your parents?"

"What's wrong with my parents?"

"Your father has a mean streak."

"No he doesn't!"

His eyes have adjusted to the light. He can see the parts of her face that jut out, eyebrows, cheekbones, slope of nose. She seems too sharply constructed, a witch woman, though she's sitting cross-legged like a child, pouring handfuls of dry sand over her thighs. "He won't let you do stuff for no reason," she says. "For spite."

Demian knows that in similar words he has complained to her about his father, who gave him a curfew earlier than that of his friends' younger brothers, frequently refused him permission to attend parties, and who wasn't planning—he'd warned him—to let him get his driver's license till he was eighteen years old. Teenagers have glop for brains, he'd said. Though as a teenager himself—his mother had told him—he'd dropped out

of college and done a lot of the drugs teenagers were supposed
to say no to these days. Demian hasn't really spoken to his father
since the day he refused to sign the learner's permit. But now
Demian says, "He has his own ideas. He does what he thinks is
right and not what everybody else does!"

She claps her hands.

"What is that supposed to mean?"

"You are so *canned.*"

He's about to stand up, leave, maybe. But she takes his arm.
"Demian, I love you."

"So you can say anything you want to me?"

She puts her arms around him, thrusts her tongue into his
mouth. He keeps up his end of the bargain. Soon he is urgent,
panting. She is, too. His fingers are wet with her. As usual he tries
to pull off her shorts. As usual she pushes away from him. Once
he questioned her, learned that her noncompliance had to do
with something apologetic she detected in his attitude toward
sex. Since then, his efforts have been mild, ritualized. She is his
first real girlfriend. He is pleased to be kissing and touching her
even at the level of intimacy she has ordained. She hurls herself
at his hand, trembling.

He has to be home by 10:30 and it's 11:35 by the oven clock
as he tiptoes across the kitchen. He has never missed curfew
before, but the evening is still warm on his skin, he feels
invulnerable. And his father is surely asleep.

He takes his shoes off in the living room. His father
is *inactive,* his mother says. The understatement of the
year, Demian thinks. Tired from working in the bookstore,
which doesn't bring in enough for him to hire a manager, his
father often falls asleep on the couch in front of the ten
o'clock news, and Demian and his mother have to prod him up
to bed.

But he's up now, standing in his PJs at the top of the stairs.
His long, thin, still young-looking face is blank; not even his lips
seem to move as he says, "You're grounded." His lips are pressed

close together, a tuck in the long swatch of his face, but the words linger in the air well after his lanky body has vanished behind the master bedroom door.

In bed Demian is stiff with fury. There is no recourse; the only question is how long. And even worse than not seeing Rachel is seeing her with the weight of his father's edict on his shoulders, making him smaller than he is, unworthy of her.

Four years from now Demian will fly home from school in time to watch his father breathe in comatose sleep, then cease breathing—feeling nothing, because from now on nothing he does for good or ill will have any impact on his father. Later he'll rage at his father for dying before he was ready for him to die, and later still he may decide that if his father wasn't ideal he did the best he could. But now Demian has hopes for what he can be to his father and what his father can be to him.

Demian is up early, hours before he has to leave for Bi-Rite's, rehearsing the speech he'll give his father at the breakfast table. He has it outlined in his head like a five-paragraph essay, and now with the sun turning the sky pink, then blue, he sits at the kitchen table while his mother, who has to leave soon to teach summer school, performs five or six brisk cleaning and cooking acts. His father sips coffee. His father butters a piece of rye toast, as slowly as an old man, though his hair is still thick, his face unlined; people sometimes think he's Demian's older brother. Demian says casually into the space between bites, "I want you to reconsider."

His father looks to the left, the right, all around the room. "Who's talking? Is somebody talking to me?"

Demian's ears feel hot. This is the first direct statement he's made to his father in several months. "Dad, I'm never late. I shouldn't be punished the first time I mess up. Give me a second chance."

"Look, you." His father's voice is quiet, but it takes up the room. "If some dude walks into my store with a gun, and I say hey now just wait a minute, do I get a second chance?"

Demian sees the illogic of his father's argument, but his father stands up, leaning forward as if about to fall on him. "If you get sick, kiddo. If your heart hurts, air sticks in your throat, you say with your last feeble breath, God, Jesus, Krishna, whoever —please, what did I do, could you please, please give me a second chance, what's He going to say to you? Tell me, Demian."

Demian wants to ask his father what makes him think he's God, but the air or something is stuck in his throat.

"Let's say you get your girlfriend pregnant, Demian. Let's say for the sake of argument you knock up your young lady. But you aren't ready to be Papa yet. You want to walk across Turkey in your stocking feet. You want to climb Mt. Tamalpais and keep on going."

His father has just said more, it seems, than he has ever said to Demian before. His hands are waving, his face is white, and Demian's mother pats his back, leads him back to the table. She gets him more coffee, hovers over him, though she's running late, till his face warms up. He kisses her goodbye a beat longer than he has to. Says nothing to Demian. Demian feels sick, choking on the words he can't speak to his father. "Mom," he whispers after the door is shut, "is he mean, or what?"

"Demian," she says, "you've got to give him some slack. The business isn't going well."

"Who cares?" Demian's voice rises. Every once in a while he's allowed to sneer in front of his mother. It's his one respite, acting like his father in front of his mother. "Mine isn't going well, either." He watches her face, prepared to shut down at the first sign of her disapproval.

"Demian," she says, "he may have to declare bankruptcy. Don't say anything to him, please. Eat your breakfast."

Her lips look blue, like the lips of little kids who have been in the water too long. Demian eats his cereal, a piece of toast, then, absentmindedly, the rest of his father's toast. It's not even eight o'clock, he has plenty of time. He eats while his mother says nice things about his father. How good he is to her. How well his friends like him, even the rich, much-respected ones. Demian is aware that people listen when his father speaks. Demian would like his own friends to treat him as his father's friends treat his father. Sometimes he quiets his voice, thins it out a little, to see if that's the trick.

"He's way too smart for what he does," his mother is saying. "He did well in college without studying. He could remember everything he'd ever read. He was a great talker, there was nothing he couldn't have done if he'd wanted to—do you know how high his IQ is?"

"Higher than mine," Demian says.

His mother doesn't protest, just shakes her head as if in wonder. "He never got time to sit and figure things out. He was too young to have a child."

"Mom," Demian says, "he was twenty-six when I was born. He's forty-two."

"He was too young," she says firmly, gathering up her books. "But he loves you like crazy, you ought to know that."

Pedaling to work Demian thinks about his father's IQ, how many points it might be higher than his own, and tries to see him as the Disappointed Man in his mother's fiction. He says *bankrupt* under his breath, trying to diminish his father enough to forgive him. It doesn't work. He tries to feel his father's love for him, remembering a ballgame his father took him to on his tenth birthday—him and his best friend, John Frank, and John Frank's father. He remembers sitting next to John in the back of their old Rabbit with his baseball glove in his lap for catching foul balls. Remembers listening to his father up front talking with John's father, John's father laughing at his father's jokes, though John's father drove a Volvo and everyone called him Dr. Frank. Demian was proud of his father. It was clear even then that although his father talked less than his friend's father, it was his father's words that thickened in the air. His father had given him and John their own tickets to hold, and jouncing along on the back seat, they squinted at the blue and white cardboard oblongs, discussing the numbers and letters that stood for what they were about to experience. SAT AUG 1:20 PM. AISLE 518 ROW 5 SEAT 242. GAME #52 CHICAGO CUBS VS. NEW YORK METS. ADMIT ONE SUBJECT TO CONDITIONS ON BACK NO REFUND NO EXCHANGE. There was one set of letters he couldn't fathom: OBST VW. He showed the ticket to John. "Obstetrician?" John asked.

"It's a beer ad. Obst Blue Ribbon!"

"That's *Pabst* Blue Ribbon!"

"I know, fart head."

Only when they got to the park and sat down in seats behind a pillar that let him see half the field if he craned to the right, did he realize the letters stood for Obstructed View. At first he didn't mind. He'd never been to a major-league game before. The smell of hot dogs and popcorn filled his mouth and nose, the stands were cool and dim like a naptime bedroom, the playing field bright green under the sun. He put his glove on, waiting for his father to sit down next to him, not necessarily to talk to him, since of course he had more to say to Dr. Frank, but just to be there so Demian could ask him questions or maybe just sit quietly beside him, watching him watch the game. But when Demian had finished taking in the brightness and darkness, and located his favorite Cub, Shawon Dunston, who could hurl the ball like the end of a whip, his father was still standing in the aisle. "We'll get you guys after the game," he called to them, holding out a five-dollar bill. "Don't eat too much." Demian took the bill, folded and folded it again as his father and Dr. Frank descended the steep steps, vanishing toward seats Demian knew had an unencumbered view of the field. Still, he wasn't sure what to make of the turnaround. It wasn't exactly what he'd pictured when he'd asked on his tenth, his double-digit birthday, not for something to ride or look at or hold in his hand, but for an event to experience with his father. The man who took his father's seat told him stories about the ballplayers' personal lives. It was lots of fun sitting with John, leaning hard one way around the pillar to watch the ball come off the bat, then the other way to see where the ball ended up. Shawon Dunston threw the ball into the dugout, and the Cubs still won. But although he and John wore their gloves all nine innings, the foul balls went to seats below them in the sun. And although he and John kept good track of the game, marking the P.O.'s, F.O.'s, K's, H's on their scorecards with their short yellow ballpark pencils, some of the balls fell where neither of them could see. The man in his father's seat said Shawon Dunston would never learn to take a walk because he was mentally retarded. When Demian's father returned for them after the game, the skin of his arms looked dark gold in the sun, and it was clear to Demian that the game he'd seen was not as good a game.

Demian leans back in his chair at the Geller breakfast table, puts his feet on a second chair, takes the cup of coffee Rachel has poured him. He's never had coffee before, and he gulps it like milk, burns his throat, swallows his grimace. Rachel doesn't ask him why he isn't at Bi-Rite's this morning. She talks rapidly, of nothing he has to respond to. She's barefoot, in a long, wrinkled shirt she must have slept in. He imagines what's under the shirt; his face burns. Her brown hair looks white blond on the side where the sun hits.

She runs into the kitchen, returns with a plate of kiwi and nectarines, and two dark blue cloth napkins. But on the gray tile of the kitchen floor she has left patches of red. She is limping. He watches, frozen, as blood wells out of her foot. She sits down, crosses her leg over her knee, eats a nectarine, while her blood drip-drips onto the gray tile. He thinks, Why doesn't she wipe it up? Should he wipe it up? Someone should wipe it up. It gives him the creeps, these bright red splashes, but the cloth napkin she presents him seems too fine for this use. He's looking around for paper when she throws a piece of broken china onto the table in front of him. "Parental carnage," she says.

It's the source of her injury, picked up from the kitchen floor—a white shard, triangular in shape, a thin gold line around the part that had been rim. The broken edge is red. "Car*nage*," she says, accenting and softening the last syllable like a French word. This morning her father had relieved some of his anger by throwing a cup at the refrigerator. Her mother relieved hers by refusing to sweep. "They need to *see* this," she says, placing the broken piece of china on the blue cloth napkin in the middle of the breakfast table. She seems thrilled almost, as if the bloody shard is the final piece of the puzzle of her life. She arranges a kiwi on the napkin, a bud vase alongside. "It's our new centerpiece! A still life! What'll we call it, *Terror at Teatime?*" She speaks with a British accent, biting off her words with her teeth. "No, something simple: *Daddy.* That's it—*Daddy!*"

He starts laughing. "That's terrific. It's really funny." He laughs more, in loud bursts. He has never laughed like this before. He tells her the story of the one baseball game his father took him to, exaggerating his hopes so that their obstruction by the pillar seems purely comic. She takes his hand, squeezing hard, and he elaborates, this time stressing his naïve reverence for his father, his father's indifference. What had his father called out, descending the stairs? Demian doesn't remember now, makes it up: "Try and have fun, kiddo!" "We'll be thinking of you, suckers!" "Look, you—you're lucky you weren't offed in utero!" It doesn't sound like his father but makes him laugh hysterically.

She starts laughing, too. "He slapped me this morning. I told him what I thought of people who can't control themselves, and he held me by the hair and slapped my face. Like this." She grabs a hunk of her hair, yanks her head to one side, giggles. "He said, 'I'll show you how I control myself.'"

He smooths her hair where she yanked. He has begun shaking a little, though he doesn't feel sad or scared. "Sometimes in the room with him I feel like I don't exist. I don't have a body. I don't know how to talk, even." He's shaking harder, down to the soles of his feet. He has never spoken like this. "He'd slap me, too, if he thought I was important enough. The truth is, I bore him. Poor Dad, bored by his son." He replays what he said, awed by what seems to be the utter truth of it. It seems reckless and marvelous saying these things about his father. He's an explorer, charting ground never before seen by mortal eyes. "I really don't need him. If he died tomorrow it wouldn't make the least difference in my life. It might improve things."

Later, with his father's blood leaking into his brain, he'll remember what he said, and even though over the years his father had grown no more interested in him, he'll think for a moment of all the things his father wanted to do that he couldn't do, couldn't ever do now, and he'll sit down in a chair by the bed, for a moment unable to breathe.

But now he's on his knees before Rachel's chair. She puts her arms around his shoulders, presses her face to the top of his head. He hears her heart beating through her T-shirt. His teeth are chattering, and to stop them he starts kissing her through her shirt—her shoulder, the two round little bones at the top of her chest, the long swell of breast. In the past he has treated this part of her body reverently, but now he sucks as if he were drinking, wetting the cloth of her shirt till it feels to his lips like rough, wet skin. He has stopped trembling. "I hate him," he murmurs, almost lovingly.

"Has he ever knocked your mother down? Called her a slut? Said he could smell it on her? I'm in the same room, here at this very table eating my cantaloupe."

He can't tell if she likes what his mouth is doing, but she has made no objection. He raises her shirt, observes her body in the daylight; thinks, *There is so much of her.* He says, "He made me sit behind a pole. He traded in his ticket and sat with a buddy. The only baseball game he ever took me to."

It doesn't sound quite awful enough. He looks at her for confirmation, but she seems not to have heard him. "Has he ever come home drunk and gotten in bed with you? And when you screamed he put his hand over your mouth? And when you bit his hand he told lies to your mother? Who still thinks you're a slut though she doesn't say so?"

"Is that true, Rachel?"

She shakes her head no. "Another example of my sick imagination."

Her voice is light but he can't shake off the terrible picture. "If it were true I'd kill him."

"Me, too."

Her last comment comes without inflection. He tries to read her face, but it doesn't help. He hugs her hard. She returns it with a slight time lag, mechanically stroking the back of his head. She seems uncharacteristically passive. He feels sure that if he were to take off his pants, she'd sigh once, then let him have her. The thought terrifies him. "Rachel, where are you?"

She looks at him, smiling with the corners of her mouth only. He wants to be gone from here, to be riding back to Bi-Rite's, whose manager is a friend of his dad's and might not question the excuse he'll make up on the way. But Rachel is sitting so still in her chair, she seems to take up no space. He imagines that if he left her, he'd never find her again. When he called, her mother would say, *She's traveling in Europe.* Her mother would say, *There's no one here by that name.*

"Rachel," he whispers. He touches her face, the curve of her arm, side of her knee, arch of her wounded foot, softly so as not to miss her faintest whispered response. Her foot feels cold, and he warms it between his hand and his face. Then he puts his lips to the injured spot, cleaning off the dried blood with his tongue, smoothing down the flap of torn skin.

Jessica Treadway

Down in the Valley

They always meet us at the door and search what we're carrying, before we can go in. It's the same for everybody —routine—but it makes me feel guilty. As if they think we'd be trying to smuggle in something dangerous.

The thing is, we don't even realize sometimes, my wife and I. What counts as dangerous, I mean. We learned the obvious things early on—they made us take Dee Dee's Far Side mug back home with us that first day, and the instant coffee we brought her had to be poured into a margarine tub. Those things made sense, once they were explained to us. Glass and ceramic, you could smash them and come up with a jagged edge. Dee Dee asked us for a jump rope, because they wouldn't let her go outside alone to run or even walk. We went to the sports store and bought one of those high-tech ropes with wood handles and a strap at the center to balance the weight. When we presented it for inspection, it got checked with the sharps.

A *jump rope?* I said, and Helen said *Honey* to me, and then I got it, too. The thought of it pulled something inside my gut and with the pull came a picture of my daughter, double-jumping between her best friends in the street we lived on, her hair bouncing in a braid. *Down in the valley where the green grass grows, there sat Dee Dee as pretty as a rose.*

Our daughter's bed is the middle one in a room of three. She faces the window when she sleeps, and on the door of the standing closet she has taped the get-well cards her friends sent her, Snoopys and teddy bears, the messages inside signed with

X's and O's. At first I thought she wouldn't want to tell anybody she was here, but my wife thinks it's healthy, she shouldn't be ashamed. "What if she was in with a broken leg?" Helen asked me. "She needs help, Tom. It's not something to hide." Still, I sense that she shares my discomfort at having people know. This is a psychiatric unit, not a hospital for bones or blood.

She has been here a week now, and unless they discharge her sooner than they expect to, she will still be here on her birthday, her twenty-fourth. Last year we all marked the twenty-third by going to a Red Sox game, Dee Dee and her brother, Dan, Dee Dee's boyfriend, Edward, and Helen and I. The Red Sox won that night, and Dee Dee and Edward got engaged. Dee Dee called it a triple play, all those things to celebrate at the same time.

They were married in December, and they moved to an apartment in town, close to the law school, where they met in Torts. It's not a great neighborhood. I told Dee Dee from the beginning that I was worried about her walking home at night from the library alone. She said they would try to study together, and most of the time, they did.

But on the thirtieth of April, a week ago, Edward was playing softball with other men from their class, and he joined them afterward for beer at the Pourhouse, across from the playing field. Dee Dee worked in the library until nine o'clock, past sunfall, and then she gathered up her books in the leather backpack I gave her for Christmas.

She stopped at the convenience store for a frozen dinner, and then began to walk down the long block, toward the apartment. When she was halfway there, a man stepped out of the alley behind the laundromat, and asked her for a light. When she said she didn't have one, he moved behind her in a single motion she felt rather than saw; he tore the backpack away from her and threw it in the dumpster. Then he grabbed her by the wrists and leaned her against the laundromat's brick wall, lifting his hand to her mouth.

He kept the hand over her lips and nose and slid her down to the cement and pushed her back, putting the frozen dinner under her head for a pillow. *Relax*, he told her, and when she laughed, so did he. But after the laugh she couldn't breathe because he was blocking her air, and she passed out, then came to sometime later, when he was finishing. He ran off, and she gathered herself together and went home.

This is what she told the police, after Edward returned to find her shaking under the covers, sucking her thumb. She had showered and dressed in a nightgown and put her clothes through the wash. She tried to convince him that nothing was the matter, she was just feeling sick, she was anxious about exams. But he didn't believe her, and finally she told him that she had been raped. Edward tried to put his arm around her but she wouldn't let him. She began rocking a little, and Edward got scared. He called the police though she made him promise he wouldn't, and then he called us. When the police got there she didn't talk until they brought in a woman officer.

Helen and Edward and I waited in the small living room, and I read the titles of books on the shelf behind my son-in-law's shoulder: *Fit for Life, Presumed Innocent, Ascent of Man.*

They brought her to the hospital. We followed, Edward driving, forgetting to brake until the last moment at every light. They took her into an examining room for questions and for tests. Helen tapped the thigh of her jeans with a tin ashtray, and Edward sat with the heels of his hands against his forehead, looking down at his feet. He was still wearing his softball clothes. I concentrated on the TV bolted to a corner of the wall, and I let myself into the world I was watching. It was tuned to *The Honeymooners,* and when I laughed at something Ed Norton did, Helen said, "Jesus, Tom. Shut up."

After a while the policewoman came out with the doctor, who was also a woman, and they sat down with us, both of them trying to smile.

"Is she all right?" Helen said, and I could tell the words had been dammed up in her throat.

"Well, yes," the doctor said.

"What does that mean?" Edward asked her. The vein in his neck gave away what he wanted to do, which was cry.

"Well, we're a little confused." The doctor brushed her hand across the clipboard she held, as if gathering to show us in her fingers what her study of Dee Dee had found. "She has all the psychological symptoms of having been raped—a classic reaction, in fact. The trauma is very real. But her medical condition isn't consistent with the assault she described."

"What does that mean?" Edward asked again. Helen tossed the ashtray onto the table, and the doctor, who was looking down, jumped.

"What are you telling us?" Helen said.

This time it was the officer who answered. "We can't be sure, but it's possible she wasn't actually aware of what happened, if she was passed out," she said. "She feels brutalized—that's clear—but there isn't any physical evidence of rape. Or of *any* sexual encounter in quite a while, is that right?" She was checking with the doctor, who nodded, looking down again.

The rest of us turned to look at Edward. "Oh, for God's sake," he said. "We've both been tired. It's exam time. Besides, she hasn't been into it, lately." He reached back to rub his neck. "I can't believe I'm talking about this."

Helen was brushing her hair. She does this when she's nervous, takes the brush out of her purse at the most irrelevant times and attacks her hair in long hard strokes.

"There's something you're not saying," she said to the doctor and the policewoman. "Tell us what it is."

The two women looked at each other to decide who would answer; the doctor gave it with her eyes to the cop, who said, "We think it's possible that for some reason, she made a false report."

"You mean *lied*?" Edward shot up out of his chair. "What the hell are you saying?"

"She would never do that," I told them. "It has to be true."

Then Dee Dee was at the edge of the waiting room, one hand against the wall, accompanied by a nurse who stood close with arms half-lifted, ready to provide a catch. "Honey," Helen said, and went to her, and I followed, but our daughter halted us with a raised and trembling palm. Edward coughed, and the sound made Dee Dee wince, her eyes remote and lightless in her flat white face.

"They're right," she said. "There wasn't anybody. I made him up. I'm sorry."

Her birthday falls on a Wednesday, and by noontime I still haven't decided what to get for her. I'm afraid of fumbling, of offering the wrong thing. Helen has bought and wrapped many gifts from us together, for this occasion—more than any other birthday or Christmas of the past, as if we could build with all the packages a fortress against the danger looking for entrance to our daughter's mind. But I always like to give a remembrance that's just from me, and walking back to the office from lunch, I pass the window at Snyder's and have a brainstorm. This is where I bought the leather backpack for Dee Dee at Christmastime, and when I go inside I find one identical to the original gift, and on my way into my building, carrying the bag, something else occurs to me. On the phone, to Helen, I say, "What about the backpack? She said the guy threw it in the dumpster. If she was wrong, does that mean she still has it?"

This is how we speak of that night, to each other: we use words like *upset* instead of *crazy*, *wrong* instead of *lie*. Helen—who keeps losing weight in her voice and body, all her energy used up in fretting, trying to figure this thing out—sighs and says she doesn't know, she doesn't know, so I call Edward and ask him, and he says no, the police did find it in the garbage, and I say, How can that be?, and he says he doesn't know, either. I suggest that this may be a clue in support of Dee Dee's story, and Edward reminds me that she admitted it was a lie.

"I hate that word," I tell him, and he says, "What do you want me to say?" He is trying to keep up with classes—Dee Dee thought she'd be able to, too, studying with the notes he copied for her, planning to ask for passes from the hospital to take her exams—but she gave up the first week and applied for Incompletes, and though Edward swears he will not, he may have to do the same. Usually we go at different times to see her, because the doctors recommend short and separate visits, so I don't know how things have been between Edward and Dee Dee, whether they suffer the same silences as Helen and Dan and I when it is our turn, or whether she has been able to explain anything to her husband in a way he can understand.

Everything here in the hospital depends on your privileges, or what the initiated call *privs:* whether you can leave the unit at all, how often, for how long, and with whom. Privs aren't issued as reward or punishment, the nurse on duty explained to us when Dee Dee was admitted. They are determined by how "safe" the staff thinks you are, and how much responsibility you can be trusted with, mostly for yourself.

"What the hell does *safe* mean?" I remember asking. Helen and I were standing with the nurse in a corner of the unit. Edward and Dee Dee were going through her suitcase with a counselor, separating out the things she could conceivably hurt herself with: they took custody of her hair dryer, her compact mirror, notebooks with wire spirals.

"Most of the people who come here have been self-destructive at some point," the nurse told us.

"You mean suicidal?" Helen said. In the car on the way over she'd made me stop, telling me she had to vomit, but nothing happened, and I thought she might be bringing it up now.

"Sometimes, but not necessarily." The nurse looked even younger than Dee Dee. She didn't wear a uniform, but instead had on a sundress over a T-shirt with rolled sleeves. Her arms were tan already, this early in the season, and I guessed she had been on vacation in the last month, someplace warm, with someone who loved her. "A lot of sexually abused women cut themselves with a razor or a knife. On their arms, mostly, or sometimes on their legs." She watched us react and then paused, like a teacher waiting for her students to catch up in their notes.

"The internal pain is so intense that it gives them a distraction, and relief, to feel something physical instead."

"But Dee Dee said she wasn't raped," Helen said, and the words seemed to choke her.

I took her hand, which was shockingly cold, and reminded her, "We don't know what happened."

"Well." The nurse looked as if she wanted to smile at us, for comfort, but decided halfway into the gesture that it wasn't the right one. "She'll be able to talk about it in therapy." She reached out to pat Helen's sleeve, and I waited to be touched too, but at that moment the counselor brought Dee Dee over with the searched suitcase, and we had to say goodbye. We would have hugged her, but they had already advised us of the hospital rule against personal contact, so I lifted my fingertips to my lips and kissed them, then turned them in a salute to my daughter, hoping she would know how much I wanted it to mean. When she picked up the suitcase to bring it to her room, I stole a look up and down her arms, to check for scars, and I noticed Helen doing the same thing; our eyes met in relief when we saw the flesh intact, and on our way out to the car we gripped each other around the waist, tightly, digging our nails in, until it hurt.

After two weeks, Dee Dee's privileges allow her only as far as the building's basement, which is divided into three rooms for visiting, laundry, and Ping-Pong. It's here, on the white tile floor, that Dee Dee stretches and jumps rope, when she can get one of the counselors to supervise. *Along came Somebody and kissed her on the nose.* ("Somebody" always changed, a different boy's name every time I heard it sung to the slap of the rope against the sidewalk.) *How many kisses did she get?*

We have a Ping-Pong table in our basement at home, but the kids never learned to play because I always had it piled with junk from my worktable, where I make things out of wood. When Dan was a baby I bought him a toy tool set, but he dropped the hammer when I put it in his hand, and it was Dee Dee I would find playing with the plastic screws and wrenches, concentrating on some close task, tongue set between her teeth.

By the time she was five she was helping me shape things, her small hands piggybacking mine as they sent boards through the saw. We would climb the stairs from our Saturday sessions trailing sawdust from our shoes, and at supper Helen couldn't understand why we weren't hungry, because she didn't know about the candy we ate in secret while we worked.

Dee Dee takes us down here, to the circle of seats around the low table scarred with graffiti, *Dr. Flembag sucks* and *Please help me* engraved in light scratches across the cheap blond wood. We give her the birthday presents, pretending this is all going on in our living room, our neighborhood outside. When I hand Dee Dee the last one, my fingers brush her arm, and she pulls back with such a jerk that the package falls.

"What's the matter?" I say.

"Tom, no personal contact." Helen gets up and moves between me and Dee Dee on the couch, as if we are siblings in the back seat of a car. Still, she is trying to preserve the mood of a party. "You two," she says to us on either side of her, but careful not to touch. "You always break the rules."

The next morning Helen and I are both dressing for work. I am still a little breathless and cloudy from the dream I was having when the alarm went off, which I remembered distinctly and with dread for the few minutes before I got up, and then forgot in the first motions of the day.

We haven't had sex in a month, since before all this began. Helen doesn't seem to miss it, and I am glad, because I couldn't touch her if she wanted me to, but this way it's not my fault. The subtlest connection of our limbs in bed makes my heart speed up, but not with desire. She has not seemed to notice that I feel this way, and I would not be able to tell her why, if she did ask, because I can't tell myself.

Dee Dee is the one we should be talking about, and we do. But after the first few days there seems to be nothing to say. We have forgone our usual meals together in favor of snacks eaten standing at the kitchen counter or in front of the TV. Dan used to come by often, to do his laundry or to pick up mail that hadn't made it to his new apartment, and before all this he stayed a while, and we talked about his job or the Red Sox or a girl he wanted to date, but lately he's only in and out, hurrying to finish his errands, moving through the house the way he would through a post office or a laundromat. He mumbles his goodbyes.

Except for when we sleep, Helen and I are hardly ever together in the same room. There is none that feels big enough for us, that can contain both our bodies and the balance between them. Helen keeps finding things to blame me for, and even if I'm not guilty, I let her. I wait for her to swear about the garbage or the dog. If too much time passes between accusations I get nervous, thinking she is storing them all up for one big strike to my blind side.

So that morning we get a phone call, the phone call, from the hospital, from the social worker assigned to Dee Dee's case, a Lolly Sheftick, which is enough to make you laugh, except that she doesn't look the way her name sounds, like a crazy grandmother with bad makeup and a wig—in fact she's pretty in a flushed and angled way, taller than Helen and slimmer, but with a smile that includes rather than threatens women less good-looking than she.

She has called us here to discuss "a matter of some urgency." This Lolly Sheftick explains to us outside her office, in a quiet voice around a table strewn with *Good Housekeeping* and *Self*. A plant in the center of the table sheds brown leaves from its pot, and I wonder who is responsible for not taking care of it. Lolly stands, and I expect her to lead Helen and me through the door that shows her name, but instead she says she would like to talk to my wife first, privately, and would I please wait here.

Helen looks at me for some clue, some secret signal, to tell her what this means. I shrug—the movement is spastic, beyond my control. They go behind the door and shut it, and I am alone in the lobby, except for a woman who sits at the reception desk;

but she is listening to something through the headset of a Dictaphone, so I am, essentially, alone.

I sit there. After some time I remember where I am, and I stand suddenly and the receptionist looks up with a startled motion, a palm flying to her chest. I lift a hand to show her I'm sorry, and I knock on Lolly Sheftick's door. She opens the door, and beyond it in a chair against the wall, I see my wife still waiting, still with the question in her eyes, and Lolly Sheftick says, "But Mr. Osborne, we're not ready yet," and I tell her, "Yes, I am."

"I want to hear this," I add. "Please let me in."

"Mrs. Osborne?" Lolly says. "Do you mind if he's here, too?"

"Of course not. He's my husband," Helen says. "Why would I mind? You're scaring me," she says to Lolly. "You'd better tell me why."

There is an empty seat next to Helen, but instead I take the one that makes a triangle among us, and I look at the four feminine legs across from me, both sets crossed at the knee, my wife's tapping the carpet with the toe of her best pumps. We both changed our clothes after we got the phone call, without discussing it. We seemed to realize that what we had on already would not be enough, that we needed to dress up.

Lolly Sheftick folds her hands on top of her knee and says, "This is not going to be an easy thing. I asked Dee Dee if she wanted to be here, but she said no. She's probably right, actually. It would probably be too much."

"Are you going to tell us why she said she was raped, when she wasn't?" Helen, I see, is wrapping her fingers in a grip stronger than prayer.

"Well," Lolly Sheftick says, "we believe it's more complicated than that. No, she wasn't attacked two weeks ago. She's told us that. We believe—and we've talked to Dee Dee about this—that she made up the attack to explain the feelings she's having now about something that happened long ago."

"Long *ago*?" Helen says, and I watch her hands come apart in her lap.

Lolly nods. She picks up a pen from her desk, and I watch the way she fingers it.

"Are you telling me my daughter was raped a long time ago?" Helen laughs. "That's impossible. Impossible. I don't know what you're saying." She looks at me and puts her hand out, palm up in my direction, to show me that it's my turn, now, to object to what she's hearing.

But I have left the office, let myself leave the body that still sits in my place, decided not to listen anymore. I make a sound that could mean anything. Helen stiffens in her chair. Lolly Sheftick lifts the cap of the pen to her mouth, pulls in between her lips, bites it, then yanks it out through her teeth.

"Mr. Osborne," she says, "this is uncomfortable, I know. It's worse than that. But I have to tell you both that what Dee Dee remembers has to do with you." Though her tone is professional, courteous, trying even to be kind because she can destroy me, I see the hatred in her face.

"It does," I say, meaning to make it a question, but it doesn't come out that way.

"What?" Helen says. She picks her purse off the floor and begins to rummage for her hairbrush, though she looks not inside the bag but at my hands, which start to dance along the chair arms.

"What, Tom?" she says, locating the brush, and in taking it out she flips a book of matches on the floor. "Wait. Wait. Don't tell me." She presses the bristles deep into the flesh of her palm.

"Stop that," I tell her, frowning at the brush, and I think of reaching over to take it from her, but my hands are still rapping and fluttering at the side arms of my seat. We watch them, the three of us.

Finally, when the hands don't stop jittering, when nobody says a word, Helen leans forward with the brush and smacks it down on my fingers. Lolly Sheftick giggles—not a long one, she stops as soon as she hears it, but it is enough to make her realize she shouldn't have, and she says, "I'm sorry."

"What happens now?" I ask, after a moment. On Lolly's desk there is a photograph of her and someone else, but it is too small to see distinctly, and I resist the urge to squint or lean to make out the details.

"Okay, tell me," Helen says, still clenching the handle. She is speaking to me, but she looks at Lolly, whose eyes send me some pity along with her contempt. There are certain things we learn by being human, and one is that we're more alike than we can bear.

"Mr. Osborne?" she asks.

But when she sees me spinning, she tells Helen herself. "Dee Dee remembers being abused by her father," she says, the words emerging at a slow, distorted speed. "I'm sorry, Mrs. Osborne."

"Oh, for God's sake," Helen says. "That's not true." She actually seems to smile. "I'm so sick of this abuse talk, it's everywhere you go. Abuse, abuse. How come you never used to hear that word? It's the latest thing. A fad, like sushi."

I wait for Lolly to laugh again, but instead she looks disturbed. I watch us from a corner of the ceiling, where I'm hanging from a nerve.

"I understand your reaction," she tells Helen. "We see it all the time. You don't want to believe it. Neither does Dee Dee." She tosses the pen onto her blotter, opens the desk drawer, and pulls out a cigarette from a pack of Merits, which she lights with the urgency of a swimmer sucking air.

"She feels them in her body," Lolly says, turning her head to exhale toward the wall above her desk, at the buzzer labeled HELP. "She's re-experiencing the sensations, as if they're happening to her now. It's not unusual. I'm sorry," she says again, dragging for dear life.

She looks at me. "Do you have anything you want to say, Mr. Osborne? I realize this is . . ." But there is no language for what this is, and she can see it in my face. When I start to speak, I choke on my own swallow, and cough to clear my throat.

Helen is waiting, her breath suspended, her body taut with dread. "I didn't abuse her," I tell them, and my wife's release is audible. Before she can turn it into words, I head her off and whisper, "I wouldn't call it that."

How do these things happen? How can you understand? It's not that I forgot, like Dee Dee—although they say she didn't, either, not the way you forget the name of someone you hardly know.

No, I remember all the nights, the darkness of her room, the way the walls held us in comfort when it was cold outside. And in summer, with the windows open, how the air would touch us through the screen, and I would lift the sheet across her shoulder and watch her fall to sleep.

When it began, she welcomed me, her body making barely a dimple in the big-girl bed. I felt such love for her, such wonder; and as I swept her hair behind the soft part of her ear, she closed her eyes and smiled. We played a game with words, *Dee Dee* and *Daddy*, whispering them to each other until the syllables got twisted and the names became nonsense. We called it tucking in.

There was no sin in it, to start with. Then the awe I felt at what she let me do overcame the *no* I knew I should be heeding; I looked into her face and saw the light there, the smile and the trust, and I changed them because I could, no other reason, I saw that I could leave a mark as long as life and so I did it. I know it and, God help me, knew it then, but only the way you know a thing in theory, with other people's proofs at the back of the book. You look them up and see how they arrived there, and you know the answers to be true; but at the test it goes out of your head, you are back to your own sad way of figuring, and you forget what you swore to yourself you would understand in time.

In the mornings it woke with me. Not as far back as the little bed, but the moments after, when I went down the hall and in to Helen. I felt like a burglar in that passage, an intruder in my home. Once I opened my eyes I sent my memory of the night to lodge in a place other than conscience, which was filled up long ago. Even so, at breakfast, I waited for my daughter to turn her head from me, and it always took me by surprise when she would plop a kiss against my forehead and ask me how I was.

Now, they tell me why: during the nights, after I left her, a cloud spread through her senses, wiping out my visits and waking her in white. Until this spring. Was it the thaw? Her class on criminals? A movement Edward made above her in the bed?

It stopped when she was twelve. She got her period that year, and when Helen came to tell me, looking proud and brave (I think she had been crying), I was down in the basement building Dee Dee a new bureau, sanding off the boards. My wife held a basket of laundry, a mix of dirty clothes from all the hampers, our underwear with the kids' gym suits, the dust rags, and the towels. She set the load on top of the washer to leave her arms free for a hug, and when I held her in it, our bodies fitting flush so nothing could have come between them, I heard, "She's not my baby anymore," and I swear to God I couldn't tell which one of us had said it.

Later, when Dee Dee came down to inspect the bureau, I offered her candy, and she took it, watching me while she ate; I hid my wrapper the way we used to so Helen wouldn't know, but she folded hers in half and dropped it in the trash bucket, where it fell without a sound. She ran her fingers over the drawers and showed me where they needed smoothing. She told me which varnish she wanted me to use. When Helen called us for supper, she waited until I went up the steps first, instead of letting me follow her, as I always had before.

That night I fell asleep with my arms around Helen, and I woke a few hours later with a jolt, thinking I had been caught, until I remembered that I belonged there, and that I wouldn't have to leave. When I realized that I expected to find myself in a bed that I had soiled, I felt more guilt than after any time with Dee Dee, and I got up and went to her doorway, where I stood and watched her sleep.

She lay curled in an impossibly small space at the edge of the mattress, and her thumb was in her mouth. She was the baby we set to nap in a laundry basket, prone on a pillow, wrapped in my flannel shirt. She was easy to carry that way, and it was all we could afford. That first summer, we took her everywhere with us—to the Esplanade for fireworks, to the beach, even to Fenway Park. She seldom cried, and she outgrew Helen's hugs before any of her friends could bear to let their mothers from their sight. On the playground, when she fell, she froze in landing, and we waited for the wail. But before Helen or I or another grown-up could move to comfort her, she got up to kiss herself on the injury—the finger or the foot—and smearing the tears away she joined the game again.

When she began to change positions in the bed I turned from the doorway, not wanting to be seen, and behind me my son was standing, with his finger on the light. He switched it off, and the hall went dark, turning us to shadows. "What's up, Dad?" Danny said, and I could feel him wanting to believe what I would say.

"Just checking," I told him, and I sent him back to bed. But I saw him waiting by his window, hugging his long arms, until I left his sister's door.

Maybe it's silly, a superstition, but I wonder if it might make a difference to Dee Dee, she might say she'd talk to me, if I brought some cherry Danish to the hospital for her. Helen will only speak to me on the phone, and just barely, after the day in Lolly Sheftick's office a week ago. When Helen started to lose control that morning, Lolly took her to another room, and I stood to make them think I would go back to the lounge; but when they had left I shut the door behind them, and sat down at Lolly's desk. The photograph I had tried to get a look at earlier was propped against the wall. It was a picture of Lolly and a man, in summer, their arms around each other's bathing-suit waists, her head against his chest. I put my hand out to touch it, and dust fluttered from the frame.

On Friday, after work, I drive back to the motel where I've been staying and change my clothes and get a dinner at the drive-through of the Burger King on the way to the hospital, and when I get there I park on the far side of the lot, and eat the dinner, waiting for my family to show up. Visiting hours begin at five-thirty, and at six Helen and Dan arrive together, and they go into the building. A few minutes later Dee Dee comes outside with them, and they walk to a cluster of wood chairs in the center of the lawn. I watch them talking; they even laugh. Then Dan picks up a stick from the ground and begins jabbing it at the grass, until Helen tells him to stop it; I can see reproach in her face, but when he drops the stick, she leans over to touch his knee.

I think about getting out and going over, but I am not even supposed to be here. Helen's made that plain. Instead I sit there with the window rolled down. When somebody walks by I put my hand over my forehead, as if rubbing out an ache. When the coast is clear I look over at the three of them, my wife and children saying words I cannot hear. Dan shakes his head a lot, and Dee Dee's face looks old across the yard.

Helen does much of the talking, and at the end of the visit, when they stand and head back to the hall, she puts a hand on each child's shoulder. They are passing near my car, though I know they won't notice it, because they don't look to the sides as they move forward, just keep on going straight, not because there is nothing to appreciate around these grounds but because there is too much that my daughter needs permission to see and touch and feel.

When they are beyond me and almost to the door, I press my horn a couple of times, trying not to sound frantic, before they can disappear. Dee Dee jumps at the first toot, and at the second all three of them turn around to stare. Then Dan and Dee Dee look at Helen, to see what they should do. I put my head out and say, "Hey, hi," and Dee Dee is the first to answer.

"Oh, Daddy," she says to me.

But no one makes a move until I ask, "Will you guys come here a minute? I'm not going to get out," and cautiously they all move toward me.

"You're not supposed to be here," Helen says.

"I know. But I wanted to see you," I tell them. "Where's
Edward?"

"He's not here," Dee Dee says.

"I see that."

Dan kicks the tire and says, "Look, what do you want?"

"Nothing," I say. His anger scares me. A breeze blows by, and
the smell of my burger carton comes up from the car floor to
make me queasy.

"Then get out of here," Dan says.

"Can I talk to Dee Dee?"

Helen says, "You've got to be kidding."

"What, Dad?" My daughter takes a step forward and pulls her
hair around her face. "Tell me."

They are all waiting for what I have to say. But I've forgotten
what it was, or if I even knew. "Sorry," I mumble, meaning that
I'm lost, but Dan takes it for something else.

"Sorry?" he says. "You're sorry?" He laughs, then spits across
the pavement.

"That's not what I meant," I tell him, but he will not
understand.

"You'd better go," my wife says. She touches Dee Dee's
elbow from behind, and Dee Dee tenses, then smiles at her
mother so she won't take offense.

"Okay," I say, and start the engine. The smell of food and the
force of my family's feelings are squeezing out my breath. I lose
control of the clutch, and the car sputters, and looking up to turn
the key again, I see my son making a face, as if he knows he
could expect no more of me.

"Wait," Dee Dee says, putting a hand out. I shift to neutral,
trying not to flinch. She leans into the car. Her face is at my level.
"I'm going to be okay, you know," she tells me. I nod foolishly,
and drive away confused. Was she trying to give me comfort? Or
claim a victory?

We used to have a date on weekend mornings. We made
trips to the bakery, even before Dan was up to watch cartoons,

and we never told anyone about our secret, about the pastries we ate on the way home and the Cokes we drank with them. The men in the bakery had a game, pretending week to week that they'd forgotten Dee Dee's name, and when they saw her coming they went into their routine, calling out "Irene!" and "Mildred!" to see how she'd respond.

At first, when she was little, she shook her head; sometimes she laughed at an odd or ugly name. They knew, of course, and before they gave us our breakfast they said the real one, and she waved goodbye, hugging the warm bag to her chest.

But on the morning that turned out to be our last one there, she wouldn't let them play. She was older then, and instead of picking out a cherry Danish, she asked for a corn muffin with jelly on the side.

"Okay, Lucille," one of the men said, as he reached into the case.

"Tell them my name, Dad," Dee Dee said.

"They know it, honey." I shrugged at the man to show I couldn't help my kid's manners.

"Tell them," she said again, and this time both of the men straightened behind the glass display.

"Honey—"

"Tell them," she said a third time, so close to breaking that the men looked at each other and then at the floor. "Tell. Tell. Tell."

Behind us a line was rustling. "Goddammit," I said, slapping a dollar on the counter. "Her name is Deirdre Anne."

"Okay," my daughter said, "let's go," and she took the bag and turned.

In the car I said, "What's wrong with you?"

She was buckling her seat belt, and her hair fell in her face. "Nothing." Her voice held more, but she contained it; I could see her swallow something down.

We pulled away and I told her, "You embarrassed me back there." She was eating her muffin and she tried to answer, but her throat was thick with crumbs.

"Hey," I said, realizing this was all we'd ended up with. I almost hit the car in front of me, with my hand out for my share. But she looked out the window as if she hadn't noticed, and I saw that she wasn't going to give me any of what she still had left.

Christopher Zenowich

Po Lives on the Y

When I saw the sign for piglets I told my father to stop the car. "I want to buy one," I said, attempting to say this with conviction. The thought of raising a pig over the summer had come as suddenly as the sign.

"How are you going to raise a pig when you're so busy reading Wittgenstein?" he asked, but he turned onto a dirt road which led up a small hill.

I wanted to read Wittgenstein's *Philosophical Investigations* all summer and somehow still be able to make some money for my senior year of college. As my father drove, I had gone on at length about how smart I was compared to my philosophy class nemesis, Peter Meltzer, the would-be valedictorian. My father listened, but after a few stabs at advice ("You shouldn't be so concerned about the guy, just yourself"), he adopted a pose which I thought of as his *film noir* self: wrist cocked over the driving wheel, eyes focused dully on the road ahead, brow furrowed in what appeared to be concentration, but was more likely a headache. I was sure anyone who grew up in the Fifties could do it. I played the role of the dame he didn't want to hear another word from.

"Meltzer's just a grind," I said. "He reads every secondary source on a philosopher before he comes to class. I swear he plagiarizes, and he's too slick at it to get caught."

My father nodded and made a throaty sound: the same he made toward my mother when she was off on a rant. That made me more determined. How could he imagine how humiliating it had been to be pitted against Peter Meltzer. Every week we took one side of an issue assigned by Professor Blackmon. We were asked to share our notes ahead of time, so that our in-class debate over some Meta-ethical issue would be more intense. Was the concept of morality a condition of rational discourse? Did distributive justice compromise larger issues of right and wrong? The topics were always immense; Meltzer's notes went on at least twenty pages, and were typed. Mine were four or five pages, handwritten, and rambling. What really pissed me off was the fact that Meltzer was such a gentleman. In debating me, he would ask if perhaps I had made a mistake, and cite the references I had bungled. He was witty, charming, and a liar. He had the professor in his hand. And when Meltzer brought up an issue discussed by Wittgenstein in *Philosophical Investigations* (one I was certain he had read about somewhere else), and Professor Blackmon said, "That's an interesting reading of Wittgenstein, Peter, but I believe the *Philosophical Investigations* is a book that cannot be read outside of a course—one I'm planning to teach in the fall," I knew then that I would spend my summer learning just what Wittgenstein wrote. I would know it backwards and forwards, without commentary; I would learn the words themselves. I would be ready for Meltzer.

"You got a job," my father said. "Your mother set you up at the hospital. In the kitchen." He maneuvered the car around several gullies that cut across the road.

"I would have found a job on my own," I said.

"Sure, but now you don't have to look." The car scraped against some rocks. He cursed.

"What does it entail?"

My father cleared his throat, rolled down the window, and spat. "It enn-tails," he said, drawing the words out, "washing pots and pans."

Just what I didn't need, a job like that. Hard work and fatigue. It would make Wittgenstein a chore at night.

The farm was a series of ramshackle wood buildings, all a weathered gray tone. Not the kind of place you expect to find in

northwestern Connecticut, where well-to-do people from New
York City were buying rundown places like this and turning
them into wineries, horse farms, outlets for native honey and
jam, psychiatric retreats, meditation centers, rehabs for one
addiction or another, or colonies for painters, playwrights, and
potters. It was hard to imagine how these locusts of good taste
had missed it. I liked it at first sight, as desolate as it was; there
was desperation here. There almost certainly had to be a
beheaded chicken in the kitchen sink, blood forming a pool
around its carcass. The barn probably hadn't been cleaned in
months. The man, when he was even there, was in a rage against
the things he didn't understand—quite possibly everything in his
life—and was ready to slaughter his family and go fishing. All
this seemed confirmed when a short, squat woman with brown
hair and a pimpled face emerged from the main house carrying a
diapered infant in her arm. There was a little kid behind her, his
dirty hands clinging to her dungaree jacket.

"How much are the pigs?" I asked.

"Twenty-five apiece," she said, and coughed. She sounded
tubercular, and didn't look much older than I was. "They're
already neutered, that's why."

I stuck my hand into my pocket and pulled out a ten and a
twenty, all I had left from my last paycheck at school. We took
two pigs, Camus and Sartre, I named them, and put them in the
trunk.

"You're just like they are," my father said as he spun out of
the driveway onto the main road. "You're just like those
goddamn New Yorkers."

Rupert, the head chef, spent fifteen minutes showing me the
proper procedure for washing pots and pans. When his voice
rose above a mumble it was whiny and nasty.

"Let me give you the big sketch here," he said, pointing to the
stainless steel tub divided into three sections. "This is your soak
sink, the middle one's your wash sink, and that there's your rinse
sink." He grabbed a white plastic bottle from a shelf and emptied

it in the soak sink. "Disinfectant. Just a bit every time you change the water. You follow?"

Like this was all so tough. I nodded without looking too smug. My new white shirt tugged at my armpits. I had to wear that and black chinos.

"What you have here are your steam pipes," he said, pointing to copper tubes below the surface of the water in each sink. "You heat the water up like so . . ." He turned a faucet on in each sink, producing an explosion of syncopated metallic hammering that made it impossible to hear him.

"What?" I yelled.

"You heat the water up as hot as you can stand it," he repeated. "The soak sink is the most important."

I pulled on my long black glove—it extended above my elbow—and dropped my hand into the water. It was hotter than I could stand. I yanked my arm out. "It's hot," I said.

"You got the sketch, then," Rupert said, and patted me on the back. "Laurie and I are the chefs today. We got baked macaroni and cheese for lunch. We need a lot of pots. If you've got any questions, see me. Your head chef is like the captain of a ship. You owe him your total allegiance. So don't ask Peejay nothing."

Peejay was the other pot washer. He showed up about fifteen minutes late, pulled on his black rubber gloves, and stuck one hand into each sink. "Naw, naw, naw," he said, turning on the steam in each.

"What's the matter?" I asked.

"Naw, too cold," he said without looking at me.

"Wait a second, I can't stand it now. It's too hot for me." I reached to turn off the steam in the soak sink. Peejay came to my side, and after I finished turning it off, he turned it back on.

"Too cold," he said. He pushed my hand away from the steam faucet. "Naw."

He was at least fifty years old, his head oddly large for his body, which was smaller than mine. He might have been five foot five. When he stared at me, he kept his mouth open. His lips were dry and cracked, his eyes suspicious, almost squashed beneath his bushy brown eyebrows. His hair was uncombed and not recently washed, full of cowlicks and snarls that gradually loosened as the steam and heat of the pot room got into them.

By ten o'clock break, I had sweated through my shirt and my skin was covered with a film of chlorine and detergent. In the hospital cafeteria I saw Rupert sitting by himself. "Take a seat," he said, kicking a chair out with his foot from beneath the table. He was unrolling a small wad of crumpled foil. Inside was a soggy, half-smoked cigar he attempted for a minute or two to relight with a Bic lighter.

"Screw it," he said, and pulled out a new cigar from his pocket. "So how's your day going?"

"Just fine," I said.

"So give me the word on Peejay."

I knew better than that. I didn't say anything without knowing where Rupert stood. "What is a word really?" I had read in Wittgenstein the very night before. "What is a piece in chess?"

"He's a little, you know . . ." I said finally, stammering into a theatrical pause.

"Retarded?" Rupert asked, blowing smoke above my head.

"Yeah, I guess." I wanted to say something wiseass, but resisted. I thought of my mother working in the Supply Office, seeing these guys every week from now until who knew when, and I didn't want her to have grief over what I had said or done this summer.

"I'll say he's retarded," Rupert said. "He's a dummy, and he's been here for fifteen years. Part of the good stuff the hospital tries to do."

I looked around for Peejay. Even though I didn't want to work with him, it would be cruel if he overheard us. "Where is he?" I asked. "Doesn't he get a break?"

"As if he even knows the difference," Rupert said. "He's outside. Look." Rupert pointed toward the parking lot in back. Peejay was there, waving his arms as if he were pleading a case before a jury.

"What's going on?" I asked.

"Get this sketch," Rupert said. "He's got some imaginary friend out there. He's had him ever since I've been here, and that's five years. I used to work as the head chef down at the Le Bon Spoon, but they didn't have retirement. This place is lucky to have me."

When Laurie said, "New guy, huh?" I knew I was slow. She was Rupert's first assistant chef, and strictly all business. Fat and expressionless, her face the color of mashed potatoes, she appeared with pots and pans which she tossed into the soak sink, saying only, "Need these back fast." This had gone on ever since break, her dirty pot-and-pan runs becoming more frequent as lunch approached. Peejay, who got on my nerves by kicking back pots for more soaking, grunted something I couldn't make out. I never saw him leave. The pots and pans kept coming in. I assumed Peejay was doing something elsewhere. I soaked, washed, and rinsed as fast as I could.

On Laurie's next visit, she said, "Peejay took off again, didn't he?"

Still scrubbing a stinking pan caked with cheese sauce, I glanced up at her, and must have looked confused.

"He's in the goddamn bathroom again," Laurie said. "I'll get him." She came back in a few minutes, holding Peejay by the ear.

"Get back to work, you bum," she said, shoving him toward the sink. "And you," she added, looking at me, "c'mere."

"Naw, naw, naw," Peejay said, turning on the steam as I walked around the corner with Laurie.

"Don't ever trust him," Laurie said. "And don't ever lend him five bucks. He hits up every new guy for five and never pays him back."

I wasn't prepared to raise pigs. But if I admitted that fact to my father it would be remembered for years, and flung in my face over any decision I reached.

I made a pen out of snow fence I got from a farmer, and a shelter from some old doors. The pigs were so small, at first I was worried they'd get out somehow. But they didn't seem to want to leave. I had trouble keeping Camus and Sartre straight in my mind, both of them Hampshires, although Sartre did have a little birthmark behind one of his ears. Gradually they developed different personalities. Camus ran to the fence first when I came with food; Sartre followed slowly and grunted more. On rainy days, he had to be coaxed by Camus's snorts of satisfaction at the trough. After one week I had spent most of my hospital paycheck on medicine and feed from Agway.

"If they die," my father said, "you bury them." I could tell he'd been working on a good lecture. He couldn't wait for me to screw up.

But I wasn't about to let them die. I wanted them for slaughter in the fall, after the first frost, the guy at Agway told me. I had found a meat locker that would do the job—how I loved the expression, "dressing them out"—and made arrangements for them to be picked up by the owner of the place. He would keep a third of the meat in return for the work. My father would pay me a fair price for his share of the meat.

Each night, after feeding Camus and Sartre, I went in, ate a cold dinner, and shut myself in my room, my cell, a dry-walled partition off the garage, to read Wittgenstein. I had read his *Tractatus Logico-philosphicus,* a work in which he asserted that whatever was the case in the world was ultimately a picture of a thought as expressed by a sentence. So all the true sentences summed up exactly what corresponded to the truth of the universe. But he had renounced this work, in part because it could not explain the truth of ethical statements or expressions of love or anger. In his later work he explored the possibility that language was a game in which situations altered the meaning of sentences. "Language is a labyrinth of paths," he wrote. "You approach from *one* side and know your way about; you approach the same place from another side and no longer know your way about." This accounted for the truth and the relativity of values. His culminating work, *Philosophical Investigations* was said to be understood by only his closest inner circle, two of whom taught at Cornell. I intended to make a pilgrimage there in the fall, to ask them questions about this man who died in a bare white room, who was born to one of the richest families in Vienna, only to give his fortune away, who lived a Spartan existence dedicated to philosophy, who was a virtuoso cello player, who had fought for Austria during World War I and volunteered to the British Armed Services during World War II, aiding a team of doctors in developing a way to estimate the severity of war wounds. I wanted to become their student. As Camus and Sartre hung from meat hooks in a freezer, their fatty flanks being cured to bacon in hickory smoke, I would be dazzling Professor Blackmon with my understanding of Wittgenstein's most complex work. "You must let me speak to his greatest students," I imagined myself saying to him.

I asked Peejay if his name was initial *P*, initial *J*, or Peejay, spelled out. He looked at me and said, "Naw," and so I decided it was spelled out. Besides his ability to trick me into doing most of the pots and pans, Peejay knew a lot about what to avoid. He disappeared whenever macaroni and cheese was on the menu. But I knew where to find him, and didn't let him get away with it. He seemed to respect that.

"The big sketch is, he's a devious dope," Rupert told me one coffee break. "I've seen his type before, and I allude to my experience with them."

But I was more interested in Peejay and his imaginary friend than in his deviousness. I learned that this friend rode with him on a ten-speed from the YMCA to work, waited for him outside during the day, and returned with him at night. "He knows me, all right," Peejay said, nodding his head.

"So what's your friend's name?" I asked. He didn't answer. One day when he reached to turn on the steam, one of his gloves hooked by the sleeve on the pipe just as the steam began pouring out. When he tried to yank his arm free, the glove held and for a second or more his wailing muted even the hammering din of the steam. I pushed his arm down, freeing the glove, turned on the cold water, and stuck the pink stretch of skin between his elbow and his wrist under it. I ran out and got ice. The water in my wash sink had been so cool it saved him from getting a severe burn. He missed the rest of the day.

When he came back the next morning he smiled at me. "He says you did good to me," Peejay said, and I knew he was talking about his friend. It caught me off-guard. Over the sinks, drenched with sweat and Wittgenstein, I ceased to look at Peejay as anyone but an acceptable companion. The chef's helpers, all three of them, thought his invisible friend was the funniest thing they'd ever seen. We played poker during break, and they couldn't believe I put up with him. The invisible buddy of Peejay was the main topic.

They would ask things like, "Does he get in your way? Do you ever bump into him?" They were the idiots. "Do you think he means it?" I asked.

"Mean what?" one of them asked.

"His friend, the invisible one," I said.

They appeared confused by my question. Sure, their expressions suggested. I grinned back at them, remembering a passage from the master: "But isn't it our 'meaning it' that which gives sense to a sentence . . . And meaning is something in the sphere of the mind . . . something private. It is the intangible something, only comparable to consciousness itself . . . It is, as it were, a dream of our language."

It was simple after all. I thought of what Wittgenstein wrote: "The results of philosophy are the uncovering of one or another piece of plain nonsense, and of the bumps that understanding has got by running its head up against the limits of language." He went on, "These bumps make us see the value of discovery."

Camus and Sartre grew at an amazing rate. Starter pellets gave way to fifty-pound bags of specially formulated high-protein prepared feeds. They went through two per week at twelve dollars a bag. When they saw me coming each night they raced to the trough for dinner.

"In two weeks, guys, we're switching to finisher pellets," I said, smiling. "And you know what that means." Camus looked up at me and grunted. He was the bigger and smarter of the two. He responded to everything I said.

Word of my project got around the hospital, because my mother talked about it in the supply room. A doctor told me one day in the cafeteria that pigs were smarter than dogs; that they could be trained as house pets. Their skin, he went on, is closest to a human's. Every pharmaceutical company is required to test new ointments and perfumes on the skin of a pig before testing it on people. That night I kidded Camus as I poured a container of sour milk on him. The clumps stuck to his snout and frustrated his vigorous efforts to remove them. "It's just a beauty paste, sweetie," I said. "Keep it there overnight." Finally I swiped the clumps off with my hand, and let him lick it. His tongue felt like it had a life of its own, prickly and strong, and I jumped back. Camus went still, as if confused by my reaction. He tilted his head to the side, and I swore he winked at me.

"The only true question for pigs," I said, "is, 'When's the first frost.'" Camus snorted back. I could tell the difference between their snorts. They spoke—not my language but their own—they expressed surprise, delight, and fear. They nudged and budged one another for position at the trough, one's nip to the ear producing a ripping squeal of anger. At the end, trough licked clean, they teased me with shakes of their snouts, skeptical that I had emptied the last drop from a pail. Looking at Sartre as sour milk dripped from the whiskers on his snout, I couldn't mistake his gratitude. Had I ever felt that way toward someone? He was hungry; I brought him food. In the growing dark, I listened to the sound of their smacking and sucking. And as the day's invisible stars emerged from the sky overhead, I thought of Peejay. It seemed a wondrous thing to create and communicate with someone invisible, far beyond anything I'd ever done. I rinsed out the sour-milk container in a pail of water and poured that into their water trough.

One time my father surprised me while I was feeding them. "Have you noticed," I asked, "how they come when I call them? They're smart."

"You call *that* intelligence?" my father asked.

"Sure."

"A meat animal that comes when it's called?"

"They trust me," I said.

"Why should they?" he asked.

When the hospital hired Cindy, a girl from a female detention center, as a tray runner, things changed in the kitchen. She had stolen things, they said. Been a fence. Been busted for drugs. "She's a slut," one of the chef's helpers told me. "She hangs out at the bars and deals dope."

"She doesn't even have a father," a tray runner told me. "Her mom's a whore on the Northside."

"What is this, hearsay?" I asked. "What are we talking about?"

"We're talking about someone we shouldn't be working with," the tray runner said. "She's gross. Just look at her."

I did look at Cindy. She didn't look like a whore. She didn't wear makeup. Her skin was clean, her eyes sharp and green. But you could tell she had lived a tough life. She stared back at you if you looked at her, turning away only after she seemed to have dismissed you. She hated all of us, I could see that. But that made her all the more appealing to me. When I stared at her straight on, the rest of her seemed to dissolve until all I could see were her eyes. It was like shining a flashlight on an animal at night. Her eyes radiated green. Until she turned her head. She had thick black hair cut short, and a way of walking that told me she didn't give a shit about anything. I couldn't wait to ask her out.

"Po," Peejay said.

"What?" I shouted above the sound of the steam pipes. Peejay had at last convinced me that the hotter the water, the easier it was to clean the pots.

"Po lives on the Y," he said.

At first, I thought he said, "Po lives on the why," and I thought of Wittgenstein: "I experience the because." *Po lives on the why?* What could it mean? I scraped a wad of burnt macaroni and cheese from the side of a silver stainless-steel pan and stared at Peejay. "What?" I asked.

"On the roof," Peejay said, as if I understood. "Po lives on the Y. You can see everything there."

I nodded.

He grinned and nodded back at me. We understood each other. His friend was Po. No one else knew that name. And I wouldn't tell anyone. The name of his friend had come to me only through hours of scrubbing. We were buddies now. I didn't tattle on him when he scooted out to the bathroom when there was bad work to do. We covered for each other. I had begun saving garbage for Camus and Sartre in the black plastic bags that otherwise went to the dumpster. Before a pan was cleaned, Peejay or I scraped its remnants into my bag. Prior to scraping a pan before soaking it, he'd ask, "Pig food?," I'd nod, and he would put it in the bag.

"Po don't like bad boys," he said. "Po said you're okay."

I liked being okay with Po. I learned that Po liked ice cream and *Gilligan's Island*. As Peejay talked, the sound of his voice left me in awe. I thought of how odd this thing was, our language, these sounds out of air and spit, by muscle hurled out the cavity opposite the one we evacuate from, the means by which we expressed love and happiness, groped and misspoke.

When Smitty, one of the chef's helpers, started at the Culinary Institute of America in July, they made me the junior chef's helper, in charge of starches and vegetables. Another pot-and-pan washer replaced me alongside Peejay. I liked the promotion. It gave me a chance to get closer to Cindy, and to get more food for Camus and Sartre. Cindy came in at eleven in the morning usually, I noticed, in a '57 Chevy driven by a creepy-looking guy older than I was. At two o'clock break, I ignored the other helpers, whose card games bored me, and sat by myself at an empty cafeteria table. I stared at Cindy. When I saw her watching Peejay out the window, I moved over to her table.

"Tell me, is that guy who drops you off each morning your boyfriend?"

Cindy peeled the top off her empty Styrofoam coffee cup. "Is that your business?"

"Why do you hang out with that guy?" I asked, aware of the other tray runners watching us from a nearby table. I was the first to sit with her.

"Get lost," she said, squashing the cup.

"I'm just curious."

"So am I. Why do you hang out with Peejay?"

"I don't hang out with him."

"But you don't try to get away from him, either."

"He's crazy," I said, hoping to strike up a conversation, setting my coffee down and pulling out a chair.

"So what?" she said. "I might be crazy."

"We all might be crazy," I said, immediately feeling like the college boy.

"Yeah, but do we talk about friends behind their backs just because we're crazy?"

I didn't know how to respond. "I guess it doesn't matter," I said.

"What do you want to do?" she said, staring at me.

"What do you mean?"

"You want to sleep with me?"

I laughed because I couldn't think what else to do. "Why do you ask?" I said.

"Because," she said. "What else could you care about—some smart boy like you?"

"Yeah, I guess you're right. That about sums it up."

She smiled and patted the back of my hand, which was flat on the table. "You're doing okay for someone who works in this dump."

When he was eight, Wittgenstein is said to have asked his father, "Why should one tell the truth if it's to one's advantage to tell a lie?" I had thought of lying to her but only in the most conventional sense. To have appeared offended at her remark and left the table. But it hit me she would have seen that for a ruse.

As we walked back into the kitchen, the other tray runners glared at me. I had betrayed them, each of them, although I knew not a one. When I saw Peejay approaching later that afternoon, I wanted to stop him. Maybe for just a quick chat. Maybe to soothe my conscience. "How's Po?" I asked as he passed. He ignored me.

"Wait a second," I said, following him.

Peejay kept on walking. He stopped at the sink and went through the routine of heating up the water.

"Peejay," I said, "talk to me. What's the matter here?"

Peejay never turned from the sink. He put on his gloves and began scrubbing. "You're out there," he said. "You left."

I said something to him about wishing him well. He didn't care. I was gone.

Camus and Sartre never ate better. *"Bon appétit,"* I said as I tipped over trays of potatoes au gratin, potatoes lyonnaise, mashed potatoes, and baked potatoes, they loved them all. Sour milk, fresh milk, cheese sauce, and cream. They came, they snorted, they ate. To Sartre I said, "Don't ask me, ask a priest." Each day I overshot the menu laid out by the hospital's dietitian. Twenty dinners of potatoes became forty. Vegetables, the same. No one questioned what was going on, not even Rupert, the captain. My expertise at the language game of lying went up, my feed bill at Agway went down. Once a week Peejay glared at me from the pot room as I tossed turkey bones into the stock kettle and added water. The steam to heat them reverberated its metallic rap reminiscent of the pot room.

Cindy, however, did not give in to my overtures. I continued to sit with her at break. I listened to her, so I claimed, as a friend.

She could talk to me, I told her. One break, I heard about her bad mother. "She never wanted me, and never let me forget it." On another break, she told me about her missing father. "My mother said every time she looked at my face she saw him." More than once she talked about the detention center. "The guards there are all dykes. They can't wait to push you around, and they always find a way to grab you so it hurts. You have to get friendly to avoid it." I didn't ask her whether she did.

I listened without saying anything, convinced silence was the only language she wouldn't suspect. A week after we began talking, a Friday morning, we were at break when she said, "Basically it comes down to this: life sucks. Just when you think things are turning around, you're back down again."

"So let's go out anyway," I said.

"You're just lonesome, you know. I'm not your friend."

"What's the difference, then?"

"Sure," she said. "What does it matter?"

As the leaves dried and scraped against one another, and the weatherman droned on about the possibility of an early frost, as the sun burned weakly on my back and I carried tray after tray of overshot menu items to my mother's car, one final supper after another for my buddies, I felt that the doctor was right: that I had never known a smarter animal than a pig, and that—and this thought stung me the most—in the grand scale of things I would always be closer to Peejay than to Wittgenstein.

When Cindy offered to buy some joints before our first date, I asked if she could also pick up a couple of ounces for me to take back to school.

"Sure," she said. "No problem."

I gave her the money. I waited for her in my mother's car, vacuumed for a good impression, and contemplated possible explanations for not returning home that night. The car broke down, I was drunk and didn't want to drive, any good lie would do.

Finding an excuse didn't turn out to be the problem. Cindy

emerged from the laundromat where her dealer worked in handcuffs. I opened the door of the car and before I could clear my head almost started to walk toward her. Then it came over me: Let her go. She's not worth it.

Cindy saw me. She smiled and shrugged as she was being shoved into the back of a police cruiser. I wondered if there was something I should do. Should I get her a lawyer? Should I see her in jail? In the end I did nothing.

"The only true question," I told Camus that night, "is whether cowardice is the better part of valor." I walked around the pen slowly, the light fading. I slapped mosquitoes and chatted with the pigs. At first they followed me around the perimeter, careful to avoid their latrine area. "You guys don't really understand me, do you?" I said. "You're not that smart. Not smart enough."

My father called me one Wednesday in early September. Someone down the hall fetched me from my room. Camus and Sartre were gone, he told me. The frost had come. But he had never seen two animals fight harder going up a ramp. He said he owed me more than $400.

"It was like they knew," he said. "They each had a noose around their neck and they fought like hell. It took three of us."

I dropped my course in Wittgenstein. Blackmon was shocked. "You had such a handle on the material," he said. "Even Peter mentioned it. He wanted to know what secondary sources I thought you'd been reading."

"None," I said.

He pressed me for more, but I kept my mouth shut.

I would never understand why I had bought Camus and Sartre that summer when my family had plenty to eat. I would never understand why the Russians sent the dog Laika into space to starve to death, or why I even thought about any of this, so minor in the context of crimes. And as I thought of Wittgenstein, I could no longer see the genius, but only the man who cruised the parks at night in search of rough love. His nature took him there as it took him to philosophy. How can such a thing be? There is no simpler way to answer than in the words the man I revered had disavowed: "Whereof we cannot speak, we must pass over in silence."

Vassilis Tsiamboussis

A Pat on the Cheek

Translated from Greek by Martin McKinsey

She had always said, "When I die, if my Angel comes and takes me for a last look at all the places I've ever lived in or been to, it won't take him more than a couple of minutes." In other words, that's how sheltered and paltry her life had been.

But that night, when her Angel carried her off from the hospital, he left her suspended above her poor little house, like a balloon, for three whole hours, looking in through the window at her only-begotten son, whose eyes were deep wells of sadness, not just tonight but from way back. He was painting their single room for the wake, lest he and his mother become objects of ridicule in town. Painting and crying . . .

Who knows what came over her all of a sudden that, without permission, she came down and dabbed off his sweat with a clean towel, put an old jacket over his shoulders to keep him from catching cold, looked the room over, said, "Nice job," and gave his salty cheek a pat. Then she returned to the Other, who was waiting for her on the glass cloud, unruffled, unsmiling, showing no trace of anger or other emotion, maybe only slightly impatient to be off, as he spread his wings and, like a stork with its young one in its arms, began to ascend.

Contributors' Notes

Susan Bergman has recently completed a Ph.D. in Literature at Northwestern University. "Imago" is part of her first book, tentatively entitled *Shameless,* forthcoming from Farrar, Straus and Giroux. Current poems and essays appear in *Antaeus, North American Review, Pequod,* and *The Pushcart Prize XVI.* She lives in Barrington, Illinois, with her husband and four children.

Mary Bush is the author of a collection of short stories, *A Place of Light* (William Morrow, 1990). Her stories have appeared in several literary journals. She currently teaches creative writing at Memphis State University.

Dan Chaon has published stories in *TriQuarterly, Story, Crazyhorse,* and other magazines. He lives in Cleveland and is completing a collection of short stories.

George Cruys's stories have appeared in *TriQuarterly, Epoch,* and *Transfer.* He is currently a participant in The Writer's Film Project in Los Angeles.

Andre Dubus's most recent book is *Broken Vessels,* published by David Godine, which has just been reissued in paperback.

Stuart Dybek's most recent collection of stories is *The Coast of Chicago* (Vintage).

Paul Griner, a recipient of the Mary Roberts Rinehart Award, has published stories in quarterlies and in *The Graywolf Annual Four.*

Susan Hubbard is the author of *Walking on Ice* (University of Missouri Press), a collection of stories that received the Associated Writing Programs' Short Fiction Prize. Her work has appeared in *Passages North, Green Mountains Review, Dickinson Review, Wooster Review, Albany Review,* and other publications. She teaches at Cornell University.

Leon Kortenkamp received his M.F.A. from the University of Notre Dame, where he worked under the direction of Samuel Adler, Valdemar Otto, and Marc Chagall. His drawings, prints, and paintings have been published and exhibited widely, most recently in a solo exhibition at Wiegand Gallery, College of Notre Dame, where he has been a professor of art for the past ten years. He lives with his family in Belmont, California.

Martin McKinsey was recently in Greece on a grant from the Greek Ministry of Culture. His translation of *The Iron Gate* by A. Frangias is being brought out by Kedros Editions.

Robert Olmstead was born and raised in New Hampshire. He is the author of *River Dogs,* a collection of short stories, and two novels, *Soft Water* and *A Trail of Heart's Blood Wherever We Go.* His third novel, *America by Land,* is forthcoming from Random House. His stories have appeared in *Story, The Graywolf Annual Four, Black Warrior Review, Granta,* and *Cutbank.* He is the recipient of a Guggenheim Fellowship and currently is Writer in Residence at Dickinson College.

Susan Power is a Native American (Yanktonai Sioux), originally from Chicago. Her stories have appeared in *Story, High Plains Literary Review, Iowa Woman,* and *Other Voices.* She is a graduate of Harvard Law School and the University of Iowa Writers' Workshop, where she was the first recipient of an Iowa Arts Fellowship. She is currently a James Michener Fellow.

Mona Simpson is the author of two novels, *Anywhere But Here* and *The Lost Father.* Her first short story was published in *Ploughshares* in 1983 in an issue edited by Raymond Carver. Other stories have appeared in *Granta, Harper's, The Iowa Review,* and *The Paris Review.* She is working on a new novel, *A Regular Guy,* and a collection, *Virginity.*

Sharon Solwitz has twice been the recipient of the Nelson Algren Award. In addition, she has won the Katherine Anne Porter Prize for Fiction, literary awards from the Illinois and Kansas arts councils, and a prize in the *Stand* fiction contest. Her stories have appeared in *Mademoiselle, The Chicago Tribune, American Short Fiction,* and other magazines. In 1991 she received a fellowship from the Illinois Arts Council and her Ph.D. in English from the University of Illinois. New work is forthcoming in *Boulevard* and with the *PEN Syndicated Fiction Project.*

Jessica Treadway's collection of short stories, *Absent Without Leave,* will be published this fall by Delphinium Books. Her fiction has appeared in *The Atlantic, The Hudson Review,* and *The Agni Review.*

Vassilis Tsiamboussis's first book, *The Vespa and Other Provincial Stories,* was published in Athens in 1990. He lives in the town of Drama, in northern Greece.

Christopher Zenowich is the author of a collection of stories, *Economies of the Heart,* and a novel, *The Cost of Living.* He is currently finishing a new novel, *The Knuckleball Pitcher's Guide to Low-Fat Living.* He lives in Morris, Connecticut, with his daughter.

About the Editor

Tobias Wolff was born in Alabama in 1945 and grew up in the Pacific Northwest. He is the author of the short novel *The Barracks Thief,* which won the 1985 PEN/Faulkner Award; two collections of short stories, *Back in the World* and *In the Garden of the North American Martyrs,* which received the Saint Lawrence Award for fiction in 1982; and a memoir, *This Boy's Life.* Mr. Wolff's work appears frequently in *Esquire, Vanity Fair, The Atlantic,* and other magazines and reviews. He lives with his family in upstate New York and teaches at Syracuse University.

Photo: Jerry Bauer

P·l·o·u·g·h·s·h·a·r·e·s B·o·o·k·s·h·e·l·f

Recommended Reading   Fall 1992

THE STORIES OF JOHN EDGAR WIDEMAN
STORIES BY JOHN EDGAR WIDEMAN
Pantheon, $25.00 cloth. Reviewed by Melanie Rae Thon

The Stories of John Edgar Wideman includes two previously published collections, *Fever* and *Damballah,* and ten new pieces gathered under the title *All Stories Are True*—an African proverb that has become Wideman's guiding meditation. For in all his works, in his stories and his memoir and his seven novels, Wideman shatters the barrier between biography and fiction.

In the 1984 memoir *Brothers and Keepers,* Wideman tried to comprehend why his brother Robby ended up being sentenced to a life in prison, while Wideman himself became a Rhodes Scholar and college professor. He discovered he could not understand or write *about* his brother's life—his childhood, his addiction, his crimes, his imprisonment—without imagining that life fully, without confronting his own life and reinventing experience. Now, Wideman goes even further, saying there is a place where memory fails, where "I'm beginning to fabricate what might have been said. Devise a history I don't know." And there are times when facts are inadequate, when they conceal the truth. In the story "Newborn Thrown in Trash and Dies," the omniscient infant tells us: "I believe some facts are unnecessary and that unnecessary borders on untrue. I believe facts sometimes speak for themselves but never speak for us. They are never anyone's voice and voices are what we must learn to listen to if we wish ever to be heard."

Wideman does listen, to this child, to all his people. His

stories open at the center, where a voice suddenly starts speaking. Sometimes it is his own: "I think I murmur their names, a silence unless you are inside my skull"; sometimes it is the voice of an aunt or grandmother, coming to him with a small gift, a piece of his family history: "What seems to ramble begins to cohere when the listener understands the process, understands that the voice seeks to recover everything . . ." Often the leaps are daring: the voices erupt, and Wideman finds himself hearing a retarded man or a murdered baby or an American jazz singer in a Nazi death camp.

No matter whose voice he hears, Wideman immerses himself. The truth can be discovered only by telling the tale, so every story is a journey, unexpected and scary, a plunge into the unconscious mind. Reading these pieces, you feel a disturbing sense of risk, the fear that Wideman moves without plot, intuitively, and might not know his way back to the surface, that he is struggling to find meaning and hope in the midst of chaos and despair, that he has asked us to come with him but can make no promises.

We follow him on faith because his vision is humane, his love for his people passionate but honest, his poetry transcendent. What these stories lay bare, what they impel us to face in ourselves, may startle and bring sorrow, but will redeem us in the end if we embrace what it means to hear other voices in our own skulls. It is the most intimate of bonds, this merging, where distance collapses, where the dead live in our bodies, where the imprisoned walk free beside us, where the brother of a crippled girl can make amends and be forgiven.

In "Loon Man," one troubled man tells another it's "really crazy not even keeping straight who you are not. Who you are is hard. But Foster, any bird or beetle knows who it is not." Yet Wideman himself is crossing that boundary all the time, *forgetting* who he is not, imagining another person's life and entering his soul, learning to see through his hands: "Look at the blood in the ropes in the backs of your hands. Think of that blood leaving you and running up in somebody's else's arms, down into somebody's fingers black or brown or ivory just like yours. And listen to those hands playing music. Now shut your eyes. Shut them for good. And ask yourself if anything's been lost, if something's been taken away or something given. Then try to remember the color of light."

Stories save us, reveal us to one another, give back memory. Writing to his brother Robby, Wideman said: "Stories are letters. Letters sent to anybody or everybody. But the best kind are meant to be read by a specific somebody."

Sometimes these letters are the only hope we have. In "Casa Grande," a father visits his twenty-one-year-old son in prison. He says he cannot bear "the terrible reality" of his son's life, cannot think of it for more than a fraction of a second. Then he discovers a story the boy wrote when he was ten, a tale of a trip to Jupiter. The father believes he had no memory of the story, that it was lost completely. But in his own journal, he finds this entry, written a year before the tale resurfaced: "He sits on a planet ten million light years away, waiting for time to change the place he is to another. . . . He dreams a forest of green creatures, some tall as trees, many man-sized, others a foot or two high." *Nothing is lost.* The imaginations of father and son tangle as one. What the father thinks he cannot do, he has done already: their lives have been exchanged; their intimacy is absolute.

But words fail. Wideman's own son was incarcerated for manslaughter. The pain of having a brother and a son in prison cuts too deep. Letters are incomplete. Understanding eludes us. Ultimately, we must trust the struggle for its own sake, must have faith in the desire to communicate and in the longing to find connections. Exploring "The Beginning of Homewood," a story that began as a letter to Robby, Wideman tries to grasp the link between his great-great-great-grandmother and his brother, both "outlaws": "I ask myself again *why not me,* why is it the two of you skewered and displayed like she would have been if she hadn't kept running. Ask myself if I would have stayed and tried to make the best of a hopeless situation. Ask if you really had any choice, if anything had changed in the years between her crime and yours."

To say, *You suffer what I do not,* is close to saying, *You suffer for my sake.* This humility, this wonder in the face of sacrifice, is a theme that haunts Wideman. Some submit by choice, others are sacrificed against their wills. The young woman in "Signs," besieged by threats and racial hatred, abandons hope of ending the abuse and finally claims she made up the story, that she is responsible for the notes in the bathroom, the scrawls on her door. Only this "confession" will satisfy her tormentors. "Could this be called fighting back. Offering up your flesh and blood until the beast chokes on your bitterness."

In "Fever," a story set in plague-ravaged Philadelphia, a man with only a first name nurses the dying and hauls out the dead. Each body he touches brings him closer to his own death, and he knows this. But he stays, and dies. People find explanations for the fever that devastates the city, and Wideman hears these voices, scientific and precise, defining Dengue and Yellow Fever, describing how mosquitoes carry disease. A mythic passage tells the tale of a mosquito biting a slave, as if the mosquito is lover, goddess, demon, liberator. But another voice speaks the simple truth. The city is a body, sick like the bodies of its people; the world is a larger body. "Fever grows in the secret places of our hearts, planted there when one of us decided to sell one of us to another. The drum must pound ten thousand thousand years to drive that evil away."

Winter comes, and frost. The mosquitoes die. Many people live, spared by the sacrifice of others. Wideman sees how capriciously some are chosen and keeps asking: *Why not me?* There is reverence for those who offer up themselves in these stories, and there is awe, a collision of tenderness and terror, sorrow and hope.

Melanie Rae Thon is the author of a collection of stories, Girls in the Grass, *and a novel,* Meteors in August, *which have just been released in paperback by Faber and Faber. Her second novel,* Iona Moon, *will be published by Poseidon next year.*

GOODNIGHT, GRACIE

POEMS BY LLOYD SCHWARTZ

Univ. of Chicago Press, $22.50 cloth, $10.95 paper
Reviewed by Robert Pinsky

Lloyd Schwartz's writing displays a peculiar combination of gifts—observation of personality; loving attention to homely turns of language, neglected as stray cats; a moral generosity that cannot be called "forgiving" because it declines to condemn in the first place; a formal aptitude for triolets and off rhymes; a way of being funny that in the old distinction favors humor over comedy; and above all, an intense vocality.

Speech is his muse. In his first book, *These People,* Schwartz created poems based on the interrogative pauses, the evasive rushes and defiant ellipses, of conversation, a method that may be most clearly brilliant in the love dialogue "Who's on First." The unpredictable alternation of extreme and domestic, sensational and ordinary, all comprehended by a sense that speaking is as natural as breathing, was another hallmark of that book.

The quality of voice achieves at least an equal variety of effects in Schwartz's second book, *Goodnight, Gracie:* straightforward pathos in the poem "Gisela Brüning," great intensity in "Simple Questions," complex layering of emotion in the excellent title poem. I have to say that in "Crossing the Rockies" the voice—as voices will do—goes on too long. But as in *These People,* Schwartz's writing always has integrity. Nothing is pumped up or dolled up. *Goodnight, Gracie* marks a significant new step in a distinctive, humane body of work.

Robert Pinsky's most recent book of poetry is The Want Bone *(The Ecco Press). He is completing a translation of Dante's* Inferno, *which Farrar, Straus and Giroux will publish next year.*

CITY OF BOYS

STORIES BY BETH NUGENT

Knopf, $20 cloth. Reviewed by Elizabeth Searle

Junkies, says the runaway girl who narrates the title story in

City of Boys, "exit right out of every situation before it's even become a situation." The same might be said for many of the chillingly detached characters in Beth Nugent's perceptive and unsettling first collection. Through ten spare, haunting stories, Nugent captures the overwhelming sense her characters share of being trapped inside dull, cyclical, insect-like lives.

In "Locusts," a family is compared to seven-year locusts that "seem capable of little other than eating." The boys in "City of Boys" are "nervous as insects, always some part of their body in useless, agitated motion . . ." A disturbed and outcast boy in another story finds solace watching "the beetles and ants fight it out over a territory smaller even than his own."

Whether the setting is the flat Midwest where "the leaves of the trees seemed somehow locked into place" or Northeast city apartments crawling with "more roaches than there are moments of love in the world," Nugent creates a bleak emotional landscape that feels strange and yet strangely familiar.

Sally, the observant young narrator of "Cocktail Hour," moves from state to state with alcoholic parents who have the "same conversation on average of twice a week." When asked by teachers to tell about her travels, Sally reflects that "the America I have seen is exactly like itself. . . . The houses and the neighbors and the streets are all just exactly alike, without difference enough even to help me make something up."

Nugent's more hopeful characters seek release from their oppressively uneventful lives through sex—looking for "someone to whom touching is all the reality of being," and yet finding this to be a different sort of trap. In the title story, the narrator who has run away from her mother becomes locked in an obsessive affair with an older woman. "That first time with her, I felt as though my mother was curled up inside my own body giving birth to me; each time she let me go, I made my way back inside her."

In "Abattoir," a woman senses that her first lover has gone through the same motions many times before. "He closes his eyes to kiss me, but I know he is thinking of his mother, and as his hand crosses my skin, what it touches disappears: my mouth, my eyes, my bones, they all disappear . . ."

Many of Nugent's characters experience the sensation of disappearing. Some resort to drastic means to convince themselves that they are indeed present. Annie, another of Nugent's lonely young girls, burns the hair off a doll belonging to her only friend, feeling disappointed when "there is no flame, only a crackle, as each hair sort of fizzles crisply down to the plastic head and goes out."

Though disappointment and boredom pervade the lives she portrays, Nugent manages to infuse her stories with a keen poetic charge. She can uncover startling imagery in the simplest domestic acts, such as tuning in a ballgame on TV ("he twists the color knob, turning the faces of the players bright red, then down to shades of black and white") or chopping vegetables ("I concentrate on the play of my fingers and the blade, my hand moving steadily back along the spine of a carrot, the knife relentlessly pursuing").

She is particularly original when rendering familiar places. In an elementary school, "children stare at figures on a dark board." In a college dormitory, "girls lie in the darkness just a few feet from the strangers who are their roommates."

Families, especially, live together as strangers. One girl wakes to "the world rushing by in a cluttered blur of objects," then remembers she is on a train trip with her embittered parents. "There was a time when her parents, having quarrelled, would turn to her with sad, shocked looks for all that they asked her to witness, but now it goes on as if she is not even there." By the end of the story, the girl looks into a mirror and finds, in fact, "no one there."

With her quietly nightmarish imagery, her dark deadpan humor, and her cold-eyed compassion, Beth Nugent vividly dramatizes her characters' profound detachment and disorientation. Her portrayals of everyday life have—in a larger sense—much the same effect as the cassette tapes made by a man in "Locusts," recording the incessant sounds of locusts outside his window: "There was something terrible about hearing it like that," his daughter thinks when he plays back the tapes. "For the first time, I realized what it was that we were listening to every minute of every day with no change in pitch or intensity, and for a few hours I could hear nothing else."

Elizabeth Searle's collection of short stories, My Body to You, *won the 1992 Iowa Short Fiction Prize and is forthcoming in 1993 from the University of Iowa Press.*

TWO TREES

POEMS BY ELLEN BRYANT VOIGT

W. W. Norton, $17.95 cloth. Reviewed by Joyce Peseroff

Twin to the tree whose fruit Eve first tasted, and visible only after she ate, is the tree of immortal beauty, "hung with sweet fruit; / fruit that made the birds nesting there / graceful, brightly plumed and musical," writes Ellen Bryant Voigt in the title poem of her fourth and most overtly philosophical collection. Voigt uses lyric poetry to address epic questions of fate and will, drawing as she has done before on classical mythology and the Bible, family life and life observed with the eye of a scientist. Truth is what she's after as she explores the hungers of consciousness, writing in "*Variations:* Thorn-Apple": "If truth is not a thing apart from me, / then I don't want it."

Two Trees celebrates and honors the life of the mind "at work, at play"—animated by the aquarium's eagle ray, by tapestries on Avenue des Gobelins, and, in Voigt's most vivid and passionate poems, by the transcendent power of music: "The day is foul—a thin sleet falling everywhere / . . . / Inside the studio, it's high summer, / eighteenth-century rational Germany. / On the open score a meadow blooms . . ." Music is vessel and pole star, magic cloak and finger-cracking harness; yet, in "*Variations:* At the Piano," Voigt observes, "After a life of music the musician said, / 'But music, music has nothing to do with life.'"

Nor can mind, however adept at transport, avoid the stall of "Priam looking down from the city wall, / Echo near the pool,

PLOUGHSHARES BOOKSHELF

Charles Bovary," or the homely strategy fixed by two boys on a playing field, "already set in their early victories, / one at the prow, one at the wheel" (*Variations:* Thorn-Apple"). Voigt accommodates the complex vision of a twentieth-century rationalist through a series of variations following several key poems. Borrowed from music, which, like poetry, can unfold only in time, the variations offer a garden of forking paths, connecting with and amplifying the lyric moment first presented in each title.

Like Keats, Voigt pants after beauty; poems like "Herzenleid" shimmer with a synaesthesia of visual images rich in sound. The moan implicit in ". . . I sat with my life-mate, the two of us / two loons in brackish water . . ." exemplifies the engagement of sound and sense which makes *Two Trees* such an absorbing series of meditations on the nature of character and destiny, life and art.

Joyce Peseroff's most recent book of poetry is A Dog in the Lifeboat, *published by Carnegie Mellon University Press.*

THE LOVER OF HISTORY
A NOVEL BY JONATHAN DEE
Ticknor and Fields, $19.95 cloth. Reviewed by Debra Spark

Jonathan Dee's prescient novel, *The Lover of History,* was published in 1990, just before the Gulf War, and save for a few brief, favorable reviews, the book was, more or less, ignored. One supposes this had something to do with the timing of publication. For though the novel is elegantly written, precisely observed, and thoughtful, its initial readers must have also found it redundant. After all, in early 1991, the details of Dee's book were being played out, with remarkable accuracy, in the morning newspapers and on the evening news. Perhaps now, with the war over, the book can be appreciated because of, instead of in spite of, its prophetic wisdom.

The Lover of History focuses on three young adults, all living and working in New York City. Kendall is a disgruntled night engineer at an all-news radio station. Julian, Kendall's lover, is a handsome, emotionally unavailable singer who specializes in commercial jingles. Kendall's roommate is Warner, a history instructor at an upscale private school. The relationships among the two men and one woman are fragile at best. Kendall and Warner are mere acquaintances who, short of funds, have rented a one-bedroom apartment together. They've put up a wall in the bedroom they share and have grown sufficiently uncomfortable with the arrangement to hate, however politely, each other. Julian, who has his own apartment, rarely offers his place up for meetings with Kendall. Instead, Warner is made to suffer through the sounds of the couple making love on the other side of the makeshift wall, and Kendall is made to understand that she is a guest in Julian's home, and in his heart.

In their very dissatisfaction with their lives and each other, Dee's characters are potentially unappealing, but they are redeemed by their capacity for change. The catalyst for these changes is an assassination that takes place during a televised press conference; the secretary of state is shot in the small, distant country of Colozan.

At first, Warner believes in the import of the event because, for Warner, the political is necessarily personal. Kendall, however, views "news as a commodity that she produces," while Julian seems to think about the event as little more than fodder for cocktail party chitchat. As the book proceeds, the characters reexamine their relationships to public events—and gradually the definition of public event expands to include the external world in general. Part of the conflation of the personal and political is moral, related to the conflict in Colozan. It's less about an objection to war than about an objection to war as image, war as reports of public reaction to war, war as evasive language. Warner responds to news reports with "a real sense of moral alarm, not only at the events he had seen and heard described but at the great edifice of image and language which had been constructed to try, he felt, to keep him from understanding what was happening at anything other than the most ambiguous, symbolic level."

But there is something beyond moral outrage here, since for these young characters, the war threatens anything like a coherent definition of self. Regarding the news coverage, Warner "felt as if someone was using his name without permission." Certainly, all the characters in the book are, without realizing it, using their own names without permission. That is, they all feel that they are not responsible for the decisions that they make concerning their lives. They excuse themselves from the very inauthenticity of their lives by persistently imagining themselves apart from the group of people who do the things they do. Julian is a small-time singer, but he doesn't complain, as others do, about his gigs, so he feels he has distinguished himself. Warner is educating the very group of people he most disdains, yet he doesn't see the irony in this. But, with the war, Kendall, Warner, and Julian *do* see themselves identified in a way that they have not specifically chosen. This is so clearly an insult when it is done by a large power that they are forced to see, to varying degrees, how they have subjected themselves to the same insult.

Early on, we see Kendall carrying two hanging plants out of her apartment building: "At the mirror by the front door, she smiled at her reflection; holding each plant by the hook palms up, she thought she looked like Justice." Of all the characters, she comes the closest to honestly choosing her own life. The alteration starts when she begins "slowly, to connect her feelings of personal dread with the general air of dread that surrounded her." When a war begins between the United States and Colozan, she thinks, "This is the way it happens." But then, because she is in the news business, she immediately realizes that "it has never happened this way before."

For all the characters, a fluctuating awareness of the meaning of larger events is coupled with an intense awareness of the look and sound of the city they live in and the mannerisms of people around them. Here, Dee is in his element. He has a gift for descriptive details and figurative language. Microphones on poles are described as waving "lazily like cattails beside a lake."

Yellow taxis dart "in and out of each other's company like fish." Buses strain along, "followed by kite tails of paper and grit." The smallest of details—a look here, an extra dollar left for a tip there—indicate everything about the characters' relationships. And when Dee leaves the physical world to describe the internal emotions of his characters, he's just as accurate. Even when we are less than charmed by his characters, we are sympathetic with them. In this way, Dee is much like Cheever, whose language echoes throughout Dee's novel.

The flaws that are here have principally to do with the abrupt resolution of the story. In truth, however, the disappointment of the ending doesn't affect the reading—for it's never been the story, exactly, that we are reading for, even though the changes in the characters and their relationships are absorbing. We are reading for the astute observations about the tensions of contemporary relationships among young people, and we are reading so we can look, with the author, at New York, and experience his frequently stunning perceptions as our own.

Debra Spark is a 1992–93 Bunting Fellow. Her work has most recently appeared in Praire Schooner, New Letters, *and* Ploughshares.

Gilgamesh

POEMS BY DAVID FERRY

Farrar, Straus and Giroux, $15.00 cloth. Reviewed by Joyce Peseroff

The poem of Gilgamesh, recreated by David Ferry from the thirtieth-century B.C. epic which is itself a retelling of an older Sumerian text, is best known by most readers for a tale of the Flood, complete with Sumerian Noah, that parallels Genesis. But the full narrative is a more troubling, darker story of a stormy-hearted tyrant-king who meets the Wild Man Enkidu, created by gods to be his adversary. Instead of destroying each other, Gilgamesh and Enkidu become beloved companions and adventurers, slaying the demon of the Cedar Forest and Ishtar's retributive Bull of Heaven. When Enkidu dies for his transgressions against the forest god, Gilgamesh grieves, "Must I die too? Must Gilgamesh be like that?" and undertakes a terrifying journey to seek advice from the only man known to have escaped mortality; rebuffed, he returns empty-handed to his city, Uruk.

Ferry's brisk narrative is carried by blank-verse couplets which give both freedom and structure to his eloquent and accessible translation. Careful to avoid language for which there is no scholarly precedent, Ferry preserves the text's austerity (there are no equivalents of Norse kennings or Greek epithets, and the wordplay in Harold Bloom's reading of *The Book of J* is absent) while writing verse of great emotional power: "Time after time the river has risen and flooded. / The insect leaves the cocoon to live but a minute. / How long is the eye able to look at the sun? / From the very beginning nothing at all has lasted."

A subtext of *Gilgamesh* is the triumph of this new human invention, the city. Enkidu, who speaks to animals and grazes with gazelles, is transformed by Uruk into an urbane dresser and civilized companion for the city's ruler. The two hew cedars of the Forbidden Forest to build new gates for Uruk, and after Gilgamesh brings down the Bull of Heaven, he calls forth the city's artisans to observe its workmanship. When the goddess Ishtar lusts after Gilgamesh, he responds with the choicest town gossip, a list of lovers she has abandoned: "Tammuz the slain / . . . / The lovely shepherd bird / . . . / whose wing you broke and now wing-broken cries; / . . . / The goatherd who brought you cakes and daily for you / slaughtered a kid, you turned him into a wolf." The epic hero's quest for fame seems possible only within an urban culture through which fame could easily spread.

Gilgamesh, Western literature's first epic hero, is also its first anti-hero. With Nietzschean will, Gilgamesh rejects his mortal fate, and is in turn rejected in his search for immortality. The poem ends as it begins, at the city gates: ". . . The journey has gone for nothing / . . . / I descended into the waters . . . / and what I found was a sign telling me to / abandon the journey and what it was I sought for." Ferry completes his book with a fragment from an earlier text interpolated with the Babylonian poem that is his source. "Gilgamesh, Enkidu and the Nether World" reiterates the epic's concern with death and the sorrows of the afterlife. In all, David Ferry's version of *Gilgamesh* draws fresh from the well of human feeling, even from the depths of two hundred fifty generations.

ANNE SEXTON: A BIOGRAPHY
A BIOGRAPHY BY DIANE WOOD MIDDLEBROOK
A Peter Davison Book/Houghton Mifflin, $24.95 cloth
Reviewed by James Carroll

When Anne Sexton died in her garage, asphyxiated by exhaust, in October of 1974, a generation of writers and readers were jolted, if not quite surprised. Death had been a main subject of hers; yes, poetry was, in Peter Davison's phrase, a "dangerous trade."

When Sexton was twenty-eight, living the hemmed-in life of an unfulfilled housewife in Newton, Massachusetts, she had a severe breakdown and tried to kill herself. With the support of a therapist, she wrote poems as a way of reclaiming her hold on life. ("I kept writing and writing and giving them all to him just from transference; I kept writing because he was approving.") That experience would lead her to define poetry as "the opposite of suicide," but death, madness, and the threat of suicide were continual themes in her work.

In 1967 Anne Sexton won the Pulitzer Prize. She published eight books of poetry, and was regarded as a peer by the best poets of her generation, including her tutors Robert Lowell, Maxine Kumin, George Starbuck, and W. D. Snodgrass. She was one of those rare poets whose work was cherished by a wide public, in part because her voice gave such powerful expression to the anger and pain of women at a time when anger and pain were sparking modern feminism.

She was linked in the minds of many with Sylvia Plath, who preceded her in suicide by more than a decade. Plath and Sexton worked together in the famous Lowell seminar at Boston

University in the late 1950s. "We talked death with burned-up intensity," Sexton wrote of conversations with Plath, "both of us drawn to it like moths to an electric bulb, sucking on it." As Sylvia Plath's poetry has been read through the lens of her suicide, so has Sexton's, as if death were what justified their work. The fact about both these poets, of course, is that their work needs no justification beyond itself. A cult of morbidity surrounded them nonetheless. Yet to others, their deaths were outrageous rejections of the exuberant if painful gift of life that their art enshrined. Adrienne Rich said, "We have had enough suicidal women poets, enough suicidal women, enough self-destructiveness as the sole form of violence permitted to women." And Denise Levertov wrote in her obituary of Sexton, "We who are alive must make clear, as she could not, the distinction between creativity and self-destruction."

In recent years Sylvia Plath has been rescued from the demeaning niche of suicide-poet, and from the limiting one of feminist-poet by a number of serious biographies (especially Anne Stevenson's *Bitter Fame* and Paul Alexander's *Rough Magic*), which have seen her work in its proper context—as some of the best poetry written in this century.

Now an acclaimed biography of Anne Sexton has appeared. When Diane Wood Middlebrook's *Anne Sexton: A Biography* was published in the fall of 1991, it generated enormous publicity, a rare thing for a work about a poet, even a popular one like Sexton. The notice included a front-page article in *The New York Times*. Of course, as one might expect in present-day America, what drew such wide attention was not poetry or fine literary biography, but the whiff of scandal.

The main scandal concerned one of Middlebrook's sources. Dr. Martin T. Orne, the psychiatrist whose encouragement gave Sexton her vocation, had turned over to Middlebrook tapes he'd made of their therapy sessions. That this violated the sacred tradition of confidentiality did not stop Middlebrook from making liberal use of what the patient had said to her doctor. Because some of the material involved tales of child sexual abuse in which Sexton described herself both as victim (as a child) and as perpetrator (as a parent), some of Sexton's relatives joined the chorus of outraged psychiatrists who denounced both Orne and the book. (Few were heard denouncing either "Dr. Ollie Zweizung," Middlebrook's coy pseudonym for another of Sexton's therapists, who had sex with her during regular sessions, or Dr. Constance Chase, who encouraged her to divorce her husband, leaving her more vulnerable than ever, and who then terminated her treatment.) Of course the Anne Sexton whose poems were so outrageously exhibitionist would have loved the uproar—all those wagging heads and offended sensibilities. But sadly enough, just as the true genius of her poetry was overshadowed by the shocks of her life and death, the worthiness of Diane Wood Middlebrook's powerful biography has been undercut by the controversy over Orne's violation.

The biography has several special virtues. Its first success is as a *literary* life. We never forget this is a *writer* about whom we are reading, and the life and writing illuminate each other throughout the narrative. Middlebrook edited *The Selected Poems of Anne Sexton,* knows the poetry well, and has constant reference to it. She also knows the work of the various poets who influenced Sexton and loved her, sexually and otherwise ("Poets," George Starbuck said, "were always in love"). Because the biography is so carefully keyed to Sexton's texts, we not only are able to see the exact experience out of which certain lines arose (the loss of her doctor, say), but then in reading them we can experience it for ourselves. ("Every one has left me / except my muse / *that good nurse.* / She stays in my hand, a mild white mouse.")

Middlebrook's biography of Anne Sexton is deeply compassionate—in the literal meaning of that word, that the author "suffers with" her subjects, and enables the reader to do so as well. In the case of Anne Sexton, of course, that is more suffering than one ordinarily wants. She never fully emerged from her madness. Middlebrook's narrative makes clear that it was closing in on her at the end, destroying her *and* her muse. (The book compares her last poems to "the senile ravings of an old woman"). Sexton had reason to dread living out her days in an institution, and it was out of that fear, Middlebrook says, that she killed herself. This biography's greatest achievement, I believe, is that it leads back to Sexton's awful death in a new way, so that we can see it neither as merely "shocking" nor as somehow "fitting," but as a sad human outcome.

The biography of an admired artist succeeds if it shows us something of the sources of the work we have made part of ourselves. Middlebrook's book does that and more. With insight and a love proper to her task, she lays bare Anne Sexton's suffering so that we can see more clearly than before the beauty Sexton drew out of it. ("Mother of fire, let me stand at your devouring gate / as the sun dies in your arms and you loosen its terrible weight.") We are left with a sense not of what a loss it was when she died, but what a gift it was when she wrote.

James Carroll is the author of eight novels, the most recent of which is Memorial Bridge.

B<small>A C K</small> I<small>S S U E</small>S
P L O U G H S H A R E S

VOL. 1/1, EDS. DEWITT HENRY AND PETER O'MALLEY
Poetry and fiction. Thomas Lux, William Corbett, David Gullette, Paul
Hannigan. 128 pp. Second printing. $5.00

VOL. 1/2, ED. GEORGE KIMBALL
Poetry and fiction. Maura Stanton, Fanny Howe, Phyllis Janowitz, Joyce
Peseroff, James Tate. 112 pp. $5.00

VOL. 1/3, ED. JAMES RANDALL
Richard Yates interview. William Styron reflections. Poetry and fiction.
Stratis Haviaras. 112 pp. $5.00

VOL. 1/4, ED. THOMAS LUX
Poetry and fiction. Richard Hugo, Bill Knott, Andre Dubus, Michael Ryan.
112 pp. $15.00

VOL. 2/1, ED. FANNY HOWE
Maxine Kumin journals. Poetry and fiction. Madeline DeFrees, Richard
Cecil. 128 pp. $15.00

VOL. 2/2, ED. DEWITT HENRY
Brian Moore retrospective. Fiction. Richard Yates, Tim O'Brien, Andre
Dubus, James Alan McPherson. 136 pp. $15.00

VOL. 2/3, ED. DAVID GULLETTE
Charles Simic and Mark Strand interviews. Octavio Paz essay. Poetry and
fiction. Richard Wilbur, Albert Goldbarth, William Kittredge. 128 pp. $5.00

VOL. 2/4, ED. FRANK BIDART
F. R. Leavis on Eugenio Montale. Helen Vendler on Robert Lowell. Poetry.
Robert Lowell, Elizabeth Bishop, Octavio Paz, Richard Howard, Robert
Pinsky. 256 pp. $15.00

VOL. 3/1, EDS. TIM O'BRIEN, DEWITT HENRY, AND HENRY BROMELL
Fiction. Seymour Epstein, Richard Yates, Tim O'Brien, Ellen Wilbur. 184
pp. $5.00

VOL. 3/2, ED. PAUL HANNIGAN
Poetry and fiction. Russell Banks, Fanny Howe, William Corbett. 144 pp. $5.00

VOL. 3/3&4, EDS. JANE SHORE AND DEWITT HENRY
George Starbuck interviews Elizabeth Bishop. Lloyd Schwartz on Bishop. Poetry and fiction. Richard Hugo, Barry Goldensohn. 304 pp. $5.00

VOL. 4/1, EDS. JAMES RANDALL, DEWITT HENRY, AND TIM O'BRIEN
Bill Knott interview. Thomas Lux on Knott. Poetry and fiction. John Ashbery, Jim Harrison, John Irving, Anne Bernays. 184 pp. $5.00

VOL. 4/2, ED. ROSELLEN BROWN
Men Portray Women/Women Portray Men. Fiction and Poetry. Frederick Busch, Jayne Anne Phillips, Ellen Wilbur. 160 pp. $5.00

VOL. 4/3, ED. DEWITT HENRY
Criticism. Anthony Hecht, Alice Munro, Christopher Ricks, Roger Sale. 220 pp. $5.00

VOL. 4/4, ED. TIM O'BRIEN
Fiction. Gordon Lish, David Huddle, Jayne Anne Phillips, Stephen Minot. 216 pp. $5.00

VOL. 5/1, EDS. ELLEN BRYANT VOIGT AND LORRIE GOLDENSOHN
Poetry and essays. Stephen Dobyns, Adrienne Rich, Elizabeth Bishop. 248 pp. $5.00

VOL. 5/2, ED. LLOYD SCHWARTZ
Peter Taylor, "Remembering Lowell." Poetry. James Merrill, Robert Lowell, Frank Bidart, Margo Lockwood. Ralph Hamilton portfolio. 184 pp. $5.00

VOL. 5/3, ED. JAMES RANDALL
Seamus Heaney interview. Richard Yates on Gina Berriault. Poetry and fiction. Andre Dubus, Philip Booth, Colette Inez, Thomas Lux. 200 pp. $5.00

VOL. 5/4, ED. DEWITT HENRY
Fiction. R. V. Cassill, Lew McCreary, Jayne Anne Phillips. Michael Mazur portfolio. 176 pp. $5.00

VOL. 6/1, ED. SEAMUS HEANEY
Transatlantic Writing. Poetry, fiction, drama, and essays. John McGahern, John Montague, Ted Hughes, Derek Mahon. 170 pp. $15.00

VOL. 6/2, ED. GAIL MAZUR
Robert Pinsky interview. Richard Wilbur on Elizabeth Bishop. Poetry. Frank Bidart, Jane Kenyon, Phyllis Janowitz, James Tate, Carole Oles, Stanley Plumly. Elsa Dorfman portfolio. 176 pp. $15.00

VOL. 6/3, ED. JAY NEUGEBOREN
Jay Neugeboren on persistence. Fiction. Sue Miller, Gina Berriault. 160 pp. $15.00

VOL. 6/4, EDS. LORRIE GOLDENSOHN AND JAYNE ANNE PHILLIPS
Poetry and fiction. Jane Shore, Marvin Bell, Mona Van Duyn, Jorie Graham, Eve Shelnutt. 248 pp. $5.00

VOL. 7/1, ED. JAMES RANDALL
Interview with Michael S. Harper. Poetry and fiction. Robert Bly, Robert Penn Warren, Russell Banks. 168 pp. $5.00

VOL. 7/2, ED. ALAN WILLIAMSON
Allen Grossman interview. Poetry and fiction. James Merrill, J. D. McClatchy. Ralph Hamilton portfolio. 172 pp. $5.00

VOL. 7/3&4, ED. DAN WAKEFIELD
10th Anniversary Issue. John Williams interview. Fiction. Richard Yates. 232 pp. $5.00

VOL. 8/1, ED. JOYCE PESEROFF
Robert Bly interview. Margo Lockwood letters. Poetry. Donald Hall, Jane Cooper, Gail Mazur, Howard Norman. 192 pp. $15.00

VOL. 8/2&3, ED. DONALD HALL
Poetry, fiction, and drama. Richard Wilbur, Mary Oliver, Philip Levine, Jonathan Galassi, Rita Dove, Carolyn Chute, John Hawkes, Raymond Carver. 288 pp. $5.00

VOL. 8/4, ED. DEWITT HENRY
Fiction. Al Young, Sue Miller, Jack Pulaski, Andre Dubus. 248 pp. $5.00

VOL. 9/1, ED. GAIL MAZUR
Frank Bidart interview. Poetry and fiction. Robert Pinsky, Czeslaw Milosz, Denise Levertov, Peter Davison, Howard Norman. Elsa Dorfman portfolio. 200 pp. $5.00

VOL. 9/2&3, EDS. RICHARD TILLINGHAST AND GEORGE GARRETT
Southern Writing. Shelby Foote interview. Fiction and poetry. Robert
Penn Warren, Donald Justice, James Dickey. 248 pp. $5.95

VOL. 9/4, ED. RAYMOND CARVER
Fiction. Tim O'Brien, Tobias Wolff, Mona Simpson, Jay McInerney, Joyce
Carol Oates. 212 pp. $5.00

VOL. 10/1, ED. SEAMUS HEANEY
Poetry and criticism. Rita Dove, Marilyn Hacker, Sven Birkerts. 216 pp. $5.00

VOL. 10/2&3, EDS. ANNE BERNAYS AND JUSTIN KAPLAN
Biography, Fiction, and Autobiography. Annie Dillard, Ethan Canin. 256
pp. $5.95

VOL. 10/4, EDS. JANE SHORE AND ELLEN WILBUR
Poetry and fiction. Stephen Tapscott, Carolyn Chute. 248 pp. $5.95

VOL. 11/1, ED. THOMAS LUX
James Tate feature. Poetry and criticism. Richard Cecil, Stephen Dobyns,
Philip Levine, Ellen Bryant Voigt, Franz Wright. 248 pp. $5.95

VOL. 11/2&3, EDS. JAMES ALAN MCPHERSON AND DEWITT HENRY
Fiction. Andre Dubus, Gina Berriault, Pamela Painter, Tess Gallagher. 256
pp. $5.95

VOL. 11/4, ED. STRATIS HAVIARAS
International Writing. Poetry, fiction, and essays. Seamus Heaney, Italo
Calvino, Raymond Carver, James Merrill, Günther Grass, Graham Greene,
Sven Birkerts. 272 pp. $7.00

VOL. 12/1&2, ED. LEONARD MICHAELS
What's a Story. Fiction, essays, and poetry. Philip Lopate, Jean-Paul Sartre,
Thomas McGuane, Mary Ward Brown, Sue Miller. 224 pp. $7.00

VOL. 12/3, ED. CHARLES SIMIC
Poetry and criticism. William Matthews, Charles Wright, Al Young, Lucie
Brock-Broido, Donald Hall. 160 pp. $5.95

VOL. 12/4, EDS. MADELINE DEFREES AND TESS GALLAGHER
Poetry and fiction. Philip Booth, Ann Beattie, Francine Prose, Mona
Simpson, James Tate. 236 pp. $6.50

VOL. 13/1, ED. DEREK WALCOTT
Poetry. Joseph Brodsky, Rita Dove, Jorie Graham, Seamus Heaney, Garrett
Kaoru Hongo, Marie Howe, Askold Melnyczuk, James Tate. 152 pp. $5.95

VOL. 13/2&3, ED. DEWITT HENRY
Fiction. Linda Bamber, E. Annie Proulx, Dan Wakefield. 228 pp. $7.00

VOL. 13/4, ED. BILL KNOTT
Craig Raine feature. Poetry. Ai, Marvin Bell, Erica Jong, Mary Karr, Michael
Milburn, Lloyd Schwartz, Charles Simic, Peter Viereck, Thomas Lux, Sven
Birkerts. 188 pp. $5.95

VOL. 14/1, ED. MAXINE KUMIN
Poetry and fiction. Marilyn Chin, Donald Hall, Howard Nemerov, Joyce
Carol Oates, George Starbuck, Eleanor Ross Taylor. 168 pp. $5.95

VOL. 14/2&3, ED. GEORGE GARRETT
Fiction Discoveries. New writers introduced by Richard Yates, Tom Jenks,
Andre Dubus. 216 pp. $7.00

VOL. 14/4, ED. PHILIP LEVINE
Poetry. Yusef Komunyakaa, Alicia Ostriker, Michael Collier. 176 pp. $5.95

VOL. 15/1, ED. MAURA STANTON
Poetry and fiction. Richard Cecil, Albert Goldbarth, Debra Nystrom,
Michael Ryan, Arthur Vogelsang, David Wojahn. 196 pp. $5.95

VOL. 15/2&3, ED. JAMES CARROLL
The Virtue of Writing. Fiction and essays. Rick Bass, Alice Hoffman, Ward
Just, Christopher Tilghman, Theodore Weesner, Annie Dillard, Robie
Macauley. 222 pp. $7.95

VOL. 15/4, ED. MARILYN HACKER
Diversity/Adversity. Poetry. Eavan Boland, Hayden Carruth, Jane Cooper,
Rita Dove, Thom Gunn, Mary Oliver, Quincy Troupe. 264 pp. $7.95

VOL. 16/1, EDS. RITA DOVE AND FRED VIEBAHN
Poetry and fiction. Marilyn Chin, Martín Espada, Marilyn Hacker, Eileen
Pollack, Steven Schwartz. 210 pp. $5.95

VOL. 16/2&3, EDS. JAMES ALAN MCPHERSON AND DEWITT HENRY
Confronting Racial Difference. Fiction and essays. Louis Berney, Robert Boswell,
Garrett Hongo, Alberto Alvaro Ríos, Carol Roh-Spaulding. 302 pp. $7.95

VOL. 16/4, ED. GERALD STERN
The Literature of Ecstasy. Poetry and prose. Deborah Digges, Jack Gilbert, Li-Young Lee, Sharon Olds, Jack Driscoll. William Kittredge essays. 300 pp. $7.95

VOL. 17/1, ED. M. L. ROSENTHAL
Works-in-Progress. Poetry. Dannie Abse, Eavan Boland, Robert Dana, Tess Gallagher, Donald Hall, Galway Kinnell, Louis Simpson. 236 pp. $7.95

VOL. 17/2&3, EDS. DEWITT HENRY AND JOYCE PESEROFF
Twentieth Anniversary Issue. Poetry and fiction. Rita Dove, Jane Kenyon, Robert Pinsky, Charles Simic, Rick Bass, Andre Dubus, Joy Williams. 294 pp. $7.95

VOL. 17/4, ED. CAROLYN FORCHÉ
Traces of Struggle and Desire. Poetry, fiction, and nonfiction. James Merrill, Bobbie Ann Mason, Daniel Halpern, James Tate, Charles Simic, Olga Broumas. 268 pp. $8.95

VOL. 18/1, ED. ALBERTO ALVARO RÍOS
West Real. Poetry, fiction, and nonfiction. Michael Dorris, Maura Stanton, Dionisio D. Martínez, Peggy Shumaker, Ron Carlson. 244 pp. $8.95

ENTIRE BACKFILE: $350.00

BACK ISSUES ORDER FORM

QUANTITY	VOL./NO.	PRICE
————	—————	————
————	—————	————
————	—————	————
————	—————	————
————	—————	————

TOTAL PRICE: ————

All prices include postage.
International: Write before ordering.

PLEASE SEND WITH CHECK TO:
Ploughshares • Emerson College
100 Beacon Street • Boston, MA 02116–1596
(617) 578-8753

MFA

Writing Program at Vermont College

Intensive 11-Day residencies
July on the Vermont campus; January on Florida's Emerald Coast.
Workshops, classes, readings, conferences, followed by
Non-Resident 6-Month Writing Projects in poetry and fiction
individually designed during residency. In-depth criticism
of manuscripts. Sustained dialogue with faculty.

Post-graduate Writing Semester
for those who have already finished a graduate degree
with a concentration in creative writing.

Vermont College admits students
regardless of race, creed, sex or ethnic origin.
Scholarships and financial aid available.

Faculty

Tony Ardizzone	Susan Mitchell
Phyllis Barber	Jack Myers
Francois Camoin	Sena Jeter Naslund
Mark Cox	Christopher Noel
Deborah Digges	Pamela Painter
Mark Doty	David Rivard
Lynn Emanuel	Gladys Swan
Jonathan Holden	Sharon Sheehe Stark
Lynda Hull	Leslie Ullman
Richard Jackson	Belle Waring
Sydney Lea	Roger Weingarten
Diane Lefer	W.D. Wetherell
Ellen Lesser	David Wojahn

Visiting Writers

Julia Alvarez	Naomi Shihab Nye
Frank Bidart	Tim Seibles
Jorie Graham	E. Annie Proulx
Maureen McCoy	Steve Stern
James Thomas	

Further information:

Roger Weingarten, MFA Writing Program, Box 889,
Vermont College of Norwich University, Montpelier, VT 05602
802-828-8840

Cohen Awards

The 1992 Denise and Mel Cohen Awards

*for the outstanding poem, short story, and nonfiction
published in Ploughshares Volume 17*

BEST POEM (co-winners)

Tess Gallagher

"from *The Valentine Elegies*"
Vol. 17/1, edited by M. L. Rosenthal

Tess Gallagher was born in Port Angeles, Washington, where she now lives. Her most recent books of poetry are *Moon Crossing Bridge*, from Graywolf Press (1992), and *Portable Kisses*, from Capra Press (1992). She is also the author of a book of short stories, *The Lover of Horses*, reissued this year by Graywolf Press, and a collection of essays, *A Concert of Tenses*, from the University of Michigan Press. Other books of poetry include *Amplitude: New and Selected Poems*, *Willingly*, *Under Stars*, and *Instructions to the Double*, all published by Graywolf. Ms. Gallagher co-authored two screenplays, *Dostoevsky* and *Purple Lake*, with her late husband, Raymond Carver, and wrote the introductions to *A New Path to the Waterfall*, Carver's last book of poems, and to *Carver Country*, a volume of photographs by Bob Adelman which documents his life and work. Photo: Marion Ettlinger.

Richard McCann

"*Nights of 1990*"
Vol. 17/4, edited by Carolyn Forché

Richard McCann was raised in Silver Spring, Maryland, and educated at Virginia Commonwealth University, Hollins College, and the University of Iowa, where he received his Ph.D. His fiction and poetry have appeared in *The Atlantic*, *Esquire*, and *American Short Fiction*, and in *Editors' Choice: Best New Short Fiction for 1987*, *Men on Men 2: Best New Gay Fiction*, and *Poets for Life: Seventy-six Poets Respond to AIDS*. He is the recipient of numerous honors, including a 1991 PEN Syndicated Fiction Award and fellowships from the Fulbright and Rockefeller foundations. He is the author of *Dream of the Traveler*, a book of poems, and is completing a novel, which will be published by Pantheon. He co-directs the M.F.A. Program in Creative Writing at The American University. Photo: Stanley Garth.

Cohen Awards

BEST STORY   **Eileen Pollack**

"Neversink"
Vol. 17/2&3, edited by DeWitt Henry and Joyce Peseroff

Eileen Pollack was born in Liberty, New York. She is a
graduate of Yale and the University of Iowa, and currently
teaches at Tufts University. Her stories have appeared in
*The Literary Review, New England Review, Agni, Prairie
Schooner, Sojourner,* and *Playgirl,* and have been anthol-
ogized in *The Pushcart Prize* XVI and *The New Generation.* She is the recipient of a
Michener Foundation Fellowship. A collection of her short fiction, *The Rabbi in the
Attic and Other Stories,* was published in October 1991 by Delphinium Books/Simon &
Schuster, and she recently completed her first novel, *Paradise, New York.* Photo:
Michele McDonald.

BEST NONFICTION   **Dan Wakefield**

"Lion: A Memoir of Mark Van Doren"
Vol. 17/2&3, edited by DeWitt Henry and Joyce Peseroff

Dan Wakefield was born and grew up in Indianapolis,
where he achieved the rank of Eagle Scout and wrote a
sports column for his high school newspaper, *The Shortridge
Daily Echo.* He fled to New York City via Columbia
College, and took up residence in Greenwich Village,
writing for *The Nation, Dissent,* and *Esquire,* and publishing his first book, *Island in the
City: The World of Spanish Harlem.* Since then, he has written his novels in Boston,
from *Going All the Way* and *Starting Over* to *Selling Out,* based on a perilous side trip to
Hollywood, when he created the NBC series *James at 15.* His book *Returning: A
Spiritual Journey* began with an article in *The New York Times Magazine,* and led to
writing workshops in "spiritual autobiography," which he conducts throughout the
country, in addition to teaching a course in the novel at Emerson College. He
incorporated his memoir on Mark Van Doren into his latest book, *New York in the
Fifties* (Seymour Lawrence/Houghton Mifflin). Photo: Theresa Mackin.

Each of these awards carries a prize of $400 and is made possible through the generosity
of Denise and Mel Cohen of New Orleans. The Cohen Awards are nominated and
judged by the advisory and staff editors of *Ploughshares.*

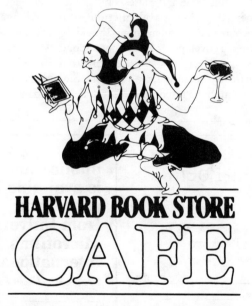

Submission Policies

Ploughshares is published three times a year: one fiction issue and two mixed issues of poetry and fiction. Each is guest-edited by a different writer, and often he or she will be interested in specific themes or aesthetics. Before you submit, you should check if we are seeking something in particular. You may either send a business-sized, self-addressed, stamped envelope and ask for detailed writer's guidelines, or call the *Ploughshares* office at night, after 8 P.M. (applies to weekends as well), for a recorded announcement (617) 578-8753. Postmark submissions to *Ploughshares*, Emerson College, 100 Beacon St., Boston, MA 02116-1596, between Sept. 1 and April 30 (returned unread during the summer). Overall, we look for submissions of serious literary value. For poetry, limit of 3–5 poems. (Phone-a-Poem is by invitation only.) For prose, one story, novel excerpt, memoir, or personal essay. No criticism or book reviews. Thirty-page maximum. Mail poetry and prose separately. Only one submission of poetry and/or prose at a time; do not send another until you hear about the first. Please write your full name and address on the outside envelope and address it to either Poetry, Fiction, or Nonfiction Editor. All manuscripts and correspondence regarding submissions should be accompanied by a self-addressed, stamped envelope, or we will not respond. We cannot accommodate revisions, changes of return address, or forgotten S.A.S.E.'s after the fact. Expect three to five months for a decision. Simultaneous submissions are permitted. We cannot be responsible for loss, delay, or damage.

Please Inform Us When You Move

The post office usually will not forward third-class bulk mail. Please give us as much notice as possible.

A G N I

The Usual Suspects
Derek Walcott, John Updike, Sharon Olds, Margaret Atwood, Leslie Epstein, Rita Dove, Joyce Carol Oates, Seamus Heaney, Ai, Thom Gunn, Marjorie Agosín, Robert Pinsky, Arturo Vivante, Donald Hall, Russell Banks

Unusual Suspects
Kate Millett, Noam Chomsky, Carolivia Herron, Andra Neiburga, Shu Ting, Natalka Bilotserkivets, Peter Dale Scott, George Scialabba, Delmira Agustini, Joshua Cohen, Marilynne Robinson, Sissela Bok

People We Suspected First
Melissa Green, Sven Birkerts, Tom Sleigh, Ha Jin, Mary Morris, Glyn Maxwell, C. S. Godschalk, Lucie Brock-Broido, Patricia Storace, Tama Janowitz, Edward Hirsch, Jane Miller, Suzanne Gardinier, Stuart Dischell

People No One Else Suspects Yet
Thomas Sayers Ellis, Merrie Snell, Sharan Strange, Rafael Campo, Carol Moldaw, Robert Polito, M. T. Sharif, Volodymyr Dibrova, Martin Edmunds, Fred Marchant, Dzvinia Orlowsky, Jeffrey Gustavson

Suspicious Subjects
Social Control and the Arts, Mentors and Tormentors, War, Spirituality After Silicon Valley, Reflections of a Non-Political Man, Robert Mapplethorpe, The Literature of Chernobyl, Latin America

Isn't it about time you investigated Agni?

- -

Please send ❑ one year ($12) ❑ two years ($23) ❑ three years ($34) of *Agni*. (International addresses add $4/year). Two issues each year.   PS

Name _____

Address _____

City _____ State _____ Zip _____

Please mail, with payment, to *Agni*, Boston University, 236 Bay State Road, Boston, Massachusetts 02215.